EMERSON

by

Mary Ann Powell

authorHOUSE®

AuthorHouse™
1663 Liberty Drive, Suite 200
Bloomington, IN 47403
www.authorhouse.com
Phone: 1-800-839-8640

This book is a work of fiction, based on true experiences. Unless otherwise noted, the author and the publisher make no explicit guarantees as to the accuracy of the information contained in this book and in some cases, names of people and places have been altered to protect their privacy.

First published by AuthorHouse 6/13/2007

ISBN: 978-1-4343-1300-3 (sc)

Library of Congress Control Number: 2007903285

Printed in the United States of America
Bloomington, Indiana

This book is printed on acid-free paper.

ACKNOWLEDGEMENTS

I would like to thank the following people who helped make this story come to life:

My family: Donna, Candi, Richard, Earl, Tammy, Sharon, Valarie, and Kaycee, for your belief in my story. To Harrison Dutton who gave his ideas, love, and dedication. To June Bond for her helpful assistance.

A special thank you to my best equestrian pal, Betty Webb, and to Theresa Fisher for medical information and advice.

To my pilot son, Richard, for flight data and information.

A sincere hug to my good friends Arden Batch and Sandra and Jerry Bass.

And last, but not least, a hearty thank you to my lunch buddies for staying with me all the way: Evelyn McDaniel, Ann Catena, Joanne Bentz, Betty Matthews, Gloria Maines, Mary Ware, Jacque Janss, Sue Bradley, and Maryanne Rosenwald.

Thank you all so much. This story could not have been told without your support.

Fantasy horse illustration on cover by: Valarie Powell

CHAPTER 1

Carol Spencer, blue eyed and golden haired, circled a big, lanky bay gelding whom its seller called Emerson.

At fourteen, Carol was already an experienced rider, but this awkward creature was like nothing she had ever seen. Would this horse be one she would be proud of having at Loafing Hills, her father Ned's farm in the Blue Ridge range in Maryland?

Her father inspected the animal and shook his head. "That's the saddest looking thing on four hooves. Carol, are you sure you ought to consider it?"

The thin, gray-haired man who was showing the colt handed the leadrope (shank) to Carol. The large, fifteen-three-hand horse attached to it observed her curiously and nudged her.

Carol and her father, Ned Spencer, had been on a trip to Georgia to visit his parents when she spied the sign:

HORSES FOR SALE.

"Oh, Dad!" she had exclaimed. "Let's go in and find out what they have to offer. You promised me a horse for myself. They just might have what I'm looking for."

"Well, all right," he had said reluctantly, "but don't you realize we're a long way from home? Anything you get would have to be shipped back."

She laughed. "Of course. We wouldn't ask any poor thing to walk all the way back to Maryland!"

Mr. Spencer smiled warmly. His daughter was dear to him because she was his only family since her mother had lost her life in an auto accident when Carol was only three. He had raised her under the care of Mrs. Donavan, their housekeeper at Loafing Hills farm. From the time Carol was nine, her father, Ned, had made a business of buying and selling horses. These included racehorses. He purchased them from racetracks and retrained them as hunters or pleasure horses. He developed a good market for them and had a brisk trade. Loafing Hills' animals earned fame for their soundness and performance. The work was rewarding, and the Spencers found it interesting and satisfying.

Carol had begun taking riding lessons at the age of ten from a very experienced equitation teacher. She had become a very good, experienced rider, and she dearly wanted a horse of her own.

When Carol saw Emerson, she was immediately intrigued. Though the ungainly colt was only three, his bones were so prominent that he looked misshapen. His belly was distended like an overloaded sack, making his dark coat that rippled over his wide-set ribs, appear to have a washboard effect.

Ned Spencer asked, "What *do* you see in him, Carol?"

"I think he shows promise." She stroked his nose. It was velvety smooth under her affectionate touch.

"You sure have a lot of faith," her father said.

"Anyone who believes in horses has a lot of faith," Carol replied.

"Umm," Ned murmured. "I dunno, Carol."

"Oh, Dad! Come on now!" She walked the horse a dozen paces. "How do you like his gait?"

"He moves nicely. Shuffles, stumbles, and is about to fall," he joked. "Better hang onto him. He may need you to hold him up."

"Oh stop, Dad," Carol laughed. "Probably he has more worms in him than an acre of ground, but a dose of medicine and a diet of grain will put him in condition. He'll be beautiful!"

Carol turned to the old man selling him and asked, "Where'd you get him? And why is he called Emerson?"

The seller replied with a toothless grin, "Bought him six weeks ago, real cheap, in North Carolina, in the Cape Fear River country, at a little town called Emerson. But it's really a coincidence because I found out his name was Emerson before he was brought to the sale. So, I bought Emerson at Emerson," he laughed. "I have to admit though," he continued, "I was going to peddle him to the slaughterhouse for dog food, but I couldn't get any weight on him."

Carol almost said, *It doesn't look like you tried too hard*, but she held her tongue. Instead she laid her hand on the horse's neck and said, "I like him, and I like his name too. In my heart I truly believe he will, with work and care, make a great show horse."

Mr. Spencer spread his hands in a gesture of surrender. He rubbed Emerson's neck. "Pack your bags, old buddy! We're buying you a ticket to Maryland."

Ned Spencer explained to Mr. Ladd, the seller, that he and his daughter, Carol, were on their way to Baser, Georgia, to see his parents who were moving back to their home in England at the end of the month.

He handed the seller fifty dollars less than his asking price, telling him, "You know you got a bargain; this horse is not a purebred. In fact, I'm really not sure why we are buying him. Please have him looked at by the sale barn veterinarian and ship him to Maryland in two weeks."

CHAPTER 2

Emerson vetted out sound; the papers arrived with him at Loafing Hills two weeks later at precisely four o'clock Saturday afternoon. A sleek van halted at the house. The driver, as wide as he was tall, bounced from the cab like a volleyball, extending a chubby hand with a cheerful greeting.

"Name's Tom Bently! I come a long ways with this here tail-swisher!" His drawling North Carolina accent hummed with a music that was delightful and unforgettable.

Ned Spencer and Carol introduced themselves and then went to the rear of the van to welcome their guest.

"It's Emerson, all right, Dad!" Carol squealed. "Isn't he wonderful?"

Mr. Bently guffawed. "He's all yores! A high and mighty one. If ya know what's good for ya, you'll call him Mr. Emerson!" he called as he withdrew a portable ramp and led the horse down using a head halter and a rope shank. "I'm surely glad this thing ain't my crittah. Took a few men t'git his rump in this heah van, and the rest of him din't wanna go in it, neither." The horseman snorted and swiped his nostrils on a scruffy cuff.

"I'm shore happy he was willin' to come out. We coulda been heah all day fussin' with his highness. Just see his fancy looks!"

Mr. Emerson stepped down the incline obligingly, saluting his new home with a melodious whinny, wheeling friskily while Mr. Bently carefully maintained a safe distance.

Ned commented, "We'll get him started soon."

"Oh," Mr. Bently whooped, sidestepping the big colt. "I'd put him away purty soon. He's a headstrong one. I tell you, people. I wouldn't turn him out to pasture till he learnt to behave like a gentleman!"

Carol took him and started for his stall with her father, while Bently drove away with his van.

She said, "Mr. Emerson looks scruffy, doesn't he, Dad?" She had to admit it to herself.

"Too late now to change your mind," Ned Spencer told her. "I doubted from the first that he'd be satisfactory."

"That isn't what I mean." She told her father, "He is just the horse I've been hunting for, but he's not yet what I want him to be. He's lost still more weight in the last two weeks. We've got to start building him up, and we've got to get going on this immediately."

Mrs. Donavan, the housekeeper, one of the sweetest and kindest people in the world, made a trip to the barn to pass an opinion on this horse. However, what she saw did not please her at all.

"Carol, dear," she wrung her hands. "I'm afraid you took on too big a job for a fourteen-year-old to handle. You're thin enough yourself, but look at this skinny nag! I can't believe you'd buy anything in such poor condition."

Carol chuckled to herself. Mrs. Donavan was as round as a butter churn and wanted everyone else to be chunky too. However, she was right about Emerson. He was emaciated.

Emerson proved to be the gentlest, appealing horse that Carol had ever worked with. He had a love for being groomed, and he adored being fussed over. He even seemed to enjoy Carol pulling his long tangled mane. When Carol did not give him as much attention as he wanted, he trailed her around and nudged her with his velvet muzzle.

In two days he was a devoted pet that trotted to the fence to greet her whenever he saw her.

Mr. Spencer teased Carol. "Whenever I judge anyone's horse and I can't find anything worth praising about it, I simply say, "Well, your animal sure has kind eyes!

"Carol, dear, Emerson certainly has kind eyes!"

Before Emerson began looking like a worthy specimen, it took tubing for worms, plenty of good grain, and six weeks of hay and constant attention. At first, his scruffy coat began to fall out; then his undercoat took on a glossy shine. Finally, he grew firm on his hindquarters, ribs, and over his backbone until he was strong and solidly built. He became a handsome, beautifully formed horse.

Ned Spencer was almost incredulous. "Carol, I swear you know your horses better than I do. Whatever you saw in him has proved itself in his development. It's taken a lot of loving care, though, and I don't believe anyone but you could have done it."

At last, Carol was ready to begin Emerson's training. The first lesson was to teach him to lunge on line, where she placed a halter on his head and then stood in the middle of the schooling ring, holding one end of the long lunge line. She snapped the other end onto the ring on Emerson's halter. She would teach him to walk, trot, and canter around her on command.

Carol took Emerson into the ring for a trial session. An hour later, she came to the barn in tears and called her father. "Dad, please come here and help me."

He left his chores and went to see what the problem was. "It can't be that bad, Carol. You're not easily upset. Now, tell me what's wrong."

"Dad, Emerson won't move. He simply stands looking at me." She nearly sobbed.

"Now, now, let's go at this real easy," he soothed her. "You hold your end of the line; the other end is attached to Emerson. Now, I'll walk him around you in a circle. Hopefully, he'll get the idea."

He took the halter and led Emerson around Carol, repeating the word, "Walk," again and again. After fifteen minutes of practice, he turned loose of the halter, but remained in stride next to the horse. Slowly he inched away, allowing the animal to continue, but when he was five feet or more from him, Emerson halted and did not take another step.

"Carol, let's change places," her father suggested. Mr. Spencer got the lunge whip and gently tapped the colt on the hocks, but the horse would not budge. He refused to stir unless Carol walked beside him.

"Well," her father said, exasperated, "I think we had better let it go for today. We'll start in again tomorrow and keep it up for twenty minutes a day 'till he finally learns what we want him to do."

Two weeks later, Emerson still hadn't gotten the idea. He would stand like a post no matter what they did to persuade him to obey. He wouldn't try to charge them or canter off, he simply froze.

In the third week, Carol led him into the yard in front of the house so he could enjoy the fresh grass there while she held the line. She was already tired from the day's lessons. She had repeated the commands: walk, trot, and canter hundreds of times. He just wasn't getting it. She finally gave up trying to educate him to lunge on the line.

"I don't understand you, Emerson," she said to him. "You can't be so dumb you can't follow ordinary directions. You're behaving like a balker, which is a horse that just won't move! Why won't you *walk* for me?"

When she spoke the word "walk," Emerson raised his head, looked at her with interest, and started to circle her at a walk.

I can't believe this, even though I'm watching it, Carol thought. *Why, he followed through like magic!*

She wanted to call her father or Mrs. Donavan to see the miracle, but was afraid she would break the spell. It was too wonderful to risk.

Cautiously, she rose to her feet, while Emerson kept circling. "Emerson," she asked him softly, "I love you for this. Will you trot for me?"

He paused for just a moment, watching her with affectionate, gleaming eyes.

"Trot," she repeated anxiously.

Instantly he moved into a springy, balanced trot, with his head down, in perfect form, moving with a rhythm that would take first prize at any show.

Almost timidly, and half out of her mind with joy, she called, "Canter."

His response was rolling, excellent, and as good as any she had ever seen. He first threw out his fine foreleg and then made the transition to a canter with a smooth grace that was positively professional. He had even picked up the correct lead.

He shook his head gloriously, as if celebrating the pride in this accomplishment; and at her command to halt, when she shortened the line, he drew up and faced her at a standstill, his ears up proudly, as if saying, *Well, my lady, how do you like that?*

Carol was as delighted as if she had taken all the blue ribbons at the state fair. She jogged with him to the barn.

"Dad! Dad!" she called excitedly.

He came running out. "What's the matter? Have you had an accident? Are you hurt?"

"No," she chuckled. "Look, Emerson is lunging like a pro. Come and watch!"

"I'll believe it when I see it," he said soberly.

She moved Emerson to their workout area, but on arriving there, he stood motionless. She tried to get him going, but he wouldn't stir.

"Just a minute," she suddenly said. "He did what I wanted while he was in front of the house. Maybe he doesn't like it out here."

"That's silly," Mr. Spencer said. "A command is a command, no matter where the order is given. He's stubborn and won't do what you tell him to, that's all."

"Oh, yes, he will," she insisted, leading Emerson back to the grassy place in front of the house. "You watch."

Here he repeated his remarkable performance of only minutes ago.

"That's strange," her father remarked. "However, I am afraid it tells me something about your horse that we are going to be sorry to find out.

He's going to do exactly what he pleases, what he feels like, and when he feels like it, and that's bad news, really bad news."

Carol discovered this wasn't altogether true, as she worked with him the next few weeks. He lunged any time, anywhere she wanted him to, except in the area where the workouts were usually given. There he stood observing her with a sulky, uncooperative stare.

Now it was time for lesson number two, to teach Emerson how to load into and out of the van. Carol was aware that she had better not attempt this procedure on her own, since she realized Mr. Bently had already had a very unpleasant experience with him. However, she had grown to trust her pet, felt sure that he would not hurt her, and saw no reason she shouldn't try.

CHAPTER 3

Early the next morning Carol schooled six of the thoroughbreds they planned to sell the following month.

It was a beautiful morning, and even though her dad was out of town that day, she decided to attempt to load Emerson into the van. She took him out of his stall, gave him his daily grooming, and then walked him boldly up to the parked van.

"Come on, Mister," she clucked to him, leading him to the van's ramp. To her amazement he followed her like a well-trained dog, right up the ramp, and allowed her to back him quietly into a stall as if he had been doing this all his life. The movement was executed without a hitch.

"You certainly surprise me," she told him, rewarding him with a pat. She thought, *Dad won't take my word for it, and Emerson will probably never do it for me again.*

When her dad returned home, Carol said, "Dad, I want to show you something that's too good to be true. Please come out and stand beside the van."

He obliged and watched in utter amazement as Carol led her horse from the barn, led him up the ramp into the van, and backed him into a stall.

Mr. Spencer said, "Well, he did it that time I'll have to admit. You know, Carol, you must have him charmed with your good looks. You'll have to agree that Mr. Bently was homely!" They both laughed as she hugged her dad.

Even though Emerson was not broke to ride, Carol felt that she wanted to break him her own way and take her time bringing him around to be the kind of horse she wanted him to be. He was only three, so there wasn't any hurry. She could tell he would finish out to be a big horse, over sixteen hands tall, and it was really important for a horse that size to be broken in right.

She began by adjusting a light bridle on him, with a special rubber bit. She then put on the saddle without the stirrups. He was left in the stall with this equipment for half an hour every day for a week.

The following week, she lunged him with the saddle and bridle on.

During the third week, Carol began driving Emerson. Walking behind him, she guided him with a long line attached to his bit on either side, running through rings on the saddle. This would be effective in teaching him to respond to the bit without having to carry a rider, which might make him nervous while he was becoming accustomed to the reins.

Carol avoided the working area. Carrying her whip, she took him to the paddock, picked up the reins, and told him to walk. He obliged. Several times, she turned him to the left and to the right. He obeyed perfectly. Then she tapped him gently on the flank with the whip and asked for a trot.

The instant he felt the whip touch him, he balked. Again she tapped and got no response.

"Listen," she said sharply, "I want you to trot!"

He swung his head around and glared at her when she tapped a bit harder, as if telling her, *Quit that*!

She straightened him several times, tapping him, and repeated her command. Again and again he turned to face her.

Carol threw down her whip in despair. Well, she reflected, here we go again.

"Mister, I'm not giving up!"

She patted him. "Come on, now, Emerson. Be a good fellow and trot for me. Trot! Trot!"

Without any warning, he launched into a delightful jogging trot, which almost tugged Carol off her feet.

"Oh, you!" she hollered at Emerson. "You are too much!"

Ned Spencer, who was observing this by-play, called out, "I've got it, Carol! I know what's bothering him."

She took Emerson to her father. "What is it, then?"

"It's the whip, Carol. Can't you see he will not put up with it?"

"I didn't hit him hard enough to make it sting," she said.

"It isn't that. He's rebelling. Don't you recall, when we were trying to teach him how to lunge, he simply didn't understand what was expected of him? About the time he got it straightened out, he got a tap with that whip. He's protesting; that's what! Didn't you notice, when you were instructing him in front of the house that he finally figured out what you wanted and did it because you didn't remind him with the whip? He has the schooling area tied in with the whip, and that's why he won't work there. He's a smart horse, all right."

"I never thought of that," she said. "The day he walked into the van, I didn't have the whip. Probably Mr. Bently lost his temper and gave Emerson a sound lashing when they were loading him in the van at the sale barn. He's letting us know he won't do anything if he gets the slightest lick with that whip. Today he was fine 'till I tapped him. Then he got balky. When I dropped the whip, he performed beautifully.

"You're right, Dad! Emerson hates that whip, and he will not let us use it without getting his temper up."

Her father replied, "Do you realize how tough a job it's going to be to train him with the carrot and stick theory? Punishment and reward are simply not his style."

"I can see that," Carol agreed. "I'll have to think up another system in dealing with this colt."

During the next few weeks, Carol drove Emerson every day on the long lines. Then she made test runs with sandbags on his back. Finally, she substituted herself for the bags. By then, Emerson was responding well to voice commands. Carol began using leg pressure on his sides to help him understand her commands. He even accepted working again in the ring. Carol could see she was making rapid advances with him. He learned how to change gaits, the walk, the trot, and the canter when called for.

He was a smart horse willing to accommodate his mistress' excellent riding ability. She had faith he would become a great show animal. She spent long hours on his training.

Carol rode Emerson every day. She loved trail riding, and it was great exercise for Emerson. Ned Spencer often accompanied his daughter and her best friend, Karen. He had the time now as his two farm workers, Mike and Dan who lived and worked at Loafing Hills, were a great asset to the farm.

Carol had taught Karen, who was just two years younger than she was, to ride. Karen loved exercising Ned's many horses, so she was always ready and willing to join them.

Early in the morning, the three left for the wilderness and rode leisurely across the lovely Sugarloaf foothills. In the bright, clear, cool mornings, the horses were frisky; they trotted along the trails, snorting and prancing. They loved these excursions and looked forward to every one of them.

Mingling with the wonders of nature, it was as though they were hundreds of miles from civilization. In the clean, crisp, mountain air, they jogged happily, entertained by the cheerful chirping of the birds, fleeting visions of white-tailed deer, and glimpses of squirrels squabbling over their buried treasure troves. Next, they knew, would come autumn, bringing trees with glowing burnished golden crowns; they would ride over woodland carpets of glorious colors. Not long after, the first snow would arrive, covering the earth's rocks and ground with garments of glistening white.

In Maryland each part of the year had special appeals and its own brand of beauty. There was nothing as exhilarating as riding in the foothills of Sugarloaf Mountain, during any season.

Carol continued polishing Emerson's working on the flat (walking, trotting, cantering). She never slacked in their efforts. In her heart, she knew he had the promise of being a superior mount. Because he moved so much like a thoroughbred, and because of his sleek, trim lines, she often wondered whether his breeding might not be as classic as the best. He was a ham actor, loving to perform for an audience. He would snort, throw his head and dash swiftly about like a young boy showing off before company.

Carol started showing the big colt how to maneuver over poles on the ground, known as cavilettis, teaching him proper balance. Although Emerson was big, he was not ungainly, but graceful, and his enthusiasm showed that he thoroughly enjoyed this work.

Throughout the year, Carol continued to school Emerson on the flat and over the caviletti poles. The young horse grew even more handsome as he matured. His temperament and personality charmed everyone. He was the most gracious and appealing animal the Spencers had ever known.

Carol, Karen, and Ned laughed later remembering how worried they had been when Emerson had to have shoes put on for the first time. Would he behave? Not to worry...

Emerson liked the experience. He displayed no more than mild curiosity at this strange procedure. The farrier, a kind and patient man, praised the big colt and patted him gently for behaving so admirably, rewarding him with a sweet carrot. Emerson reveled in every moment of being in the limelight, getting lots of attention.

They also worried needlessly about how he would get along with other horses. They kept him separated from the other horses for a while because he acted as though he was going to bully them all, running up and down the fence line, neighing and swinging his head as if he was a mighty stallion.

One day Mike led Frosty, a small quarter horse, out to pasture and let him loose. Mike thought Carol and Karen were out together riding. When Mike got back to the barn, he heard lots of squealing and neighing, but still thinking that Emerson was out on the trails, he didn't go check what the racket was about. Later Carol came into the barn leading both Emerson and Frosty. They had become best of friends. Emerson was not a bully nor mean; he just wanted a friend!

CHAPTER 4

Leading into his fourth year, Carol realized it was time to face the serious business of perfecting Emerson's training.

Carol's ambition was to eventually show him in horse shows as a "Hunter over fences." To accomplish this with any horse, she would usually work the horse over fences using the lunge line. This taught the horse to control his balance before he had to carry weight while leaping an obstacle.

In order to succeed with this method, a lunge whip was required at times. Of course, Carol knew this was not going to be acceptable to Emerson. One crack of the whip, and he would surely quit.

One evening over dinner, Carol asked her dad and Karen to give her some ideas on how she could teach him to jump.

There were many ideas discussed, but none sounded really good until Karen asked about running Emerson through a narrow area to get to his feed. That way he would be more willing; the feed could be his reward.

Mrs. Donavan, their housekeeper, then proposed that they build the run from the pasture gate across the grass, ending in the barn lot, where they could hang his bucket of grain.

“That’s a great suggestion,” said Ned. “We all know that it wouldn’t take Emerson long to realize that he has to go through the run in order to eat!”

The next morning Ned, with Karen’s help, built the run using snow fencing. They erected two fences a hundred feet long and ten feet apart, which led into the barn paddock area from the outside schooling ring. When a horse was led into the schooling ring and Carol opened the gate at the ring, this left a clear passageway into the barn paddock.

They then laid poles on the ground, spaced about twenty feet apart. A horse that came through the passageway from either direction would have to step over these poles.

For the first week, each day prior to feeding time, Emerson was led into the outdoor ring along with his well-trained friend, Frosty.

At feeding time, Mr. Spencer at the barn, would call the horses by whistling and knocking two buckets together. Carol, in the ring, would open the gate. Frosty would take off immediately, going down the passageway to the barn paddock. Emerson would follow.

This was an everyday event for Emerson and Frosty. Both animals seemed to enjoy the excursion from the ring to the barn paddock.

Every day Ned would raise the poles several inches. By the end of the third week, both horses were jumping two and one-half feet over each pole.

Next, Ned placed a few of the poles a foot or two apart, this making them spread fences. This was to teach the horse to extend himself over a jump. These were then carefully nailed to present a solid barrier that could not easily be knocked down. Horses clear a solidly built barricade more readily than one that will topple when barely hit, since they soon understand that they cannot become lazy and careless in their jumping, but must go over the top in order to make it. Through this practice they learn not to drag their feet, but to tuck their hooves. Several jumps at this time were raised to three feet, and one was raised to three and a half feet. Both horses excelled.

Emerson was fast to benefit from the program. He used himself correctly, jumping off his hindquarters and snapping up his front legs like a professional.

The next step was to diversify the barricade, to make it more interesting and challenging for the horses. Hedges, barrels, panels, tires, or loose equipment from around the farm was added to the poles, so the jumps were different every time.

Emerson was not to be outdone. When he saw his buddy, Frosty, sail over a strange-looking obstacle, he was not going to be humiliated by being left behind. He learned to fence without even knowing it.

Emerson's first trip over the jumps with a rider on his back would be the final test of his skill. If he could not successfully carry a person through these exercises, all his training would be for naught.

Carefully, Mr. Spencer let the posts down to the two-and-a-half-foot level. Carol mounted. First she worked Emerson on the flat, circling the ring about twenty minutes; then she casually turned him into the long passageway. Quickly he moved towards the paddock, clearing five fences without any difficulty. It was certainly a rewarding day for the Spencers.

The crowd standing at the paddock, Ned, Carol, Karen, Mike, Dan, and even Mrs. Donavan, all applauded the stunning performance. Carol, wearing a beautiful smile, dismounted and gave Emerson a huge hug.

The same afternoon Karen, Carol, and her dad left for a cross-country ride. Ned and Karen were astride two of Ned's schooled horses. Carol, of course, was mounted on her astonishing steed, Emerson.

When they approached the first two-and-a-half-foot-high coop (wooden structures for horses to jump in order to enter or exit a field), her father took the lead, urging his horse over the coop. Karen followed. Emerson, without hesitation, followed faithfully behind, as though he had been accustomed to jumping them all his life. Carol knew they wouldn't always be following a rider over fences; she also knew that Emerson couldn't be tricked forever into making his leaps, but it was a reassuring start and a good beginning toward the time he would be doing them on his own. The rest of the ride they went over four more coops. No problem.

Ned suggested to Carol a few days later that she should try him in the ring with a few commonplace jumps. She hesitated at first.

"Well, we'll have to teach him someday, and it might as well be now," she said as she climbed aboard.

Emerson cantered to the first jump and went over it neatly. He continued efficiently to the second and then to the third. On the fourth fence he was off stride, and he slid into it. Carol was nearly pitched off, but she stayed on and brought him around for another attempt. This time he snorted and stopped short. He wouldn't go over. He deliberately quit.

After he rebelled for the third time, Carol knew that she had to either master the horse or give up the year of work she had devoted to his training. He had to realize who was in command and that he would not be allowed to be willfully disobedient.

"Come along, now!" she called impatiently, pulling her crop from her boot. She smacked him smartly, twice on his quivering flank.

At this, he balked angrily. He would not budge an inch, but planted his front hooves rigidly on the turf.

Crack! Crack! She snapped him two times more.

Emerson stood still as a statue. He refused to stir forward, or backward, or to either side. He froze in position and stubbornly remained there.

Carol, sobbing, dismounted and led him from the ring. "Oh, Dad," She cried, "in five minutes, I've ruined everything it took us months to achieve! Oh, what will I do? How will I ever get this hard-headed character to come around?"

Ned Spencer comforted his daughter in a soothing voice. "Now, Carol, it's going to be all right. It's a setback, of course, but you've still got the horse, and you love him. It's only a temporary problem. It has to be worked out. I've always found it's not a good idea to quit on a bad note. Go ahead. Take him to another field and work him quietly on the flat and see what comes of it. It won't hurt, and it could help."

She shook her head sadly. "Well, Dad, I guess I don't have anything to lose, so I'll do it."

It didn't settle everything, but at least she was in the saddle, with the pleasure of putting him through the paces that he knew.

On her return she asked her father, "Is there any way I can undo the damage to his ego?"

That evening over supper, Carol asked Karen and her dad what they thought she should do next.

Karen suggested, "I think, Carol, you should start his training over fences all over again."

Ned agreed. "Let's go back to using the passageway tomorrow; then lets ride across country again. After seven days of this, he may be in the mood to do what he should. Then we'll give him another chance at the jumps. After all, he did jump three fences in the ring, so we know he can make three, four, or forty, if he wants to."

They all laughed at that, even Mrs. Donavan as she placed a very pleasing aromatic cherry pie on the table.

The next week, Emerson performed well in the passageway, jumping everything clean. He was also very good going across country. On the seventh day, Carol was nervous when she rode Emerson into the big ring and apprehensive as to how he would behave.

For about twenty minutes, she warmed him up on the flat before turning him toward the first fence. He took the first, second, and third fence gracefully, but when he reached the fourth, he seemed to remember that he set a limit for himself and had reached it. He stopped.

"Carol," her father called, "circle him around the ring for a few more minutes, quietly, as though nothing has happened. Show him you trust him. Make him believe you are counting on him and not doubting his performance. That counts a lot with a horse. He won't want to bring you disappointment. Now, before you try that jump again, I have a clever idea."

Ned Spencer vaulted into the ring, and moved the fourth barrier to a new location. "Now," he waved his hands, "give it another go!"

Carol urged him forward. Emerson went over all four fences in perfect style.

"Dad! Dad! He did it! He did it!" She cried excitedly, as if her father hadn't seen it for himself.

"Okay," he smiled. "Now, don't push him. He's scored for today, so let it go at that."

Carol agreed. She dismounted and walked Emerson to cool him and then quartered him in his stall.

Carol's father took her aside that evening after supper. "Carol, you know there are two alternatives you are facing with Emerson. Either sell him right now as a good trail horse or keep him and see whether you can develop him the way you want. Remember, my dear, there's a strong possibility he will not finish out. You could lose all you've put into him, and in that case, it would be useless to go on."

"Don't you have faith in me, Dad? Or do you have doubts about Emerson?"

"I don't lack confidence in either one of you," he assured her. "I do believe you can do it, and he can do it, but you have to be realistic too. Do you want to take the chances?"

"I've already taken a lot of chances, and I'm not going to give up now!"

"That's the spirit," he said. "That's the spirit!"

"I have to stick it out," Carol answered. "It's not just a matter of admitting defeat. I feel I have to do this. I must!

"I'm not trying to prove that Emerson is a great horse. That's half of it; it's true, but I've got to prove I'm a good trainer. I can't give up on myself. That's the bottom line in all of this."

"I never thought of that," he murmured.

"Yes, and in spite of all his ridiculous balking," Carol continued, "I can't help but like the big goof, and I'm not about to let him fail on me!"

Several days afterward, Carol put him over four fences again. It was a flawless performance. Her father and Karen applauded as they set up several additional jumps in the ring. Emerson once again went over every one of them as though he had been doing this for years. Carol quickly learned that when he approached a fence at the wrong gait or angle, which could be expected of any young horse during the training stages, she must not allow herself to be upset, but should quickly steer him away from that location to other fences and then back once more to the one which was causing the problem. When she learned not to fight with him, he behaved smoothly and was even eager to make jumps.

At last, everything was going well. One day, however, they had an unexpected experience with him. While turned out to pasture, Emerson managed to get into the ring. The gate blew shut and enclosed him. Ned whistled for the horses to come in from the pasture for their evening feed, but hadn't noticed that Emerson was missing.

Carol's horse was not going to give up his dinner. Although the gate at the passageway was shut and was five feet high, he cantered around the ring to get up speed and before Ned, Mike, Dan, or Carol could move from where they stood, Emerson cleared the gate with a beautiful leap. They were speechless with astonishment as he continued through the passageway jumping all the remaining low fences. He trotted grandly into the paddock area as though he was lord of the manor.

With mouths open, the crowd at the barn stared at the wonder horse. Hardly crediting what they had seen, they strolled in silence to the gate and inspected it.

"There isn't a scratch on it, Dad," she whispered, running her hand along the top edge.

He nodded. "The rascal didn't even nick it. You have an open jumper there, Carol. I've never seen a horse go over an obstacle any better than that. He was sailing! It was fantastic."

Carol laughed, "Yes, it was fabulous, Dad, but I'm afraid Emerson will never make a performing jumper. If he doesn't feel like jumping, he won't. In the show ring, he'd balk just like he does at home. It would be awfully embarrassing, particularly if it were his first fence. I'd be ashamed of both of us."

Emerson's jumping began with that episode. A few days later, Ned took Emerson's best buddy, Frosty, out on a trail ride. With no apparent thought or effort, Emerson invited himself along by leaping the four-

and a half-foot pasture fence and joining them. After that outing, he simply went anywhere he wanted to go.

One day, Mrs. Donavan reported he jumped over the six-foot gate behind the house. "I never imagined he could do anything like it," she exclaimed, wiping her face with her apron as she called Karen to come see. They both watched as Emerson went trotting around the outside of the house, his head high in the air, as though he were leading a parade. Then he topped the gate back into the pasture easily, as if it wasn't even there.

Karen missed Emerson's first jump over the fence into the yard, but witnessed the second one, going back into the pasture. "I think the only reason he went back," she laughed, "was because his buddy Frosty didn't follow him out, so Emerson had to re-jump the fence to get back into the pasture with him. Frosty just stood there looking at Emerson like he'd lost his mind!"

Later at the supper table, they told the family, including Mike and Dan, this story. Mrs. Donavan added, "I'm really glad we don't have close neighbors; he might just turn up on their doorstep."

Mrs. Donavan laughingly told Carol, "Do you realize you turned that horse into what he is? You taught him to jump when he wanted to. Now, he could become the terror of the Blue Ridge Range!"

Carol and Karen both giggled at the idea.

CHAPTER 5

Another year passed by, Emerson was now five years old. Beautifully muscled, he was a magnificent animal who attracted the admiration of every visitor to Loafing Hills.

Carol moved slowly in bringing Emerson up to her goals for him. She never pushed him, and above all, she never fought him. It took all the horse psychology that she, her dad, and Karen possessed to cajole him into performing, as she wanted. At every step Carol had to outmaneuver, outthink, and outguess him; and with the intelligence he possessed, this wasn't easy to do. He was clever and challenged them every step of the way.

"Dad," said Carol, "we've learned more from Emerson than we've taught him. He's one of us. He's beginning to think like us. He's pretty close to outsmarting us."

"True," her father assented. "You'll have to work out your every move, like playing a game of chess with a champion. He forces you to be alert every minute. If you're not ahead of him, he'll soon leave you behind."

A local church group was holding a regional horse show that summer. Carol realized this was going to be a golden opportunity to present Emerson to the world of show horses. It was not her intention to exhibit him, but merely to introduce him to the sights and sounds and let him mingle with equine friends.

The event was being held only a mile from Loafing Hills, so Carol rode Emerson alongside her dad and Karen, who were riding horses in training. They rode cross-country to the grounds.

A hundred or more horses, two hundred people, and scores of vans and trailers were already at the church.

This was an excellent turnout. If Carol thought the bustle would excite her mount, she was mistaken. He acted as though he had been to a hundred shows and was as calm as he was standing in their paddock back home.

This show was for beginner riders only. All exhibitors had to be under sixteen years of age. Carol, who had just turned sixteen, could not have participated anyway.

Karen, two years younger than Carol, a good rider and very knowledgeable regarding horses, spoke up.

"Carol, I'm fourteen; I qualify for riding in this show. Please let me show Emerson; I've worked him on the flat for you several times, and he won't be at all skittish with me. It would be a great experience for both of us. And look at me: riding breeches, boots, hardhat, and a spotless white shirt," she smiled. "I'm ready," she concluded enthusiastically.

Carol and her dad consented, agreeing that it would be excellent practice for both Emerson and Karen. Carol took off her riding jacket, handing it to Karen.

"Please be careful, Karen," Carol begged. "If he gives you trouble, don't hit him. Just exit the ring, please."

Karen mounted Emerson. "Just one thing, Carol," Karen pleaded, "please don't enter him as Emerson. Whoever heard of a show horse with a tag like that?"

Carol strolled to the secretary's booth and wrote down Emerson, without mentioning it to Karen. *It's my horse*, she thought, *and that's his name. I'm not going to change it now. If it's good enough for the town in North Carolina where he came from, it's plenty good enough for him, and it's good enough for me.*

The first class she entered him in was Pleasure Horse Under Saddle. Even though Emerson took his new surroundings in perfect form, he tried curiously to see everything in the ring at once because it was unfamiliar to him. Although his gaits were smooth and all his transitions were well done, and though he picked up the correct leads both ways, his head acted as though it were on a swivel.

Whenever a horse passed, Emerson bent his neck to see what animal was going by. Karen did her best to keep his head straight, but Emerson was too curious to look good to the judges.

The second class of events, Baby Green Hunter Under Saddle was more in line with Emerson's abilities. Although he still appeared to have lost something and was glancing in all directions, he was beginning to settle down and look like a promising entry. Since the contestants in this particular section were also baby green, at least Emerson fit in better. It counted when the ratings were tabulated. Emerson won the class. He ranked first out of sixteen. For his first show, it was a superb triumph!

Karen wobbled out of the ring and moaned to Carol, "Good grief, they called him Emerson, right over the P.A. system! I felt like a fool! Couldn't you think of anything else to call him? Like Minnehaha's Littlest Baby Snookums Boy? Or, Persian Alligator's Aftermath?"

Carol laughed. "Sorry, but I have a real stubborn streak about that name. It's his hometown, and likely he's as proud of where he's from as the people who live there. It wouldn't be fair to switch names on him now."

A number of other classes were scheduled before the last one in which Emerson would compete, which was an equitation event. This was judged strictly on the performance of the rider.

Karen suggested, "Carol, wouldn't you like me to show him in just one open jumper competition? There'll be only eight fences, each three and a half feet high. I've watched you school him over higher fences at home."

"I don't know. You're a talented rider, but what if he cuts off on you? What could you do?"

"I'd leave the ring, Carol. I promise. I know nobody can fight with Emerson. All I could do would be to simply leave. However, what's the harm in giving it a whirl? The opportunity to be in the ring will be good for him," she enthused.

Carol nodded. "I'll bet you'd like to see how well he can do, yourself," she said.

"So okay, go to it, but if he cuts off, Karen, just remember, come out immediately. Don't monkey around with him. He might get out of hand. We'll do what we can to correct any problem after the show."

Karen promised to do as Carol asked.

Several horses were competing in this class. Emerson was scheduled to come on last. Only three of the others had clean rounds. When Emerson's turn came, Carol held her breath and whispered a prayer. *Oh, please, please! Emerson, take the first fence, at least!*

Emerson certainly felt like jumping. He went over all eight fences, topping them like an expert. The last of the fences was at the far end of the ring. He wasn't accustomed to the crowd, and the sudden outburst of cheering startled him. Before anyone realized what was happening, he was over the five-foot high ring fence. This disqualified him.

Karen stayed on his back, though she was tossed and thumped. The throng cheered louder than ever and demanded that he be allowed back again in the ring. By the time Karen rode around the outside of the ring to the entrance gate with him, he had settled down. He evidently realized that the uproar was a salute to his performance.

Emerson reentered the ring, pranced to the center, and turned toward the crowd. As the onlookers applauded, he posed with ears forward, neck arched, and tail high. He studied his admirers for a full two minutes. Carol and her father, delighted at his performance, cheered wildly along with the rest.

Karen rode from the ring, her face beaming.

"Boy," she gave Emerson an affectionate pat as she dismounted, "I wouldn't have been surprised at all if he had reached down and bowed out there. Your horse is a sweetheart, but my gosh, Carol, is he ever a ham!"

Later in the day, Karen took him into the last class, which was to be judged on the horse's way of moving. Emerson went smoothly through the routine until the last call for a canter. He had picked up the correct lead and was proceeding nicely until all of a sudden he noticed something or someone in the bleachers. As soon as his attention was distracted, he stopped and looked.

"Go, Emerson, go," she urged him, getting him in hand again and pushing him forward into a canter.

He finished the class nicely. Among sixteen entries, Karen earned second place. Except for the untimely stop, the judge told Karen she would have won the class.

Carol, her father, and Karen were approached by a man in a riding habit as they prepared to leave for home.

"Hello, Mr. Spencer. I'm Robert Simmons," he identified himself.

"Yes," Ned answered, "I recognize you. You're a famous stunt rider and showman."

Simmons smiled. "Thank you, sir. I really like that horse you have. What do you want for him?"

Carol spoke up. "He isn't for sale, Mr. Simmons."

"Come on, Miss Spencer. Don't try to drive the cost up by saying that. Just name your price."

Ned broke in, "I'm sorry, Mr. Simmons, but Carol meant what she said. Emerson is not for sale."

Simmons' face fell. "Well, I'm sorry too. If you change your mind, please call me," he said. Then he handed Ned his business card. He started to walk away and then glanced back wistfully. "Mighty fine animal you have there...the very best!"

Emerson's next chance to perform at a horse show came only a month later. Carol and Karen took Emerson and one of Ned's horses, Pepper, to the show. It was a Baby Green Hunter Division open to all age riders. They both placed in the Baby Green Under Saddle class, Carol winning the blue and Karen close behind with the red. The last class they both competed in was Baby Green Handy Hunter.

Emerson was everything but handy (versatile). Although he took the first fence easily, he got in wrong on the second. His jump made him resemble a Lipizzaner doing a capriole, and he cleared the fence by at least three feet. The last fence consisted of a hedge with a rail on top, leading out of the ring.

This jump confused Emerson, and he almost halted and sat down in front of it. Carol circled him about, and he cleared it this time without a hitch.

Carol's father, watching from the sidelines remarked jokingly, "Emerson doesn't like to jump over a jump to leave the ring; he'd rather jump the ring-fence to get out!"

Karen was ecstatic. Her day with Pepper brought her two second-place ribbons, which was extremely good for a young horse in training.

Carol entered Emerson in two more local shows during the following month. He performed well. His collection of ribbons began to fill a display wall in the barn's show room. Karen was excited that Pepper had come along so fast too and was sorry when he was sold. But she knew, and was proud, that she had helped train the horses to sell.

CHAPTER 6

One of the largest shows in Maryland would be held in August, and Carol eagerly awaited it. It included a Baby Green Division, in which she planned to enter Emerson. She put him through hard daily workouts in preparation for the forthcoming event.

Two weeks before the show, Ned Spencer called the horses in from pasture for their morning feeding. Two of the small herd, Santana and Emerson, had been rubbing in a strand of scrub saplings during the night. Their legs, necks, and lower bodies were sticky with streaks of sap. Carol and her father scrubbed them both with soap and water, but the resin would not come off. When they tried to work it out with their fingers, tufts of hair came off, exposing the raw skin. By the next day, Santana's legs were slightly swollen, but were not too seriously affected. Emerson's were much worse. They were swollen and sore, and he appeared to have a case of hives from nose to tail.

Doctor Harper told Carol, "We'll try an antihistamine shot. You'll be busy for the next two weeks with baths, salves, and shots if you want to have a well animal."

That mishap put an end to Carol's hopes to compete in the August show.

By September, Emerson and Santana had recovered from their bouts with the allergy. Then Emerson encountered trouble from a different source. One of the Spencer mares in training, called Lady, which she definitely was not, decided she was going to show Emerson she did not hanker for any of his company. She demonstrated her lack of affection by kicking him soundly on the shoulder. Fortunately, no bones were broken, but he was terribly sore and swollen and required six weeks of rest from training. Before he was back in condition for further workouts, the show season was over.

Another fall and winter went their way. Carol or Karen rode Emerson almost daily on the back trails when the weather was seasonable. Emerson, upon turning six, was beset with another affliction. He became allergic to his straw bedding, developing a hollow cough. To foster his recovery, he was transferred to a stall outside. The straw was then replaced with wood shavings. Carol lavished much care and medication on her ailing pet, and finally the cough subsided under her devoted treatment.

That spring brought out the best in Emerson. He looked more beautiful than ever. He was a picture-book animal. Maturity lent him special dignity, which was quite impressive. Even Carol's father now admitted he had much more than "kind eyes."

In May, an outstanding show was scheduled which would bring in exhibitors from the eastern shore of Maryland, Virginia, and Pennsylvania. This horse show was the event of the season, but Emerson could no longer be shown in the Baby Green classes; he would have to meet the challenge of older, more experienced horses. Carol pre-entered him in the First Year Green division, and to qualify him, she rode and hunted him in a local fox hunting club through the winter.

Emerson got a good scrubbing the day before the show with soap and water. Carol added half a cup of cooking oil to the final rinse to help put the gloss back into his coat. When he was dry, she used a small pair of clippers to trim excess hair from around his ears and face, and then, with a larger pair, she groomed his ankles and fetlocks. She then pulled and trimmed his mane until she was satisfied it was just the right length to braid.

On show day, Carol was in the barn at dawn, braiding Emerson's mane and tail and completing the last touches. At last she led him out for inspection by her father, Karen, and Mrs. Donavan. His mahogany coat and dark dapples over his hindquarters, glistened in the sun. Tiny braids accented his gracefully arched neck and the grandeur of his head. Morning sights and sounds sent his small ears pricking forward, while his wide-set eyes took in the motion of every leaf and the flight of every bird.

Ned, Karen, and Mrs. Donavan slowly paced about the splendid horse, nodding their approval. "You both deserve a triple A plus," Ned said.

"He's wonderful," Karen declared.

Mrs. Donavan added, "Carol, I never saw a lovelier horse."

Mike and Dan came up from the barn to see, and they agreed that Emerson was one beautiful animal.

Carol took Emerson back to his clean stall where Mike had thrown down a bed of clean brood shavings. Carol ran to the house to get herself ready to go. Karen and Ned went through the horse van that had been packed the night before to make sure it contained everything that would be needed at the show: tack, riding attire, hay buckets for water and grain, a tack box with brushes, surrey and mane combs, hoof pick, rub rags, fly spray, and medical supplies.

Ned said to Karen who was helping him, "Good grief, it's as easy to pack stuff for six horses as it is to plan for one."

Karen laughingly agreed.

Departure time was eight o'clock, and they were ready on time. Ned, who was driving, and both girls waved goodbye to Mrs. Donavan.

Since this was an indoor show with classes for Carol scheduled in the late afternoon, they would have ample opportunity to settle in at the location with Emerson, even after the four-hour journey.

Only Carol was showing today. The young horse that Karen was now exercising at the farm was not ready to show.

"I'm sorry you aren't showing today, Karen," Carol spoke, "but I'm glad that you are going with me anyway. You help my nerves."

Both girls laughed.

They arrived on the show grounds at twelve-thirty. It was several hours before Emerson was unloaded and comfortably housed in his stall, and everything had been unpacked. Once they felt that Emerson was settled, they opened, and greatly enjoyed, the boxed lunches that the amazing Mrs. Donavan had sent along. Ned agreed that she was a true saint.

After lunch, they checked the show's program. It was fun to meet other entrants and talk over the rules and requirements for the classes. Before they knew it, the afternoon classes were ready to begin.

Emerson won the Hunter Hack class (judged on the horse's way of moving). He moved with the grace and elegance of a thoroughbred.

After his performance, Carol's father came up to her while she and Karen were un-tacking him.

"Honey," he informed her, "I've just been to the secretary's booth. They have the open jumper courses posted and are accepting post entries. The courses don't seem hard at all to me. Emerson has been over the same type of fences at Loafing Hills. You ought to take a crack at it, Carol. You'd have a chance to take a ribbon."

"Okay, let's do it," she answered excitedly.

"Karen, would you please go enter him for me?" Grinning, she gave Karen and her dad a big hug and then turned and stroked Emerson lovingly.

Karen had entered Emerson in the Warm-up Jumper class. It was only one class away.

Emerson sailed over the big fences as though it was his everyday exercise. On the first round, fourteen other horses also came through clean. Each was then ridden again and tested for timing. Emerson had never before been pushed over fences at a gallop. It was a new experience for him, but he responded like a veteran to Carol's leg pressure against his strong sides, and he had an impressive round. Carol was surprised when they beat all opposition, and she beamed when they won first place.

Hunter Over Fences was the next class, and it was awful. Emerson took the course, but his behavior was doggy. On the last fence, he pulled a rail.

"Really," Carol apologized, "I had a heck of a time just keeping him going. He acted plain uninterested in the whole hunter course. I know he's as fit as a racehorse, and I'm sure he isn't tired. It just didn't work, that's all."

Karen agreed with Carol, "He looked absolutely bored!"

Mr. Spencer entered them in the next open jumper class. Emerson excelled there. He obviously loved it; sprinting nimbly and boldly, he cleared every fence. He put on a prize performance, winning the class handily. Carol was proud of him.

She confessed to her dad and Karen, "I can't really figure the big rascal's game. He's so uncoordinated in a Handy Hunter class, but when it comes to the timed open jumper class, he heads the list. It certainly puzzles me."

"I think you already had the answer earlier, Carol," Ned grinning, said. "I think he's made it plain that hunter fences bore him."

"Yes," Karen exclaimed, "the fences are too low for him. He's just not interested. There's no challenge in it for him. It doesn't call for any effort."

They put this theory to the test. In the last Hunter Class Over Fences, a plow horse could have done as well. Emerson didn't even give them a decent try.

"Carol," her dad said, "I told you a year or so ago that you might as well accept it. You have an open jumper, whether you like it or not."

"Go for it, Carol," Karen called. "You've got two jumper classes coming up. Let's see what he can do."

Emerson took the two remaining jumper classes like a champion. Carol was delighted to get the winning purse, the trophy, and the ribbons, but her greatest thrill of all was Emerson's excellence. He had proved himself a formidable competitor, and he had won.

The next two shows coming up that season were only repetitions of that event, minus the hunter divisions. Emerson was never shown hunter again. He easily took every jumper class in which he was entered.

A near-tragedy took place early the following winter. Ned, Carol, and Karen were out for an early morning trail ride. Ned was on a young thoroughbred he had recently bought from the racetrack, after allowing the horse a "letting down" period of six weeks. Carol was astride Emerson, and Karen was up on one of the horses that she was schooling. They were cantering across an open field, where winter weeds grew thick and tall.

Two very young deer lay concealed in the growth, where their mom had evidently left them. They did not know the horses were approaching until they were upon them. Suddenly the deer bolted from cover and cut across in front of the riders. The deer were too startled to know where they were going, so they nearly collided with the mounts. Ned's horse reared and came down on top of Carol, slamming her to the ground. Emerson, off balance, slid and fell into a shallow gully.

"Oh, Dad!" Carol screamed. "I think I really hurt my arm. Then she asked, "Is Emerson okay?"

Ned dismounted and climbed into the gully and helped Carol up on her feet. Karen looked at Emerson's legs, "Looks like a front leg is slightly injured," she called to Carol.

Ned agreed it didn't look too bad. Karen volunteered to lead the three horses back to the barn. Emerson was hurt, but could walk slowly. Ned, using his cell phone, stayed there with Carol. Even though it was a tragic accident, they couldn't help but smile when they noticed the fawns peeping at them through the brush.

Ned said, "Bet they'll have a story to tell their mom when she comes back for 'em." They both laughed.

Ned took Carol to the hospital to check out her hurting arm and called the veterinarian to come and check Emerson's leg. The doctors said, "Nothing broken in either case, but their injuries will take time to heal."

Both Carol and Emerson were laid up most of the winter, but by early spring both were whole again. Now came the job of reconditioning. Weeks were spent in practice, therapy, and exercise. Karen helped Carol everyday, and by show season they were ready to compete again.

"Dad," Carol said one evening after dinner, "I've been thinking how strange it is that Emerson always bounces back. He balked and sulked through a harrowing training period, refused to accept correction with the whip, and dealt with coughs, allergies of the skin, and a bummed up leg. Yet he put down all the difficulties and emerged victorious. It seems to me he's telling us he's destined to be a great achiever. He won't be defeated. He's a winner."

Carol and her big horse had an extraordinary year. Traveling to every important show on the east coast, they won every single jumping class they entered. It proved that Emerson was a prize animal because they were in competition against the best jumpers in the nation.

Larger and larger throngs assembled to watch him perform. They nicknamed him "Pegasus, the undefeated open jumper." According to the radio, television, newspapers, and the equine periodicals, they were well on their way to becoming a legend.

CHAPTER 7

Stabling facilities on the road from show to show were sometimes excellent, but at other times indescribably bad. The horses were put up in tents at an event in Ft. Lauderdale, Florida, and it proved to be a serious mistake.

About two in the morning, a rumble of thunder went ripping through the sky and nearly tore it open.

Ba--a-roooo-ooomm!

Tethered horses reared and neighed and shrieked with fright. Workers tried desperately to evacuate the animals to the indoor arenas, but they had to fight every inch of the way through torrential winds and a pounding downpour. The rain descended so fast, and the gale was so strong that the tents collapsed and were swept away like paper.

"Turn 'em loose! Turn 'em loose!" yelled the managers, hoping the freed horses could escape from the falling canvas that threatened to trap them.

Carol, Ned, and Karen ran half-dressed from their trailer to witness an incredible scene of chaos. A howling wind snarled at them with such fury they could not hear each other a few feet away, while the torrents blinded them.

Men were shouting everywhere. "Get 'em outta here. Help, help! Look out for that pole! It's going to drop!"

Terrified horses thrashed about in the darkness, struggling against men, shredded tents, and hurtling debris. Those trying to lead the panicked animals to safety were falling over wind-swept rubbish, or jerked to their knees by their fear-crazed charges. Horses galloped loose up and down, wheeling and kicking, and adding to the danger and pandemonium.

"Dad! Dad! What are we going to do?" Carol shouted.

Emerson's tent was in shambles. It was like a bad dream. Carol and Karen both collapsed in tears.

Her father led the girls to safety in one of the indoor arenas. "There's no use in you two wandering around out there," he told them. "Stay here and help calm the horses that are led to this shelter. I'll get back out there with the men and see what else can be done."

Carol and Karen were speechless with dread, but they knew that Ned was right. They would only expose themselves to further hazards in the stampede that raged outside in the blackness. They remained inside until morning to assist the hysterical humans and horses that came in.

By dawn the rain had subsided, and the worst of the hurricane had passed. Most of the animals had been collected inside the arenas.

Finally, Ned Spencer returned. Mud streaked him from head to foot. A gash bled on his forehead; his clothes were torn, and he was soaked through.

"Oh, Dad! Dad! Thank God you're all right! But you've been hurt!"

"It's nothing," he said. "A Band-Aid will fix it. The only thing I need is some rest. I'm dog-tired. We gathered all the horses we could find."

Carol's countenance changed. "You mean...you mean you didn't... good grief, Dad, has Emerson been found?"

"I'm afraid not, Carol." He took Carol in his arms as she wept.

"Oh, Dad! Do you suppose..."

"I don't suppose anything. He isn't injured or dead that we know of. He could be found, and we might as well believe the best as think the worst."

Taking Carol's hand, Karen whispered, "Carol, please let's not get upset when we haven't any news that's bad. Your dad looks terrible. Let's get him someplace for rest and some food."

They took him to a stand set up by the local Ladies Auxiliary. They served hot coffee, sweet rolls, toast, and fruit drinks. Afterwards, they cleaned up with buckets of fresh water and paper towels supplied by the show sponsors.

The storm had blown over. A pale sun began peeking through the gray cloud cover.

"Dad," Carol said, "Why don't you rest here while Karen and I go out to look around?"

"I can't rest yet," he answered. "Let's go."

The three had just started to leave the arena when a man came in leading Emerson.

"Carol! Look! There he is!" shouted Karen.

The farmer leading him said, "I'm glad I found out where he belongs. Why, folks, I live five miles away, and I found him in my front field this morning, grazing with my sheep! It's crazy. There's a five-foot, chain-link fence around my property. I don't know how he got over it without a ramp. I heard about the horse show and the storm on TV and figured he got carried to my place and dropped over the fence by the wind, but that hardly seems possible, does it?"

They all laughed heartily.

"He's an open jumper," Carol told him, fondly patting her horse. "He could have cleared your fence if it was six feet instead of five."

The man listened to her with open-mouthed amazement while she inspected Emerson for injuries. She was crying and laughing in the same breath, she was so happy.

Karen led Emerson further into the arena while Ned and Carol circled him. They found him to be fine, except for a few minor scratches and a lot of dirt. Carol hugged him and sobbed for joy. All three thanked the kind gentleman immensely for bringing him in.

Miraculously, all the horses were well and accounted for, but the show had to be postponed for three days to give the committee time to reorganize. Ft. Lauderdale was a close-knit community, and they overwhelmed the visitors with offers of assistance.

Horses were taken care of all over the area; lost equipment was replaced through charitable contributions, and everyone who needed aid was helped. Everything was put back in order, and arrangements for reopening the show went smoothly.

Emerson was apparently unshaken by the whole affair. When events began again, he stepped out in front by taking the Open Jumper Championship title and trophy.

Emerson was like a popular athlete. He was a crowd-pleaser. He had to be both to be successful, since he was not a born performer. Whatever he did was done out of his love for doing it. Frequently he competed with jumpers that wore dropped nose bands, tie-downs, curb bits, martingales, shin guards, or other accessories, and then were shipped over every fence by their riders. Emerson wore only a simple snaffle bit and saddle. It had been a few years since the gallant animal had felt the stroke of a whip on his flank, when Carol had given him a few licks on his refusal to top a fence. He wouldn't tolerate coercion then, and she was sure he would not accept it now.

Carol realized that if the day should ever come when he did not want to jump for her on his own initiative, he might as well be retired. Nothing could force him to obey. He had a free spirit.

"All right, Carol," Karen remarked, "we've got to face it. Emerson is a showoff and loves to put on his stunts in front of a crowd. The bigger the crowd, the better he jumps. Naturally, Carol, your riding ability has a lot to do with it too," she added. "You ride him like you were his second nature. It's really like music to see you perform with him in the ring."

Karen continued, "The pair of you have a perfect cadence and accurate timing, but I know he's not a show horse that everyone could handle. He works beautifully with you, and that's the whole story."

Karen pretended she was bawling and yelled, "I am *soooo* jealous," she cried, and laughingly stomped away.

Carol was still laughing when a man approached her. He looked curiously at Emerson.

"I beg your pardon, Miss," he said politely, "but did you happen to purchase this horse at White's Sale Barn a few years ago?"

"Why, yes," she answered, taken by surprise.

He cleared his throat. "I thought so. I read an article in the paper about you and Emerson, and since there aren't likely many horses going by that name, I figured it was the same one. Do you remember me?"

She shook her head no, puzzled.

"Well, I'm Bill Ladd, the fellow who sold him to you." He waited for this news to sink in and then added, "You got the biggest bargain that ever stood on four hooves. That big old colt really turned out to be a windfall, didn't he? Well, you've done a fantastic job with him, Miss Spencer. It shakes me up to think how close he came to turning into dog food."

Carol winced at his remark. "Mr. Ladd, I'd be much obliged to you if you could tell me more about his former owners, his background, breeding, and so forth. How could I get this information?"

He scratched his chin. "All I can tell you is, I picked him up at White's Sale Barn in Emerson, North Carolina, about six weeks before I turned him over to you. You could contact them."

"All right, I will. Thank you." She was relieved when he walked away.

Two more shows that season won them two additional championships. Then Ned, Carol, and Karen started back to Loafing Hills for a much-needed rest.

As soon as they got back to the farm, Karen turned Emerson out with his pal Frosty, who was very glad to see him. She and Karen then unpacked the van and the truck. They were exhausted when finished, but later lounging in the kitchen while sipping a cup of Ned's homemade apple cider made it all worthwhile. They both agreed, the horse show circuit was great fun and rewarding, but it was always a nice treat to come home.

Carol wasted no time writing to White's Barn at Emerson, North Carolina. It was located northeast of Whitesville and was on the seaboard Air Line railroad.

Karen had been at Loafing Hills farm most of the time since she had turned twelve years old. When she turned sixteen, she received permission from Ned and her grandmother to move in with the Spencers. Her granny had raised Karen from the time she was six, shortly after her mother's death. Karen, "horse crazy," met Carol, who gave her riding lessons. The two girls finished high school and then attended a small local college, not far from Loafing Hills. Karen said meeting Carol and living at Loafing Hills Farm was a dream come true.

Carol and Ned were working a new horse, when a car pulled into the drive. A young man stepped out. He was attractive and well built with a shock of brown hair that fell over his forehead.

"Hi," he called to them from the side of the ring, "I'm John Quill. I'm Emerson's original owner."

Carol couldn't put the horse away quickly enough. She hurried out to meet the visitor.

"Tell all," she gasped, hardly able to get her breath from excitement. "Tell me about Emerson!"

He laughed and sat down in a swing on the porch.

"The sale barn in Emerson sent your letter to me. I happened to be planning a trip to Washington, DC, so I decided to stop by Loafing Hills for a personal visit."

Ned and Carol told him how happy and pleased they were by his visit. They were really anxious to learn everything they could about this horse.

Before Mr. Quill got started with this information, Ned called Mrs. Donavan and Karen to join them so that they too would learn more about Emerson's beginnings.

"Where are you from, Mr. Quill?" Karen asked excitedly.

"My wife and I owned a small farm in North Carolina," he began, "and that's where Emerson came from. But I need to start at the beginning."

He leaned forward. "One night, one of my thoroughbreds, an unregistered, but well-bred mare, jumped the fence and visited a neighbor's farm. Running loose on that farm was a young nondescript stallion. Eleven months later, Emerson was born. Thankfully, he was the image of his lovely mother. My wife, Pat, kept him for her own and took great pride in raising him. She was spending a lot of time with him, grooming and teaching him to lead. The colt was not quite two when Pat came down with a terminal illness."

His face was sad, and his lips quivered. As he wiped his eyes, the group nodded understandingly and waited patiently while he regained his composure.

Their young caller continued, "Pat was confined to a hospital during the next year. A little boy of eight was hospitalized there with the same illness. He and my wife became very good friends. This lad was deeply interested in horses. He kept a picture of my wife and her young colt beside his bed. She promised him she would let him ride the colt as soon as he got better, although all of us knew it was a vain hope because he could not recover.

"The ride never came. Four months later, while Pat sat up through the night holding his feverish hand, the boy died. He was a courageous soul." Mr. Quill choked up.

"Sorry...I still have a hard time talking about this," he apologized, "but I want you to know the whole story. The boy's name was Emerson. Pat named the colt after him, saying she hoped he would grow up with the same wonderful spirit that our little friend had. Two months later, Pat died, too, and...." He broke off in a sob.

"I...I'm sorry, but I go to pieces every time I think about it. My bravery couldn't match either of those two. It was...well, a bit too much to lose my wife and her young friend.

"Meanwhile, the colt had been turned out without receiving much care. He looked awful. It's too bad, but I have to say I lost all interest in everything, and I didn't care.

"A very good friend of mine and his wife knew what I was going through. They came to look after me. They sold all the horses on the place for me. It was the only thing to do." He again paused briefly.

Mrs. Donavan took the opportunity to offer coffee to all, allowing Mr. Quill a quiet moment to take a few breaths before continuing.

"Almost a year later," he continued, "I began to take myself in hand. I suppose time heals all wounds. Anyway, it's over. I'm so glad Emerson has a home——and a good one."

Carol said, "It's remarkable. By pure chance, we were passing through Georgia when we found him, and I took a liking to him at once. Isn't it strange that Mr. Ladd bought him from the sale barn at Emerson...the same name as the colt? It seems, well, providential."

Ned said quietly, "I believe the Almighty has a hand in all our affairs. None of this was an accident."

John rose to leave. "Pat would be happy to know her horse is at Loafing Hills, and so would the little boy. Emerson has got to be good. He has a namesake to live up to."

Carol and Ned walked him to his car. He thanked her for what she had done with the horse. "Since I received Carol's letter," he told them, "I investigated a bit and found out how remarkable an animal he is. Looks like he's winning at all the shows. I know you've put a lot of work into him, Carol, and I know you must be very proud of him."

He also made them promise to stay in touch with him and to keep him posted on Emerson's progress.

When he drove away, Ned remarked to his daughter, "There's a fine young fellow, who loves people, and who knows his horses. Too bad he's had such luck."

CHAPTER 8

Another Maryland winter was upon them, followed by spring, and preparation for another show season. Emerson was maturing nicely. He was a strong, noble animal, and professional in both his bearing and performance. He made his mark again that year and took a box full of ribbons, a dozen fine trophies, and several valuable purses home.

In his eighth year he won every open jumper class in which he was entered. With Carol on his back, Emerson could do anything, it seemed. He was featured on TV, and a movie firm put out feelers for a film that was in the planning stages, which would feature prize horses.

A year later, Emerson was invited to Lennox, Virginia, to participate in one of the largest and most prestigious shows in the United States. There he was awarded the best in the United States Open Jumper Loving Cup. This was the highest honor in the category.

At the end of the day, the exhibitors had a party for the presentation of the awards. Carol and Ned made Emerson comfortable in his stall and returned to their hotel to dress.

Ned, Carol, and Karen were on their way to the party when Carol said, "Dad, let's go by the barn first. I have a strange, unexplained fear that something's wrong."

Ned and Karen tried to calm her. "There's no reason for you to be apprehensive, Carol," Ned said.

But Karen, looking into Carol's face, pleaded, "She really is afraid, Mr. Spencer. I think we should go to the barn first too."

"Okay," he answered, "if it will make you feel better, we'll check on him on the way to the party."

Carol felt immensely relieved to find Emerson gazing peacefully from the door of his stall.

This is ridiculous of me, Carol thought. *I've never had a feeling like this before. Everything's all right. Why am I so nervous?*

Betty and Don Johnson had their horse stabled in a stall next to Emerson's. They were busy setting up cots. Like many exhibitors, they slept in front of their horse's stall, keeping a close watch.

The Johnson's small child was already asleep on a little folding bed. Although most had already gone to the party, they had remained behind to be with the child.

Betty called, "Ned, Carol, Karen, come have a cup of coffee with us? It will only take a moment to perk."

They sat down to chat and sip the savory drink for a brief time.

Soon, Ned looked at his wristwatch. "It's time for us to leave if we're going to make that party."

Carol hesitated. "Dad, somehow I don't want to go. I know it's unreasonable, but I don't think Emerson should be left alone. I'd like to be at the party personally to accept the cup, but could I ask you or Karen to do that for me? Maybe it's not Emerson that's worrying me."

She continued, "He looks fine, but I may be just too tired. I'm not up to it; that's all."

"All right," her father agreed, "but perhaps I had better take you back to the hotel before I..."

"No, no," she cut him off. "Please, Dad, I want you and Karen to be at the party and to arrive on time. I'll be all right. The Johnsons are here; I'll visit with them.

"Karen, would you please accept the trophy for me?" Carol asked.

"Yes, of course," Karen answered, "but I'd be glad to stay here with you, if you want me to."

"No, Karen, please go with Dad. Just come back and pick me up after the party and thank you so much for standing in for me."

When Ned and Karen left, Betty said, "Sit down and we'll enjoy your company."

"First, let me check on Emerson once more, Mrs. Johnson," Carol insisted.

She was beset by a premonition she couldn't describe, even to herself. Slowly she went into the stall with Emerson.

Something is the matter! He hasn't touched a bite of grain!

It wasn't like Emerson not to feed well. Carol's heart began to pound. She looked at him anxiously.

I've got to get control of myself. He looks fine. Maybe he's just exhausted from the day's activities. He could be too tired to eat.

Deep down, she knew this conclusion was mistaken, but it comforted her for a fleeting instant. Then, as she stood beside him, she observed him shiver. *Oh, no. It's got to be my imagination. I'm just overwrought from all the excitement of winning. I'm upset and just being silly.*

However, she went to her medical supply kit with trembling fingers and removed a thermometer. Emerson's temperature was normal.

Quickly she ran her hands over his body and down his legs. Everything was as it should be. Although his hooves felt warm, she knew he hadn't foundered, and he showed no signs of colic.

"Take a few steps for me, Emerson," she said gently, trying to lead him. He drew back. She could instantly sense his strong reluctance to move. Carol glanced up at him and saw his eyes were taking on a rather shocked look.

"Betty!" she screamed, running to the stall door, "Don! Betty! Come quickly! Hurry up! Emerson is taking sick!"

They ran in, responding to her cries, and as they entered, Emerson's knees buckled. He tumbled heavily to the floor without a sound.

"Oh, oh, oh," she cried. Ignoring her good clothes, Carol dropped beside him, groaning. She took his head in her lap and stroked his neck. It was beginning to perspire.

"Dan," she pleaded, "please go as fast as you can and call the exhibitors' party. There'll surely be a veterinarian there. Tell him to get here as fast as he can. This is serious. Please hurry!"

As Dan dashed out, she called after him, "Please tell them to let my father and Karen know and ask them to come to the barn, *now*."

Emerson started shaking violently. Betty snatched up a blanket and covered him. Helplessly they waited for the arrival of medical aid.

Twenty minutes ticked by. Tears were trickling down Carol's cheeks. Her gown was wet with Emerson's saliva. His eyes were glazed.

Dr. Fuller's car screeched to a halt outside stall number twenty-three.

Carol thought to herself, *Dear God, I'm twenty-three years old, sitting on the floor of stall number twenty-three with Emerson. How weird is that?*

Dr. Fuller ran into the stall and made a quick examination, drew back, and sighed.

"Carol, from all the symptoms, he has suffered a massive cerebral hemorrhage. He's suffered a major stroke."

Ned and Karen came in breathlessly, just in time to hear the veterinarian's diagnosis. Ned carried the magnificent silver loving cup, but found himself too weak to hold it any longer. He set it on the stall's windowsill and knelt beside the dying horse.

Emerson raised his head pitifully. He seemed to recognize his mistress. He even looked at Ned and Karen. But then his head fell back into Carol's lap like a dead weight, and he lay strangely still.

Dr. Fuller held his stethoscope against Emerson's chest, listened a moment, and removed it. "I'm sorry, Carol, he's gone," Dr. Fuller whispered sadly.

She uttered a cry, "He's only ten," she cried and then wept quietly.

"The only condolence I can offer you," the doctor went on, "is that Emerson didn't suffer. It was a stroke, the same kind that kills people.

We have no conclusive answers as to why and when. Sometimes there are warning signals. In this case, there were none. He died without any pain."

Carol asked them to leave her alone with Emerson a few minutes. "Don't worry," she assured them, "I'll be all right. There's nothing to be concerned about."

Karen knelt beside Carol, ran her hand down Emerson's neck and whispered as silent tears fell from her eyes, "I'm so sorry, Carol." Then she quietly stood and left the stall with Ned, leaving Carol alone with Emerson.

Carol sat with Emerson's head still in her lap, stroking his neck. Tears crept silently down her cheeks and fell into her beloved horse's face. From the silver cup in the window, bright reflections rose in a halo that cast a sacred light around it.

"Emerson," she whispered, "oh, Emerson! You've truly made your namesake proud!" She was no longer able to curb her pent-up grief. The deep hurt overwhelmed her. She buried her face in his mane and cried until she was spent.

After awhile Mr. Spencer entered softly and stood silently. Then he lifted her to her feet and took her back to the motel.

The next morning, Ned made arrangements to have Emerson's body taken back to Loafing Hills.

Word of Emerson's death spread quickly throughout the show grounds. Hundreds of grooms, contestants, exhibitors, judges, and owners flocked to stall number twenty-three to pay homage to one of the greatest jumpers who ever lived. Many of the mourners silently left a floral tribute at the door. The show committee sent a splendid spray of red roses, shaped like a horseshoe, which was hung above the stall door. Beside the stall, a permanent plaque was later erected. It read:

Emer*son, Owner: Carol Spencer.*
He Would Enter
He Would Perform
And the Cheering Crowds
Would Start!

He Was Bold
He Was Courageous
He Will Live Forever
In Our Heart!

Radio and television newscasters saluted him by retelling the story of his career and sudden death. On their return to Maryland, Carol, Karen, and her dad received calls, letters, and telegrams from all parts of the nation, relaying condolences. Mrs. Donavan wept as she read the following heartfelt message:

To Carol Spencer and Family,

> The time and effort you have invested in your remarkable horse have not been given in vain. Emerson will always be remembered by the people. You are certain to possess the cherished and lasting memories of an unsurpassed athlete, a noble animal, and a true friend.

Please Accept Our Deepest Sympathy.

It was signed by the president of the Horsemen's Association.

Carol found it especially hard to adjust without Emerson around. She had spent so much time with him in the past that she felt forsaken and alone. For a long time after his death, she found herself wandering frequently into the trophy room to look over his prize ribbons and awards. The silver loving cup was housed in a fine display case in the center of the chamber.

Emerson, she thought, *let me thank you from my heart for all those rewarding years. I've been so fortunate to have been important in your short life. You asked nothing of me, my friend, except my sincere devotion and understanding, yet you gave all you had of yourself. You were hammy, handsome, fun, and beautiful. I loved you every moment, and I will ever cherish your memory. I am thankful you were given to me and thankful that you loved me just as much.*

Carol recognized how ironic it was for her to have a part in a horse's life that had already meant so much to a wonderful woman and a small, courageous boy. She felt sure that the three would unite in heaven, and the young boy Emerson would finally get to ride this famous animal that had been named after him.

I'm sure that Mrs. Quill will have a happy smile on her face too.

Some things, she surmised, *are not ours to question or explain.*

She also felt comfortable in the knowledge that her horse Emerson did not suffer either in life or death. He enjoyed good health and high spirits all his days.

"Oh, God, I will miss him so."

CHAPTER 9

Two weeks after Emerson's death, Carol was standing at the kitchen sink washing breakfast dishes. She glanced out the window as a station wagon pulled up to the front of the house. She did not recognize the gentleman who emerged from the vehicle as he approached the front door. Mrs. Donavan answered the doorbell. There was a moment of silence as she led the gentleman into the kitchen. Carol turned and then immediately recognized him. It was Emerson's first owner, John Quill.

He spoke first. "Carol, I am so sorry to hear about Emerson. I read about his death in the newspaper yesterday. I had to come see you."

Carol, drying her hands answered, "Thank you so much for coming. I don't think that I will ever get over losing Emerson. I truly loved that beautiful horse."

John walked to Carol and put his arms around her. She returned the embrace. They stood together quietly for several minutes.

Carol told John that she had picked out a beautiful spot at Loafing Hills where Emerson was buried. It was at the top of a hill overlooking the farm. The spot was covered with bright green grass and surrounded by tall oak trees. She had not yet decided what to have inscribed on his gravestone.

Ned, Carol's dad, entered through the kitchen door. He was glad to see John again. He felt that Carol needed all the support she could get at this time.

Mrs. Donavan came into the room and offered coffee to all. They sat and talked for an hour. Ned insisted that John stay for dinner, which he did.

CHAPTER 10

John had planned to return to his farm in North Carolina, but decided instead to stay at a local hotel for a few days. This would allow him time to help the Spencers catch up with some things that they had fallen behind with at Loafing Hills.

Ned and Carol, both feeling comfortable with John, agreed that they would love to have him stay to help, but would prefer that he stay with them at the farm.

He finally agreed to this. He could only stay a few days because he had purchased twenty-five Black Angus cattle, which were to be delivered to his farm in North Carolina the following week.

The next several days John and the Spencers worked hard to catch up with things that had been left undone since Emerson's death. Several fences were replaced; two water troughs were relocated; hay was brought in from the fields; grain was picked up from the town mill, and Ned's horses received much needed attention and schooling.

On the fifth day Carol led her dad, Mrs. Donavan, Karen, and John up the hill to Emerson's grave. She wanted to show them his gravestone with the inscription that she had, after much thought, decided on.

While climbing the hill, Carol announced to everyone, Please bear with me. I've thought about this and have finally decided that no words can ever express how I've felt about this horse. The only fitting message would be a humble one, which would reveal the deepest feelings of John Quill and myself," she concluded.

Arriving at the gravesite, they were struck with the three words etched on the stone that meant so very much. Simply stated was *I Knew Emerson*.

John awoke early the next morning. It was Sunday and time to leave Maryland and head back to his farm in North Carolina. His cattle would be arriving at his farm Tuesday morning, and he needed to do some work in preparation for their arrival. When he came downstairs, he was surprised to see Carol already up and busy in the kitchen.

"Good morning, Carol. I hope I didn't awaken you," he whispered.

Carol turned and smiled. "Oh, no," she answered, "I couldn't let you get away without breakfast. We are so very thankful for your assistance this past week."

She continued, "I still can't believe that we are actually caught up with the farm work now." She smiled as she handed him a full breakfast plate. The mouth-watering aroma of bacon and eggs filled the kitchen. He did not need to be asked twice.

Carol sat with John, sipping her coffee. "I don't mean to be nosy, John, "but we have all been so busy working here this last week, we really didn't get to ask you about your life. Are you a full-time cattleman?"

"Yes," he answered, "I am. Lots of things have happened in the eight years since Pat died," he answered quietly. "I sold my old farm and purchased a hundred and fifty acres in North Carolina and built a large log cabin, which I now call home. I built a good-sized barn and erected lots of fences." He chuckled at his fence remark because that was what he and the Spencers had been doing a lot of lately too. Carol joined him with a quick understanding smile.

"You never married again?" Carol asked.

"No. I've dated some, but nothing serious. I guess I'm just too busy," he answered.

"You sound like me," Carol laughed. "I think the last date I had was two years ago," she continued. "I go out with a guy three times, and he thinks he owns me! I can't play that game...I just don't have the time. I guess, John, we're just two lost souls."

John got up from the table, came around, and gently pulled Carol to her feet, hugged her, and said playfully, "No, Carol, you are not a lost soul. Maybe I am, but not you!"

He continued, "Let's look at a calendar before I leave and set up a real date, just for us."

Carol, laughing answered, "Well, maybe we better wait for that one. You have lots of work to do at your place, and I have Dad's three horses to work on here."

John looked almost hurt. "Okay, Miss Spencer," he said jokingly. "I think that you feel that I may be too old for you, huh? But I'm not, you know! I know that you are twenty-three years old. I read it in the newspaper. So, now listen. Carol, I am only twenty-one. Just kidding," he chided. "But, I really am in my prime. I'm a healthy thirty-two year old gentleman looking for a first date with a beautiful friend named Carol. Know anyone named Carol who just might be interested?" he asked.

Carol, giggling now, reached up, patted him on his cheek, and answered, "Oh, wow, I guess we'd better find that calendar now and decide on that date."

Studying Carol's calendar, they both agreed that the date would take place on October the 15th. That would give them thirty days from now to decide when, where, and how.

CHAPTER 11

It was time for John to head home. Carol walked him to his car where they talked for several minutes. Then John, without hesitating, pulled her into his arms and kissed her goodbye. It was not a long, romantic kiss, but it made Carol's heart flutter, and as they parted, both looked and felt pleased.

The next day, after enjoying a wonderful breakfast prepared by Mrs. Donavan, Carol, her dad, and Karen headed to the barn. They saddled Ned's three horses, two mares and a gelding: Selina, Lady, and Blackjack. The horses were in training to become show horses. They rode across the open field to an adjoining trail leading up the Blue Ridge Mountains. It was a beautiful September morning, perfect for exercising horses. They rode for two hours enjoying the fresh air and the beauty of the wilderness surrounding them. When the ground leveled, the horses were put through their paces, trotting, cantering, and galloping. They kept this up for several miles before coming down to a walk and then returning to the barn. The horses were sponged off and walked until dry.

After turning the horses out into a grassy pasture, Ned, Carol, and Karen then walked to the house for showers and a change of clothing.

Later, they met in the kitchen to help Mrs. Donavan prepare lunch. Mrs. Donavan said to Carol while handing her items from the refrigerator, "You missed a call from John Quill this morning. He said to tell you that he arrived home safely and is busy preparing for the arrival of his cattle. He also asked me to be sure to tell you that he is contemplating October 15th. He said that you would know what he meant."

Mrs. Donavan waited for a response from Carol, but none came. However, Ned asked Carol what that was all about.

She replied, "Oh, nothing really, Dad. John is just being funny; he thinks that we should stay good friends and maybe get together next month."

"Well, I don't see anything wrong with that," Ned said. "John is really a nice guy, and you do need to get out and do some fun things, away from this farm."

Mrs. Donavan and Karen agreed. "I can take care of the horses for you, Carol," Karen offered.

Mrs. Donavan said, "Yes, Carol, we know that you love your horses, but do try to plan some visits with John. He is a wonderful young man."

Carol appreciated what they were saying, but it was hard because she truly loved her life as a horsewoman and would always remember the exciting and fulfilling life she and Emerson had shared for eight years. She felt sort of lost right now. But, maybe her dad and Mrs. Donavan were right. She really liked John and was definitely looking forward to seeing him again.

The following week, Carol and Karen rode every day, schooling their mounts over cavallettis, giving the horse physical exercise, which developed muscles and balance. It also developed ease and rhythm of stride with impulsion and engagement of the hindquarters. This was just one of the training steps for hunters and jumpers.

All three horses in training showed promise. Carol liked and admired the prospects, but she knew that they would never measure up to Emerson. Her dad and Karen agreed with her, but they were also sure that with training, all three animals would make the grade and become admirable mounts.

Of course, Ned was hoping that Carol would take a special interest in Blackjack. *This three-year-old gelding*, thought Ned, *shows the most promise.* Ned also had several well-schooled horses now on the show circuit. Karen was showing two, and the other ones were being ridden and shown by prospective buyers.

Carol loved being around horses, especially training and showing them. But since losing Emerson, she just couldn't seem to sustain the interest and excitement once associated with it. However, she knew that she was a horsewoman; it was in her blood. She hoped she would never have to give it up.

One evening the next week, Carol received a card from John. He enclosed pictures of the new cattle, which were younger and smaller than the old herd. Carol was impressed. They all, young and old, looked very healthy and quite handsome wearing their shiny ebony black coats. John also enclosed a nice note to her. It read:

> Hi, Carol, the cattle are finally feeling at home. The first few days were very hectic because Black Angus are quite jittery in unfamiliar surroundings. But, good grain and hay works wonders. They are beginning to settle in nicely now.
>
> I want you to know that I am really looking forward to our *big* date! You know, Carol, even though our work on the farm there was tough, it was also fun, and I really miss you. Hope you feel the same. Tell your dad and Mrs. D "Hello" from me.
>
> Love, John.

Carol smiled as she read the note and felt a chill run up her back. *What's the matter with me*, she asked herself, *John and I are both too busy to get involved right now.*

Carol was reading over the note one more time as she sipped her coffee. She glanced out the window and noticed a Bluejay, the color of the sky, perched on the feeder as though he had nothing better to do.

"Lucky you," she smiled, "you're just strutting around out there in your beautiful blue suit gobbling up birdseed."

Just then her dad walked into the kitchen, noticed the happy smile on Carol's face, and asked, "What are you looking so happy about, Miss Carol?" he joked.

"Oh, Dad, I was watching Mr. Bluejay out there strutting around."

Ned, however, noticed the note lying on the table, looked at Carol, and said, "Sure, unh-huh."

Carol blushed. Ned took Carol's hand and asked her to sit down. "You know, Carol," he began, "life is more than horses. We need more in our lives than animals; and if someone makes you happy, then you have to admit it and help it along."

"Dad," she answered, "I don't think I'm ready for a serious relationship right now."

Ned stood up and whispered to her, "I'm not talking about you, honey. I'm talking about me. I want you to understand that you need more out of life than dealing with animals, and now that I've raised you to be a lovely young woman, I need more too. This, what I'm about to tell you, is somewhat of a surprise to me too, Carol. Mrs. Donavan——Ellie——and I plan to marry. Neither she nor I recognized the love that we had for each other until just recently. As you know, we have been together since you were a small child. She has been a good second mother to you and loves you dearly."

Carol was so surprised at her dad's announcement that she had to sit down quickly.

"Dad, I'm flabbergasted," she cried. "I don't know what to say." Tears filled her eyes, but she was wearing a gleeful smile. "I can't think of anything better that could happen to you both. You know I've always loved Mrs. Dona...I mean Ellie, all my life. And I'm thrilled at your news. Now tell me what are the plans?"

"Well, we haven't gotten very far with our plans yet. Ellie wanted me to talk to you first, to make sure you're okay with it. As you know, honey, you are our only immediate family."

Of course, Carol knew what he meant. Her grandparents on her mother's side had passed away several years ago. Her dad's parents had left Georgia to return to their original home in England where they now resided. When Carol and Ned had made their trip to say goodbye to Ned's parents, it had been a sad event. However, it had also proved to be a joyful one. It had been on that trip where Carol had met and fallen in love with her wonderful un-broken, unschooled horse, Emerson. And, she had even convinced her dad to purchase him!

Carol, returning to the present, continued, "Dad, I really could not be happier for you and Ellie. You both have been wonderful to me, and I love you both so much. Now it's your turn to have a life of your own, have some fun. As you've always told me, Dad, follow your dreams."

"Well, I'm sure going to give it my best shot," he answered with a laugh.

Carol asked, "Have you told Karen and the farmhands yet?"

"No, you are number one to hear the news," he answered as he bent and kissed Carol on the top of her head. "Thank you, honey, for understanding."

When her dad left the room, Carol ran through the house looking for Mrs. Donavan, calling out the name "Ellie" at the top of her lungs... This felt really good to Carol.

Ellie came out of her bedroom meeting Carol in the hallway. Carol almost knocked her down with a hug.

"Wow," Ellie laughed, "you haven't hugged me like that since you were a little tyke."

Carol, smiling from ear to ear, cried, "Well, I just got the good news about you and Dad, and I couldn't be happier. You know I love you, always have, always will. I cannot think of anyone more perfect than you for Dad and he for you."

Ellie hugged Carol back and whispered, "Carol, I love you too. You have been like a daughter to me for twenty years, and I couldn't ask for a better one. Your dad and I falling in love was a surprise to both of us. We couldn't believe it. It's such a wonderful feeling, and I am so happy. And even more so now that I know you are all right with it."

"All right with it?" Carol cried. "My gosh, Ellie, you have been the perfect mother to me for as long as I can remember and now the perfect partner for my dad. I think I must have died and gone to heaven...and you know something else," Carol continued, "I just love calling you Ellie!"

Holding hands, they walked down the stairs giggling like two schoolgirls.

Reaching the bottom of the steps, they found Ned standing there, hands in his pockets, a grin on his face. They ran to him with a family hug. The three danced in a circle, laughing and crying at the same time. It was truly a memorable moment.

The next day, Ellie and Ned invited the farm workers and Karen to the house for a small dinner party. Later, as dessert was being served by Carol, Ned stood and announced the marriage plans. Everyone was surprised, but also very happy to hear the news. Congratulations from all were extended along with best wishes of luck and happiness to the smiling couple.

Ned then announced, "Ellie and I have decided to have a small wedding right here at Loafing Hills in early November. Everyone on the farm and our neighbors will be invited. We are also inviting Ellie's sister Jean, who now lives in California, and my parents, in England. We hope it will be possible for them to join us."

Ned continued, "The wedding is planned for outdoors and will be held at two o'clock in the afternoon. We all know how beautiful this farm is in early November, so Ellie and I have high hopes that on our special day, the Maryland trees will still be bathed in their spectacular fall colors. This will surely add to the beauty and grace of our wedding."

Everyone understood and wholeheartedly agreed with him. "Great idea," they chimed. Before departing, there were many heartfelt hugs, kisses, and handshakes.

As Carol and Ellie were cleaning the kitchen that evening, the phone rang. Carol answered. It was John Quill. "My gosh," she exclaimed, "I was going to call you this evening, as soon as Ellie and I finished the kitchen work."

"Who is Ellie?" he asked.

"Oh, John, so much has happened within the last two days," she exclaimed. "I need to tell you all about it. Ellie is Mrs. Donavan's first name, which by the way, we are all going to use from this time on. Now, John, the big news is my wonderful dad, just yesterday, asked the nicest lady in the whole world to marry him...Ellie Donavan!"

For several seconds there was no comment from John. Then he asked, very slowly, "Carol, are you telling me that after twenty years of living in the same household, your dad and Ellie now plan to marry? Egad," he continued, "why didn't he ask her a long time ago?"

"I know, John, it is such a surprise, but I truly love the idea. They just realized their love for each other a couple of weeks ago." She continued, "They plan to marry here at Loafing Hills next month, November 5th. Believe me, John," she bubbled, "this was a wonderful surprise for me too. Honest, they are so cute together, so much in love, absolutely priceless.

"And, listen to this," she continued. "Ellie has even lost weight and now plans to lose thirty pounds more. She says that's what true love can do for you! I just love her."

"Well, I'm really glad for both of them," he answered, "and, of course, for you too, Carol. Your dad and Ellie surely know by now what they want and what is best for them. Their marriage, I believe, will be good for them both, and for you too. Please offer them my most sincere congratulations."

He continued, "Now, Carol, I know the wedding is the most important thing going on in your life right now for you and the family, but may I ask you something concerning our big date coming up in two weeks?"

"Of course, John, please do."

"Well," he answered, "I've been trying to think of something exciting and different to do. But then I thought maybe you might know of something that you really want to do, so I thought I'd better check in with you first. Now, if you don't have any ideas, I think I have a couple of cool ones," he concluded breathlessly.

"Oh, John, I would love for you to arrange our date. I promise I will be up for just about anything you can think of. Just let me know."

After hanging up the phone, Carol was upset. She realized that she had babbled on and on to John about her dad and Ellie's wedding plans and had absolutely no idea what he had said to her. Wow, She must have sounded absolutely pathetic. She felt tears come to her eyes. *I really goofed*, she thought. *I will probably never even hear from John again!*

Early the next morning Carol, astride her gelding, Blackjack, and Karen, on her favorite mare, Penny, set out on a trail ride through the wooded fields of Loafing Hills. The air was crisp and clear. The beautiful trees surrounding them held just a hint of the coming fall colors. The peace and quiet was broken only by an angry crow calling in the distance.

Both girls felt so mesmerized by nature's beauty that they whispered to each other. They did not want to break the tranquil spell of the morning. However, after an hour in the woods, life began to awaken. First, there was the fluttering of the birds and then the busy little squirrels, all adding joy to the delightful morning. Carol finally told Karen about her telephone call from John and how upset she felt with herself for being rather rude.

Karen did not agree. "Carol, I think that you are overreacting. John's a super nice guy. I'm sure he understands that you are very excited about your dad and Ellie's plans."

"I hope you're right, Karen. I just felt like such a dummy."

"You are not a dummy, Carol. You are in love!"

"Karen, I'm not in love; I'm in...like!" She giggled.

"Yeah, right," Karen laughed, as she turned her horse towards the barn, dug in her spurs, and yelled, *Carol's in love. Carol's in love.*

Carol, surprised, leaned over and whispered to Blackjack, "Okay, boy, let's go get 'em!" She turned her horse, galloped out of the woods, down through the south pasture towards the barn. Passing Karen, she stuck her tongue out at her best friend in jest. They were both giggling like kids by the time they arrived at the barn paddock.

Ned, standing at the barn door with farm workers Mike and Dan, saw the riders approaching. He had not heard Carol laugh so much since before Emerson's death. He was delighted to see both girls wearing smiles as they led their mounts into the barn for unsaddling. The horses were a little warm, so they needed walking in order to cool off before being returned to their stalls. The girls led them along, still in a merry mood, joking and laughing.

Three days later, no calls had come from John, and Carol was becoming anxious. Twice she picked up the phone to call him, and twice did not make the call.

What's the matter with me? she wondered. *I just can't call him...maybe he doesn't want to talk to me; maybe he doesn't even want to continue with our first date. And I don't blame him,* she thought.

"Good grief," she said aloud to Karen, "I'm going out to the barn to groom a horse, and I don't even care which one." She pouted.

Karen jokingly sang, "Nobody wants me, nobody loves me, going out to the garden, to eat some worms."

"Very funny, Karen," Carol answered, but she couldn't help grinning at her friend. She remembered the little song that they used to sing to each other when things hadn't gone the way they had planned. "*Nobody wants me, nobody loves me, going out the to garden, to eat some worms, great big squashy ones, little bitsy gooey ones, going out to the garden, to eat some worms.* Yikes," she concluded, "I'm hopeless!"

Entering the barn she found her dad and Mike working on one of the horses.

"Just sold her," Ned said to Carol. "She's going to Senator Myers. She'll get a good home, and his wife plans to show and hunt her."

Carol had schooled the thoroughbred mare many times and liked her very much. They called her Selina, a pretty four-year-old, mahogany-bay, sixteen hands tall. She was very quiet with excellent manners.

"Oh, I will miss you, Selina. You are a joy to work with and to ride," she spoke as she ran her hands down the mare's beautiful head and neck.

She helped her dad and Mike ready the mare for the trip to her new home in Pennsylvania. Carol placed a shipping blanket on the mare and carefully wrapped her legs to protect them from bumps and bruises. She then led Selina up the ramp into the trailer, patting her gently as she cross-tied her to the front bar. Mike, who was going to drive, brought in a net full of sweet timothy hay, hanging it up by the mare's head. He closed the ramp, climbed up into the truck, and slowly eased out of the driveway. Carol and her dad waved goodbye as he headed northwest towards Route 91 for the three-hour drive.

Carol was not ready to go back to the house so she saddled Blackjack and rode him up to the south pasture to visit Emerson. When she dismounted there, she led Blackjack to a beautiful ancient oak tree. The shade covered Emerson's burial plot. She brought with her a halter and shank to put on Blackjack so he could nibble the succulent green grass while she sat and spoke to her old friend, Emerson. It was the first time that she had come back since placing his engraved headstone. Several times she had tried to, but she couldn't. She had not been ready. She still missed the horse terribly, but knew that it was time to let go. And, she was glad to know that she was at last at peace with it in this beautiful pasture.

She sat and talked to Emerson for almost an hour. She told him about her dad and Ellie, about the farm, Karen, Mike, and Dan and, of course, about John coming back into her life.

She then arose from her shady spot, placed a kiss on Emerson's headstone, and whispered goodbye. She placed the bridle back on Blackjack, mounted, and quietly rode back to the barn. She spent the rest of the afternoon grooming the stabled horses.

CHAPTER 12

It was Friday evening, several days later, and it was Karen's 21st birthday. Ellie fixed a special dinner for Karen that evening and gave her a horse-grooming kit with her name imprinted on its side. Mike and Dan surprised her with lots of grooming tools for the kit. Karen's grandmother, who had raised her from the time she was five years old, gave her a neat suede jacket. Carol presented her with a snaffle-bit bridle with braided leather reins.

At the end of dinner, Ned stood up, walked slowly around the table, and handed Karen a piece of paper.

"What's this?" she questioned.

"Open it," he replied. "You know you are only twenty-one once." He laughed.

Karen unfolded the paper and read it. Immediate tears came to her eyes. "I can't believe this," she said softly. She stood, walked to Ned, hugged him, and whispered, "Thank you so much." She was still struggling not to break down and cry.

She turned to the family. "Did you all know about this?" she stammered.

All, in unison, nodded their heads yes. Carol reached out and placed her arms around Karen; she too was teary-eyed. The paper that Karen held was a thoroughbred registration form with the mare's name, Penny, printed on it. This was Karen's very favorite horse. The ownership had been transferred from Mr. Ned Spencer to Miss Karen Dodd.

Again Karen thanked everyone and added, "This is the best birthday ever, and I will never forget it. Nor will I ever forget this family."

Carol answered, "Karen, as far as all of us sitting here are concerned, you and your granny are part of this family."

Later Carol, talking with Karen, mentioned that she hoped it was all right with her grandmother that she had included her as one of the family!

Karen laughed. "Carol, she loved it. She enjoys living in her retirement village, but she truly cares for everyone here at Loafing Hills. She loves to visit here because, as she says, it's *always* fun. Of course, that's when I get her. I tell her it ain't all fun, Granny. Go out there and muck those stalls, groom that dirty horse, clean that tack, fix that fence. Then, come tell me how much fun you're having!" She continued, "But she knows I'm just kidding and so do you. Someone would have to shoot me to get me out of here."

"Karen, you are awful," Carol laughed.

Carol told Karen that she hadn't finished her 21st birthday celebration *yet.* "It includes a Saturday evening visit to the Corral Grill, a country bar, located a couple of miles away in town," she said. "We're gonna see some wildlife in the city. So, get all dressed up fancy tomorrow evening. We are going in," she declared.

Carol left to go help Ellie clean up after the birthday dinner. Karen offered to help too, but Carol said, "No, you're the birthday girl; you just sit and enjoy the solitude."

Karen thought about what a nice day this had been and how much she admired the Spencer family and Mike, Dan, and, of course, her super grandmother. She thought about her parents. They had divorced just a year before her mom died. She had not seen her dad in years. She didn't even remember him.

When Karen's mother had become ill, her granny (her mom's mom) had taken her in to live with her. Karen was almost six when her mom died. Her grandmother lovingly raised her. Karen was only ten when she met her best friend Carol and realized that she, like Carol, was horse crazy.

She was invited by the Spencers, with Granny's blessings, to live at Loafing Hills when she turned twelve. The Spencers helped her through school and had been like her second parents. Karen repaid them by helping on the farm.

Karen couldn't sit still any longer. She wanted to go hug her new horse, Penny. She packed up her new grooming box and carried it and her new bridle down the path to the barn. Walking through the barn to Penny's stall, she heard the mare's friendly neigh.

"Hi," she called to the chestnut horse. She thought Penny was beautiful. Of course, she was the color of a penny coin and had four white stockings. A brilliant white star sat right at the middle of her forehead. Her eyes were big, brown, and expressive. *She is a delight*, thought Karen.

Karen had ridden, schooled, and shown many of Loafing Hills' horses over the years, and she loved them all, but Penny was definitely her favorite.

"And now, she actually belongs to me," she murmured happily. She figured that Ned and Carol knew how much she cared for the mare; they had never even tried to sell her. *Gosh*, she thought, *I'll never be able to thank them enough for this gift*. It was truly a fantastic surprise.

It was feeding time for the stalled horses. Karen fed all seven horses in the barn and watched while they ate their grain. She led Penny out of the stall, cross-tied her in the barn aisle, and then spent the rest of the evening grooming and talking to her mare.

Carol awoke early Saturday morning. She planned to meet her dad and Karen at nine in the morning to school several horses. Ellie was up and helped Carol prepare a quick oatmeal and juice breakfast. She told Carol that her dad had already eaten and had gone to the barn to feed the horses. Karen came in and joined Carol for breakfast. When they finished and had cleaned up, they hurried to the barn. They heard the banging of buckets as Ned was finishing feeding.

Mike was cleaning stalls, and Dan was in the paddock loading Sport, a gelding purchased from Ned the day before. Dan planned to transport the five-year-old to the Williams' farm in Laurel, Maryland. It was always hard for Loafing Hills to say goodbye to the horses as they were sold, for each horse had received at least a year of good schooling, training, and care. However, today's goodbye was a little easier as they knew the Williams family well. They knew that Sport, a thoroughbred Quarter Horse cross with good manners, would be an outstanding mount for this buyer. They also knew that the horse would receive excellent care from them.

Carol and Karen helped by blanketing and leg wrapping, while Dan busily placed the feed bucket and hay bag in the front of the trailer. The gelding entered the trailer with no problem. The girls waved goodbye and then crossed the dusty paddock into the barn. Ned had two young horses saddled and had placed halters over the rubber-bit bridles. Both were three-year-old gelding colts, and they were just getting used to having someone crawl upon their backs. They were not too happy about it either.

Carol led the colt, Storm, to one of the Loafing Hills' schooling rings. Ned snapped the long lunge line onto Storm's halter, holding the other end just in case of a problem. He held the colt close while Carol placed her left foot in the stirrup and swung up. Even though Storm snorted and threw his head a bit, he was relatively okay. Carol had been working him for several weeks from the ground, driving him from behind. Later she added weights to the saddle. Karen joined them and walked beside Carol and the horse. She did not touch them as Carol used the reins to direct Storm.

The colt was slowly getting it. He learned that when the reins pulled the bit in his mouth, he slowed to a stop. When he felt the rider's legs pressure into his sides, he slightly picked up his pace. When one rein was pulled gently, he turned in that direction. He was learning. They didn't want to overdo, so they worked this way for only fifteen minutes. Carol dismounted and patted Storm on his neck all the way back to the barn.

Now, it was Karen's turn. With Karen mounted, they repeated the same procedure on the second colt, Corky. He, too, behaved relatively well, but only because of the past week's training, as Carol had done with Storm. It was a good morning workout for the colts. Ned, Carol, and Karen were very happy with the results.

After lunch, the girls decided to exercise two of the farm's trail horses. They walked, trotted, and cantered across two grassy pastures, and then went on through a heavily wooded area, finally ending at a bubbly creek. The day was quite warm for October, so the girls dismounted, unsaddled their mounts, and rode bareback into the creek. The horses had worked up a sweat from the afternoon exercise and thoroughly enjoyed splashing in the cool water. The girls, becoming soaked too, simply enjoyed the horses enjoying themselves.

After the horses were led out of the creek and were dried in the sun, the girls saddled up and headed home. They would help Ned feed this evening and help Ellie in the kitchen with dinner. Then they would dress and head into town to the Corral Grill, thus ending the celebration of Karen's twenty-first birthday. They both were looking forward to this adventure.

Ellie stopped the girls when they entered the house. "Carol," she called, "you have mail from John. Hope it's not bad news."

Carol opened the envelope and read the enclosed card. "This is strange," she said. "The note reads simply, 'Hi Carol, I will be phoning you next Tuesday evening with complete plans for our *big date*. Love, John.'"

"Wonder why he didn't just include the plans in the note," Karen asked. "The fifteenth is only eight days from today."

"Got me," Carol answered. "I have no idea!" she exclaimed as they ran up the stairs to get ready for the evening. "But at least he's planning to speak to me!"

"That's good news, Carol. And I'm sure whatever he's planning will be really cool. Now, let's you and me get ready for tonight," Karen called as she ran to her bedroom.

An hour later, Carol and Karen came downstairs dressed in western wear. "You ladies look great tonight," Ned said as they entered the living room. "But you forgot your cowboy hats and spurs," he jokingly added.

Not to be outdone, Ellie laughingly called to them, "If you give me a minute, I could whip up two colorful bandanas to liven up your outfits."

Both girls, rolling their eyes impatiently, yelled in unison as they ran out the door laughing. "Thanks, but no thanks, Ellie."

At nine o'clock they pulled into the Corral Grill parking lot. They could hear the country band already playing. Upon entering, they were surprised at the crowd.

"Wow," Karen exclaimed, "we gotta get away from the horse farm more often!"

They didn't want to sit at the bar and finally located an empty table close to the band. "I'm sure glad we dressed western tonight," Karen said as she looked at the other patrons. "We look pretty darned good compared to some."

Carol agreed. Most of the folks at Corral Grill were dressed in jeans, plaid shirts, and sleeveless jackets. And they, both ladies and gentlemen, were wearing boots and cowboy hats.

It wasn't long before two nice-looking guys escorted them to the dance floor. There were lots of folks there for the dancing, and they kept both girls on the floor most of the evening.

About ten o'clock a gentleman came to their table and spoke. "Karen Dodd, is that you?"

"Yes," she replied. Then looking closer she realized that it was Jim Boland. "Oh, my gosh, Jim. How are you? I haven't seen you since high school. Jim, this is my best friend, Carol Spencer. Carol meet Jim Boland. We were a steady couple in high school."

"Good to meet you, Jim," Carol replied. "Why don't you pull up a chair and join us?"

"Thank you. I have a buddy with me. Do you mind if I bring him?"

"No, of course we don't mind; bring him over," both girls agreed.

Several minutes later a good-looking man about Carol's age joined them. Jim introduced the young man. "This is my good buddy, Mark Long. Mark, I want you to meet two of the most gorgeous, and nicest, ladies that I know. My best friend Karen, from past days, and my new friend, Carol."

Mark and Jim both were good dancers, and the four danced the evening away.

The band stopped playing at twelve-thirty, and the four decided that they were hungry. They left in Jim's car and drove to an all-night diner for breakfast.

For two hours they enjoyed good food and fun conversation in the almost deserted diner. On the way back to the Corral, Mark asked Carol if she would see him the following Saturday night. Carol told him she couldn't; she already had plans. Being persistent, he asked about Sunday. She had to say no again because she was not sure about Sunday either.

"Okay, Carol," Mark tried one more time. "Well, then, how about tomorrow?"

"Well...I guess so. What do you have in mind to do?" she questioned.

"Oh, maybe a movie. The new Clint Eastwood movie?" he suggested.

"Well, I do love Eastwood. Okay," she answered, "but let's ask Karen and Jim to join us."

After being dropped off at her car, Carol talked with Karen on the way home about the next day's movie date. "I don't know, Karen, I feel guilty accepting Mark's invitation for tomorrow, knowing that John has big plans for us next week."

"Egad," Karen quipped, "you and John are good friends. You aren't married to him. Besides," she continued, "if I remember correctly, you declared that you are only *in like* with John! Remember?"

"Okay," laughed Carol. "I guess you're right. John and I may have one date, period. A movie with you, Jim, and Mark would be fun!"

Sunday morning, Ellie woke everyone up. Attending church was very important to Ellie, and she insisted that everyone in the house attend too. Carol and Karen were both dragging, but they grouchily pulled themselves together and went with Ned and Ellie. Karen fussed because Mike and Dan almost always got to stay home, using caring for the horses as their excuse. However, that did not deter Ellie. She would then make sure to play a taped sermon at the dinner table that evening, just for them. Actually, they both seemed to appreciate and enjoy it too. Karen said that was because of all the attention that they received from Ellie and Ned. The girls knew that they had several jobs to do at the barn today, so they got busy as soon as they got home and changed their clothes.

First, they helped Mike and Dan clean stalls, at the same time kidding them about the sermon they missed that morning and how, now, they would all have to sit and listen to it again tonight. The guys threw it right back at them too, saying that Carol and Karen needed the preaching more than they did. This, of course, went into all sorts of things that they accused the girls of doing. Nothing sordid, just funny things, some true, some made up, but all funny.

"Those two guys are a comedy act," Karen said.

It was 5:30 p.m. when Ellie heard the doorbell. She graciously opened the door and invited Jim and Mark in. She called upstairs to the girls. Several minutes later they came downstairs. No one was in the living room or the parlor, but they heard laughter coming from the kitchen. There in the kitchen sat Ellie, Jim, and Mark, drinking coffee and laughing. Ellie loved company and always had a joke to share.

"Hi, guys," said Carol. "I see you met Ellie, the most wonderful woman in the world." She smiled.

"Oh, I agree," Mark, said rising, "she is a treat, and she made us feel quite at home."

Jim agreed with Mark and stated, "But we'd better get moving if we plan to eat before going on to the theater."

Ellie spoke up and invited them all to stay there for dinner. "I have a big chicken roasting in the oven right now, just waiting for four hungry folks to come along."

"Ellie," Mark protested, "thank you so much, but we have dinner reservations in town at 6:30, and we don't want to be late. May we take you up on that offer at another time?" he questioned.

Ellie answered, "I'll hold you to that. Bye now, kids, have a nice evening," she added.

The movie, dinner, and conversation were entertaining and fun for all four. Carol enjoyed Mark's interest and attentiveness towards her. He was a gentleman and quite handsome too. He asked her when he might see her again. She told him that she would like to see him again also. They then agreed that he would call her in two weeks.

Later, she told Karen that she felt rather strange because she had not dated in such a long time. She'd actually forgotten how to act in mixed company, especially when no horses were involved! These past years, she had been so wrapped up with the farm and Emerson, working and showing every weekend.

"I just gotta learn how to relax," she concluded.

Karen, who found herself very attracted to her old boyfriend Jim, really understood what Carol was saying. She too had been caught up in the horse show world and felt rather out of the mainstream also.

That was when the girls made a decision. From this time forth, they declared, they were going to take Ned up on his suggestion for them to: *Get a life!*

CHAPTER 13

It was Tuesday. *Will John call?* Carol wondered. *Thank goodness,* she thought, *I will be so busy today, I won't have time to worry about it.*

Two new mares Ned had purchased during the last week would be arriving at Loafing Hills that morning. Stalls had to be readied, water and feed buckets hung, and timothy hay placed in racks. Everyone was busy cleaning stalls and feeding the kept-in horses.

About noon, they would work the two colts again. Ned would help Carol on Storm; Mike would assist Karen on Corky. Both colts were performing well, but both still needed a lot of work. Three of the pleasure horses also had to be exercised. Everyone was kept busy all day.

Ellie rang the dinner bell at six p.m. The barn work was done and so were the Loafing Hills' crew. All the inside horses, including the two new mares, were peacefully nibbling at hay.

Mike called out to Carol, "The colts have finished their grain now; let's take them out to the corral and turn 'em loose." He added, "Can't keep them young'uns up too long; they need to kick up their heels."

The barn was so clean it sparkled, and all the riding equipment had been put away in the tack room. It was time to quit for the night. The crew walked wearily to the house.

As soon as they arrived in the kitchen, Ellie informed Carol that John had called. "I told him that I'd transfer the call to the barn, but I was sure you were out riding. He said he would call back and asked when would be a good time. I told him after supper, around seven."

"Thanks so much, Ellie," replied Carol. "Sorry I'm causing you so much trouble. I promise I will be right here until bedtime."

Ellie answered, "Don't be silly, Carol; I'd rather be here answering the phone than working in that barn all day. You guys look totally exhausted. But, I bet you'll feel better after supper. Come on now, sit down and eat," she directed.

The phone rang ten minutes after seven. Carol took the call. It was John; she was glad to hear his voice. They spoke together for twenty minutes, mostly about what was happening at Loafing Hills and at John's place, which he now called New Start. All he would say about their coming date, October 15th, was that he would be at Loafing Hills to pick her up at ten o'clock in the morning. The rest would be a surprise.

"John," she chided, "you have to tell me more. What kind of a surprise?"

"Well, now," he answered, "seems to me I remember someone, named Carol, saying that she would be up for anything! Sound familiar to you?"

"Okay," she said remembering those words she had said to him and also the promise she had made to herself to "Get a Life." She answered with, "Yep, John, you're right...I'm up for anything you plan."

"You won't be disappointed, Carol. I promise."

After hanging up the phone, she noticed that she was being scrutinized by her family. "What?" she asked.

"Oh, nothing," her dad answered and sheepishly walked away.

"Ellie, what's going on?"

"Oh, we just are glad that everything is working out for you and John," she answered as she too left the room.

In fact, Carol noticed, the whole family seemed to have disappeared from the room, like a puff of smoke.

Tuesday, Jim came to Loafing Hills and helped Karen prepare a dinner for the family. Karen had found an old recipe of her granny's, which she wanted to surprise the family with. It was an old-fashioned meat-and-potatoes concoction her granny used to make for her. It wasn't difficult to prepare, and she loved it. Jim chopped up the salad fixings. Karen set the table. They insisted that Ellie, who always did the cooking, retire to the parlor and sit back and relax until dinner. Ellie enjoyed being sent away, but not knowing what those three were doing worried her a bit.

At six o'clock, Carol went to the back porch and rang the dinner bell. She knew that her dad and Mike had gone out to work on the farm's tractor. She hoped that they were at a good stopping point. She saw Dan come out of the barn and head up the hill to the house.

Dinner was a success. Delicious, everyone agreed. Carol opted to clean the kitchen. It was a very nice evening spent with the family. Karen and Jim left to go bowling. Carol was asked to join them, but declined. She had worked four horses earlier in the day and just wanted to shower and climb into bed.

Responses for Ellie and Ned's wedding set for November 5, two o'clock, were already coming in. Attending would be their Loafing Hills family, Granny, and a few other close neighbors. They had heard from Ned's parents in Delabay, England. His father was planning to attend, but his mom had been sick with a horrible cold; she wasn't sure she could make the trip. Ellie's sister, in San Diego, California, accepted her invitation and would be arriving on the fourth of November, one day before the wedding. The only others asked were Carol and Karen's friends, Jim Boland, Mark Long, and John Quill.

The rest of the week passed along smoothly enough. Every day Carol and Karen spent time training the two colts and schooling the kept-in pleasure and trail horses.

In the morning, after graining, they would turn the two new mares out to pasture and return them to their stalls in the evening. This practice would continue until early spring when both mares would be bred to Loafing Hills' thoroughbred stallion, Sky Cloud. Then they would be moved to the broodmare barn.

During the last few days, Carol and Karen had talked a lot about Mark and Jim. Mark owned his own construction business. Jim was employed as an athletic director at the same high school that Carol, Karen, and Jim had graduated from. Both guys had graduated from Virginia University. Carol and Karen had worked their way through a small Maryland state college just ten minutes from Loafing Hills. The close location had allowed them to live at home and work on the farm.

On Friday, Karen planned to leave the farm in the early evening. She, Carol, and Mark had been invited by Jim and his family to their home in Frederick, Maryland, for a Friday night dinner. Carol politely bowed out, feeling that she needed preparation time to prepare for Saturday morning's date.

Before leaving, Karen gave her friend a big hug at the front door. "Sure hope you enjoy your big date with John tomorrow, Carol. I'll keep my fingers crossed for you for a day full of fun surprises."

Carol responded quietly with, "Thanks, Karen. Enjoy your evening, and please tell Mark I'm looking forward to hearing from him next week."

"He'll be happy to hear that," Karen answered.

Well, here it is, thought Carol, *Saturday morning. John will be here in two hours.* She hurried to shower. Not knowing what they were going to do or where they were going, she laid out an all-occasion, Sag Harbor pantsuit. It was comfortable, looked nice, and its blue color matched her eyes.

After dressing, she went downstairs to the kitchen. Ellie and her dad were at the table eating breakfast. Both gave their hearty approval of her clothing choice, saying she really looked like a beautiful cover-page model.

Carol waited nervously in the parlor, gazing out the window onto the driveway. *Why am I so apprehensive and jumpy?* she asked herself. *It's just a date.* But her stomach was not listening to her. A car came up the drive to the house. *Well, I don't think it's John*, she said to herself; *he drives a silver Buick. That's a Taurus.*

But it was John. He stepped from the car and proceeded to the kitchen door. She heard Ellie and Ned greet him. The three talked quietly. Carol was so nervous she didn't go to the kitchen for several minutes. Looking in the mirror she whispered, "For goodness sakes, girl...get a grip!"

She walked very nonchalantly down the hall, planning to make a grand entrance. Instead, she stubbed her toe, lost her balance, and dived into the room like superman, landing right on John's shoes. John quickly knelt down to help her up. Carol was really embarrassed. However, when she looked up at the three faces staring at her in total disbelief, she lost it and burst out laughing.

"Oh, John," she choked out, "I was trying my best to impress you. I sure did it, didn't I?" Now, seeing that she wasn't hurt, they all laughed with her. "I bet I've come down that hall a million times and never ever stumbled before," she exclaimed. Still laughing, she said, "Must be all your fault, John."

"I take all blame," he laughed. "But, I'm sure glad you're not hurt." Finally standing, she realized that she had torn the elbow on one of her sleeves.

"Well," she declared, "now I have to change clothes. Please excuse me." Still laughing at herself, she left them and ran upstairs.

Carol returned fifteen minutes later wearing a pair of black jeans and a coral sweater. She still looked beautiful, thought her family and John. She said to herself, *I am such a klutz, but yet I'm feeling better now. I'm actually over that terrible giddy feeling I had before literally falling for John!*

Upon leaving, the two waved goodbye to Ned and Ellie.

"John, you sold your Buick?" Carol asked.

"No, this is a rental," he answered. He quickly changed the subject by asking about the new colts that she and Karen were working with.

"Oh, they're coming along great. We love working with them," she replied. Then she told him about selling Sport, a favorite gelding, and Selina, a neat mare, going off to Pennsylvania with Senator Myers.

The casual conversation continued, both feeling very comfortable with each other.

They left the highway and pulled off onto Belby Road, about ten miles from Loafing Hills. "John," Carol asked, "do you know where you're going? This road only leads to a small family-operated airport."

"Are you into flying?" he asked her.

"Yes, I love to fly. Dad, Karen, and I do a lot of it during show season. Mike or Dan take the horses in the van."

"Well, I'm glad to hear that. First surprise, Carol," he continued, "I don't think I ever told you that I'm licensed and have been flying for about ten years."

"Do I dare ask where we are flying to?"

"Our first stop will be at New Start so you can see my beautiful cattle," he joked.

They arrived at the small airpark and walked to a handsome four-seat Piper twin Comanche. "Is this yours?" Carol asked.

"Yes, I love to fly, but I really need it for the ranch."

After turning in his rental car and filing a flight plan, they climbed aboard the Comanche. John very carefully checked out all of the instruments before taking off.

An hour later after a smooth flight, they landed on the airstrip at New Start Ranch. Carol turned to John. "Hey, mister, how impressive is this?" she smiled. "What a pastoral sight."

They taxied up to a small hanger and stopped. John ran around to help Carol down from the plane. Jokingly, he asked her not to jump on him! She answered, "Ha! Ha!" Then they both laughed as he placed her gently on the ground. John's Buick was parked beside the hanger. They drove up the lane to a beautiful log cabin house.

"My gosh, John, this is charming," she exclaimed.

Inside, she was introduced to Dora, John's housekeeper. Dora, in her late sixties, had been with John and his late wife for years. She and Carol hit it off immediately.

She took Carol by the hand and led her through the rooms. The house was truly a masterpiece. There was a large living area with two stone fireplaces and a cozy family room with a large built-in television. The bay window in John's office faced the front of the house and offered a scenic view of the ranch. On the far side was an immaculate kitchen opening into a sunroom, stretching across the whole back of the house. There were two large baths, one on each side of the living area. Dora, not letting go of Carol's hand, led her up the stairs.

John called to her, "Carol, watch out now, Dora will never let go of you."

Dora hollered back, "John, behave yourself!"

"Come on, Carol," she continued, "I am so proud of what John has done here that I just have to show it off."

Carol was amazed; the upstairs was even lovelier than downstairs: four large bedrooms and two full baths. Carol, noticing French doors at the back of the house, left Dora's side and proceeded outside to the railing. She saw that every bedroom had access to this veranda.

Wow, what a sight, she thought.

Below her was a magnificently landscaped backyard. Farther out, she could see giant oak and hickory trees totally surrounding lush pasturelands. There in the tall green grass was a herd of Angus cattle, peacefully grazing under the warm October sun.

Upon returning downstairs, Carol excitedly whispered to John, "This place is exquisite, John. Dora showed me pictures of the house when you first bought it. You have totally redone it. It is really gorgeous."

"Thank you, Carol. I'm so happy you like it. Now you know the main reason I needed those thirty days. I wanted it finished before I brought you here. Another surprise for you!" he added.

Dora, coming into the room said to Carol, "I can tell you, John and his crew worked long and hard on this project. I'm so proud of him."

Carol answered, "After viewing the old pictures of this place, I'm positive that everyone, including you, Dora, put lots of effort into this. Everyone should not only be satisfied, but genuinely proud."

John agreed. "Without Dora, it would not have gotten finished."

Dora smiled at John's remark, but Carol could see that she was proud of her accomplishments too.

"Okay," John said, "I have to be excused for a business telephone call that I must make, but I'll be back with you shortly. Carol, I know that Dora has prepared a lunch for us. We'd best eat before heading out to check the livestock."

John went off to his office, and Carol and Dora walked into the beautiful kitchen. While Dora was setting out the lunch, Carol, interested in Dora's employment with John, asked her about it.

Dora, who loved to talk, told Carol a story that started many years ago. John had hired her and her husband, George Hill, to work in their home. George did landscaping and odd jobs until his death, just a year earlier. Dora took care of the house and John's wife, Pat, who was sick for three years with a terminal illness. When Pat passed away eight years ago, it was a very sad time. A few years later John lost contact with her parents when they moved to the west coast.

John did visit his mother, Lilly, frequently. She had since remarried and was living in Washington, DC.

"Oh," Carol interrupted Dora's story, "I remember he told me a long time ago that he had relatives in DC."

"Yes," continued Dora, "his mom and her husband, Clark Sanders. John even invited them to come live at New Start. They are both wonderful people, but much too citified for ranch living." She laughed. "Even though the Quills are a wealthy family, due to early years of profitable stocks and investments, they never put on airs."

Carol listened to the interesting story that Dora was telling and agreed with her. John, even though living favorably, did not flaunt his wealth. She told Dora about John staying with them and helping at the farm. "He never, even once, suggested that wealth was a part of his family," Carol said.

"I'll share with you one more fact before John gets here," Dora whispered. "You are the first lady that he has shown any real interest in eight years!" She smiled.

John appeared in the doorway. "Sorry about the phone call, but it was important. I'll tell you about it later, Carol; it has to do with your next surprise!" he concluded with a mischievous wink.

The three ate a delicious lunch. Carol listened attentively to John and Dora tell amusing stories about the rebuilding of New Start. It was interesting and fun.

At the conclusion of the lunch, Carol and John left the house and walked a short distance to a very old, updated red barn. The inside was immaculate. Carol, thinking she was going to find cattle within, was startled to see instead, two horses standing in the aisle. A ranch worker was busy tacking them for John and her.

John, seeing Carol's questioning look, told her, "We have a couple of horses here on the ranch to help us keep check on the grazing cattle."

"Good idea," Carol answered. "They look like Quarter Horses."

"Yes, one is; the other is a Morgan. I'm sure you've noticed they're both wearing western saddles. I know that's not your style, but both horses have beautiful gaits; no posting needed with these guys."

"That's fine with me. I love western riding, especially for pleasure," she answered.

They headed out to the south pasture, soon locating a herd of cattle. They circled around them, making sure all was well. Then, they continued to the northwestern pastures to check the largest herd. When they arrived and located the cattle, they spotted a steer lying down, seeming unable to get up. John dismounted and discovered the steer had badly injured his right foreleg. Using his cell phone, he called for help from the barn, and then called his veterinarian. A ranch hand brought a low-bed trailer to the pasture. He brought help with him to load the steer. The veterinarian would meet them back at the barn.

After loading the steer, John turned to Carol. "See, Carol, all in a day's work on the ranch," he grinned.

They rode the horses back to the barn behind the horse trailer. Checking the cattle had taken up most of the afternoon.

Dr. Lawrence, the veterinarian, sewed up a nasty gash in the steer's leg and wrapped him. "He must be kept quiet in a stall for at least two weeks," he told John.

Later back at the house John took Carol's hand, saying, "This evening I would like to take you to Meadows, South Carolina, to a restaurant called Garrison's. Earl Garrison is an old college buddy of mine, and he is also the one who helped me greatly after my wife died to sell off my farm animals, including Emerson, and the farm. He stayed by my side, seeing me through a very difficult time in my life. I'll never forget what he did for me, and I want you to meet him."

John continued, "The food at his restaurant is excellent, and the decor is strictly geared to equestrians. He is a horse lover and owns four Lipizzaner horses. After dinner you, Earl, and myself will attend a horse show at nine o'clock at the horse arena in Meadows. Earl's trainer and rider will open the show exhibiting the Lipizzaners. Are you game for all this, Carol?"

"Are you kidding me?" she responded happily. "I love the Lipizzaner horses. I've seen lots of videos and movies about them, but I've never been fortunate enough to see them perform live!"

"Well, then, you will tonight, and I know you will enjoy the unusual restaurant and the fantastic show," he said.

Carol suddenly realized that meant they would be flying home around midnight. She wasn't sure how she felt about that. She asked him, "John, I do like to fly, but isn't that going to be a bit difficult to be flying home so late?"

Carol immediately noticed a funny look on John's face. "What's the matter?" she cried.

"Well, I guess I'd better tell you the next surprise," he uttered. "This is something that I cooked up with your dad and Ellie. I was afraid that you might misunderstand my intentions if I asked you to stay the night, so I talked it over with your family. Ellie packed an overnight bag for you and gave it to me while you were upstairs changing your clothes this morning. Your dad was going to ask you to run to the barn for something to give us time to organize it, but, as you know, it wasn't necessary."

"My dad said it was okay, without even asking me first?" Carol questioned.

"Yes, only because he spoke with Dora several times and felt comfortable about it. I hope you're not upset or mad at me or your dad,

Carol. I know I planned too much to do in one day. Dora promised your dad that we would take good care of you," he concluded, "and we would get you back tomorrow. Promise!"

Carol was still not sure how she felt about this surprise. It was okay, but she felt a little hurt that she had not been asked or told. But, looking at John's face now, she didn't want to hurt his feelings. He'd done so much planning for this date.

She went to him and hugged him. "Of course, it's okay, John. I trust you completely. I was just a little surprised and a bit confused!"

"I am really glad you aren't upset with me," he replied. "I've been worrying all day about how you would react when I asked you to spend the night at New Start." His smile was charming.

Carol responded, "At least now I know why my family was acting so weird this past week. Secret plans," she laughed.

John picked up Carol's overnight bag and carried it up to the guestroom. When he returned, they all three had a good laugh at John's covert plans.

John and Carol left New Start at 4:30 in the afternoon. The drive would take an hour and a half to reach Garrison's Restaurant in South Carolina. Upon arriving there, Carol was awed by Garrison's decor. There were many terrific horse pictures and statues everywhere.

She was introduced to Earl Garrison and liked him immediately. He joined John and Carol for dinner. The meal was a real treat: southern grilled T-bone steaks smothered in onion gravy, a potato dish called Potato/Bacon Go Down, and tasty southern-style string beans. A fresh salad accompanied the delicious meal. Carol declined the dessert only because she was completely full.

John and Earl, however, said, "Bring it on." They both enjoyed a huge piece of freshly baked pumpkin pie adorned with whipped cream.

"Wow," John said. "Can't do this kinda meal too often, one would surely explode!" He laughed.

A little before nine, the three left the restaurant and walked just two blocks to the horse arena. They all three joked about feeling the need for the exercise. In the arena they were taken to a center box seat protruding into the show area. A friend of Earl's brought them coffee and creamer on a tray.

Carol exclaimed, "This is great...I feel like a celebrity!"

At nine o'clock, the lights dimmed and the entrance doors opened. Into the arena stepped four gorgeous Lipizzaner horses, each with a rider sitting straight and tall in the saddle. The first rider, Earl's horse trainer, Clayton Horner, led them majestically into the center of the arena to begin the quadrille. There was a noticeable hush from the surrounding audience as the white stallions, with necks arched, seemed to glide forward without a trace of command from their rider, making the men and their mounts appear as one.

Watching them, thought Carol, *is like seeing a dream*. The horses, when trotting, seemed to be suspended in air. Their high knee action and the stately carriage of the horses' heads offered an exciting aesthetic picture. The horses then halted with no visible cue from the riders.

The next movement was performing the parade paces of piaff. This was sophisticated walking and trotting on the spot. The passage gave the impression of being suspended in air.

Then came the classical movements called "airs above the ground": the *levade*, *courbette*, and the *capriole*. In the *levade* the horse stood up on his hind legs balancing on bent hocks. He then leaped forward maintaining a horizontal position in the air, called the *corbette*. At the same second, he kicked out his back legs while still maintaining the horizontal position. All four feet were off the ground at the same time. This soaring movement was called the *capriole*.

Carol nudged John, and with tears in her eyes, told him that she had never in her life seen a performance more artistically done. She felt that these four white Lipizzaner stallions were not only magnificently trained, but truly tops in the equine world.

At the close of the Lipizzaners' performance, the mesmerized crowd immediately broke out in a hearty cheer. They all seemed to be as affected by the wondrous performance as was Carol.

Carol, John, and Earl stayed for the next exhibit, which was a first year over fences, hunter class. When the class was finished, Earl said to

Carol and John, "Would you two like to take a short break to go to the stabling area, meet Clayton, the riders, and the horses?"

Without a moment's hesitation, they eagerly agreed.

The stabling area was connected to the show-room building; it took several minutes to arrive. Proceeding down the barn aisle, Carol and John were absolutely in awe of these beautiful animals. They got to pet and whisper to each one, congratulating them on their wonderful performance. Carol and John both knew that the horses could not have cared less, but it was pleasing for them to tell them that anyway.

Even though the riders were busy packing and assembling equipment, Earl introduced Carol and John to Clayton and the other three riders. They stopped what they were doing and spoke with Earl and his guests for several minutes. All were, of course, happy to hear the high praise coming from Earl and his guests. Clayton and the other three riders thanked them profusely.

Earl asked John and Carol to join him back at the arena to enjoy the rest of the events. The three walked back to the show area. It was a good exhibition, performed by many talented horses and riders. Many equestrians happily came away with distinguished ribbons and trophies.

After thanking Earl for a delicious dinner and a most delightful evening, they started back to New Start shortly after midnight. They arrived at two o'clock in the morning. Both were exhausted. They had put in a long, full, but very exciting day.

John escorted Carol to the guest bedroom. At the door he spoke softly, "Carol, I hope you sleep comfortably and I'll see you tomorrow. Before we fly you home tomorrow, though," he continued, "I'd very much like to take you on a cruise down the Neuse River. Does that sound okay to you?"

"Yes, that sounds like fun, John, thank you. I'd love to."

John gently took her in his arms, kissed her on her forehead, and whispered, "I guess by now, Carol, you've figured out that I care for you very much."

"Yes, John, I have feelings for you too. It's been marvelous being here with you. This Big Date that you have planned has been absolutely flawless. And you, John, are by every score, a perfect gentleman."

She looked up into his eyes; their lips met as if magnetic. It was a surprise, but also very nice. "Goodnight," she said softly.

"Goodnight, Carol," he answered as he let her hand slip from his.

She went into the bedroom, changed into her nightgown, and climbed into bed. She was asleep almost immediately.

John went downstairs and ran into Dora in the kitchen. "Dora, what in the world are you doing up at this time of the morning?" he asked.

"Well, John, you know you are like a son to me, and I really want to hear how the evening went."

John related the story of the evening. Dora looked pleased and happy. "Now go to bed, Dora, it is very late," he ordered. "You need your sleep."

With a smile on her face, Dora answered, "You also had better get to bed, and I'll see you in a couple of hours for breakfast.

"And, John," she continued, as she walked from the room, "you and Carol are so much alike. I love her...and I know in my heart, you feel the same!" she winked at him as she closed her bedroom door.

A funny noise woke Carol. *What's that scratching sound,* she sleepily wondered. She got up, put on her robe, and cracked the door. It was Piggy, John's little Pekinese dog, and he wanted to come in. "Well, come on in, Piggy," Carol called to the little guy. He followed her back to the bed where she picked him up and scratched his head. "Are you up early this morning or am I up late?" she questioned as she looked around the room for a clock.

"Good heavens," she said as she saw the clock on the bureau. "It's eleven o'clock. Piggy, you better go downstairs now, 'cause I gotta get going." She put him outside the door, much to his disappointment. Carol jumped in and out of the shower and threw on her clothes, taking exactly fifteen minutes. She listened for voices as she descended the stairs, but heard none. The house was quiet except for little Piggy who was dancing around, thrilled to see her again. "Come on," she said to him and picked him up. They moseyed into the empty kitchen and found coffee brewing. She helped herself to a cup and took it to the window. Dora was outside watering the flowerbed.

Carol, carrying Piggy and her coffee, walked out to join her.

"Good morning," Dora called.

"Good morning to you too," Carol answered. "I'm embarrassed." She continued, "I can't believe I slept 'til eleven o'clock. It's now almost noon."

"Well, honey, don't feel embarrassed. You got in late and evidently you needed sleep this morning." She and Dora walked back into the house. "I planned to wake you at noon. John just left a few minutes ago with Dr. Lawrence to look at the injured steer. He asked me to check with you about leaving in about an hour for the trip to the Neuse River and to advise you to dress comfortably."

Carol was dressed and ready when John came in from the barn. It was almost one-thirty.

"Give me ten minutes," he called to her. "A quick shower, clean duds, and I'll be ready."

Wonderful Dora had packed them a chicken lunch to eat on the way to the river. The pungent aroma filled the house.

"Why don't you come boating with us today?" John and Carol asked Dora.

"Oh, thank you for asking, and I love boating. But I've got some baking to do for the church social this evening. You two run along and have fun. I promise I'll go next time." She smiled.

John and Carol drove out the lane, but didn't get far. They were both hungry and the scent of the chicken was just too much. John pulled to the side of the drive and parked. Hand in hand they walked to a spot under a tall dogwood tree. Carol handed him the cloth that Dora had included in the basket. Finding a pleasant spot under a tall tree, he spread the cloth over the soft grass. Sitting side by side, they laughingly blamed Dora for the unscheduled chicken stop. The chicken aroma was just too enticing. They couldn't wait any longer.

When they finally had enough, they again started out for the Neuse River.

Finally arriving, they were both thrilled to see the boat still tied to the dock. Carol was pleasantly surprised to see the craft that they were going out on. It was a vintage paddleboat named Lady Luck. The crew was ready to go, and there were several other couples already aboard. Everyone was in good spirits; the weather was beautiful with just a soft gentle breeze blowing through the colorful fall leaves bordering the banks of the river.

The boat's paddle gently probing the water allowed serenity to settle in for everyone. The magnificent homes along the shoreline, the birds, the ducks, and the geese all added a peaceful flavor to the excursion.

Carol felt as though she had known John forever. They comfortably talked with each other like old friends, making the trip down the Neuse a most enjoyable adventure.

After saying goodbye to their newfound friends on the paddleboat, John and Carol began the short drive back to New Start. Within a few minutes, John received a call on his cell phone. It was Dora. She told John that she had tried to call him several times, but they must have been out of phone range because she couldn't get through. "I'm at the church," she continued, "preparing for our bake sale. I checked the home phone for messages earlier today. There was a message from Mr. Spencer. He asked that Carol call him at Loafing Hills, as soon as possible. That's all he said, John. I don't know any more than that. I'm still at church, but if you need me, please call. I can be home in ten minutes."

Alarmed, John handed Carol his phone. She attempted to call Loafing Hills, but the connection was so bad she couldn't even hear if the phone was ringing.

"We'll be home in a few minutes, Carol," John said quietly, "you can call him from there."

CHAPTER 14

Upon arriving at New Start, Carol raced to the phone. "I'm afraid something's happened at Loafing Hills, John," she whispered. "I hope it's not bad news."

Ellie answered the phone. "Ellie, it's Carol. Dad left a message for me to call him. What's going on?"

"Oh, Carol, I'm so glad it's you. Karen took a real bad fall off her mare, Penny. She left to go riding about six this morning. An hour later, Penny came galloping wildly into the barn lot without Karen. Mike caught the mare, placed her in a stall to check her over, and Ned and Dan jumped in the jeep to look for Karen. They found her lying on a pile of rocks in the woods. She was unconscious. She's in the hospital, still unconscious. We don't know, Carol, how bad it is. Your dad and Granny are at the hospital with her. I'm waiting for their call." Ellie's voice cracked.

"Oh, no," Carol exclaimed. "Ellie, I'm coming home as soon as I can get there." She hung up the phone. John heard most of what was said.

"Carol, go get your clothes together," he directed. "I'll leave Dora a note and meet you at the car in five minutes." John hastily wrote Dora a note and pinned it on the bulletin board in the kitchen. He quickly let Piggy out and secured his flight bag. Carol ran upstairs and literally threw her clothes into the overnight case and ran back to the kitchen. They let Piggy in and then jumped into the car. John drove them quickly across the field to the plane hanger. He made a quick call to reserve a rental car for their arrival in Maryland.

The hour flight back to Loafing Hills was uneventful. The weather was good, and the billowing clouds rode high above them. To Carol, it seemed much longer than one hour. She was terribly worried about her best friend, Karen.

They landed at the airport, picked up the rental car, and called Ellie. She had not yet heard from Ned since earlier in the day when he had told her that Karen was still unconscious and in intensive care. Ellie sounded quite upset.

John suggested to Carol that they go first to Loafing Hills instead of directly to the hospital; that way they could take Ellie with them.

Just a few minutes after arriving at the farm, the phone rang. Carol picked it up, hoping that it was her dad. It was Mark Long.

"Hi, Carol, I'm so glad you're home," Mark spoke quickly. "I know you just got back from a trip, and I want to hear all about it, but first you and I gotta get to the hospital. Jim just called me...He, Granny, and Ned are at the hospital. Jim sounded terrible. They have no updated news on Karen, and they're all worried. How about if I pick you up in about twenty minutes?" he ended breathlessly.

"Thank you for the offer, Mark," she answered, "but I have a ride. We're leaving right now, and Ellie's going to meet us there."

Once in the car and on their way, Ellie's cell phone rang. It was Ned.

"I'm sorry that I haven't gotten back to you sooner, Ellie," Ned said, "but the cell phone didn't work in the hospital, and I've been with Karen in intensive care most of the day. I'm standing outside the hospital calling you."

"Ned," Ellie answered, "John, Carol, and I are on our way to the hospital now. We'll be there in about twenty minutes."

"I'll meet you in the emergency lobby," Ned said before hanging up.

John pulled into the emergency entrance driveway, stopped, and let Carol and Ellie out. Carol told him they would wait for him in the lobby. He left the emergency area to locate a parking space in the garage.

Carol and Ellie walked through the entrance door to the hospital. Carol spotted her dad immediately. "Dad," she called, "have you any news?"

"No," he answered as he walked to meet them. "But let's go to intensive care to see if we can talk with her doctor."

"Yes, Dad, but we need to wait for John. He's parking the car."

At that moment Mark came rushing though the door, almost knocking into them. He took Carol's hand. "Hi, glad you are here," he spoke to all. "I'm really worried about Karen and Jim. Have you heard anything?" he asked.

"No, not yet. We're waiting for John to join us before going up," Ned answered.

"John?" Mark questioned. "Who's he?"

Now it was Carol's turn to answer. "John is a very dear friend of mine, Mark. I spent this past weekend with him on his ranch in North Carolina. He's also a good friend of Karen's and my family's."

"Oh, Carol," Mark said as he gently dropped her hand, "I knew that you were away on a trip this past weekend. I don't know the details, but I sincerely hope you enjoyed yourself. And I'm so sorry that the weekend ended with Karen getting hurt."

John came into the lobby and walked to the group. A few seconds of uncomfortable silence prevailed before Carol introduced John to Mark. John shook hands with Mark and Ned. He asked about Karen's injuries.

"Okay," Ned responded, "let's go see what we can find out."

They left the elevator on the second floor and followed the hall to the intensive care unit. There they met Granny sitting with Jim in the ICU waiting room. She told them that Karen had just returned to the ICU from radiology. "She's still unconscious," she cried.

Carol walked over and hugged her. "She's going to be okay, Granny," she whispered.

Ned walked to the nurse's station and asked the nurse if she had any news regarding Karen. The nurse shook her head no and replied that Doctor White was awaiting test results from radiology. She suggested that the family wait in the ICU lobby while she attempted to reach the doctor in hopes of obtaining additional information for them.

Ned returned to the lobby and sat with his friends and family. Everyone was worried and quiet except Granny. Carol tried her best to console her, but Granny had been there all day. She was upset, hungry, and very tired. Ned and Carol decided to take her downstairs to the cafeteria, where she had some juice and a muffin. Meanwhile upstairs, Ellie asked the nurse if there was a place where Granny might lie down and rest.

When the three returned, the nurse escorted Granny to a small room off the ICU ward. It had a cot where she could lie down and rest a while. She gave her a mild tranquilizer and made her comfortable. Granny, of course, did not want to do this. She was afraid that she would not hear how Karen was doing. The nurse assured her that she would wake her the minute that they received any information. Granny was asleep before the nurse left the room.

All six, Ned, Ellie, Carol, John, Mark, and Jim gathered quietly in the ICU lobby to await information about Karen. Several minutes later the elevator door opened. Doctor White stepped out, chart in hand, and approached them. He apologized for taking so long getting back to them, but explained that he had just received the results from the MRI. He sat with the group while carefully examining the results.

"First, let me tell you that Karen is still unconscious. She has a fractured left scapula (shoulder), three fractured ribs, and her left arm is fractured in two places. Of course, I'm not happy with these injuries," he continued, "but, her being unconscious worries me the most. The MRI, which is Magnetic Resonance Imaging, tells us that there is blood on the left side at the back of the brain. Karen is receiving a medication called Dilatin, which will help to prevent seizures. We are hoping that the blood will dissolve by itself. We must wait and see. If it doesn't, it will be necessary to go into the skull to take care of it."

No one spoke for a moment, and then all six began asking questions at once. Before the doctor could answer, there came a noise from the hall. It was Granny running towards them. "Come quick," she shouted. "Karen is waking up."

Doctor White was the first to reach Granny. "I woke up and decided to go into the ICU and look at Karen," Granny cried. "I took her hand and was rubbing it. Karen's eyes opened up, and she looked right at me. She asked me what I was doing here. I was so surprised, I didn't answer her. I just backed out of the room. Please come quickly, Doctor."

Ned was the only one allowed to go into the room with the doctor. Doctor White asked the rest to please wait until he could look at her first.

They obeyed the doctor's orders and returned to the lobby. Granny asked for the group to please hold hands while she recited a short prayer for Karen. They did this and at its conclusion, all in unison, uttered a quiet and thankful, "Amen."

A short time later, Ned returned to the lobby and told them that they could go in, two at a time, and only for a couple of minutes. Carol and Granny went first. Carol was scared. Karen looked so fragile lying there, hooked up to so many strange looking IV fluids and monitors. She looked so alone and helpless.

Karen opened her eyes, focused on Carol, and tried to smile. Carol felt better immediately. "Hi, Karen," she whispered cheerfully. "Granny and I are only going to stay a minute because Jim, Mark, John, and Ellie want to see you too. We are all so glad that you're awake."

Granny leaned and kissed Karen on her forehead. She felt tears come to her eyes, so she quickly told Karen, "I'm going now that I know you're okay. I love you, honey, and I'll see you tomorrow."

Carol knew that she too was close to tears, so she held her hand up in a gesture of goodbye. Karen could not lift her arm because of her IV, but she did manage to circle her fingers, giving Carol the sign of "I'm okay."

Mark and Jim went in and stayed for just a minute. Ned and Ellie wished her a restful night.

Later, all agreed that Karen had looked into their faces and definitely recognized each one, but she was so tired, she was having a hard time keeping her eyes open.

The doctor talked to them when they came back to the lobby. "What Karen needs now is lots of rest," he began, "and I strongly suggest that the family go home now and get some rest too." He concluded by promising to call them early the next morning at Ned's house.

Jim invited Mark to spend the night at his house, which was a few miles closer to the hospital. They bid the group goodnight and started home. Ned promised to call them here as soon as he heard from the doctor.

Ned took Granny and Ellie back to the farm in his car. Carol and John followed.

Once home, they sat at the kitchen table and relaxed with a soothing cup of hot chocolate.

It wasn't long before Ellie and Granny, both tired, took the bedroom with twin beds. John retired to the bedroom that he had stayed in when there a month earlier. He gave Carol a hug and a light kiss before going upstairs.

Ned left a message on the barn phone for Mike and Dan to let them know what had transpired at the hospital. Carol helped her dad lock up the house. They walked up the stairs together, whispering their happiness regarding Karen. They both felt that she would be fine after a good night's rest.

Ned and Ellie were up and preparing breakfast when they received the awaited call from Dr. White. He assured them that Karen was awake and was resting comfortably. He informed them that she was in Intensive Care and would be there for several more days.

"If you would like to see her," he added, "please plan to arrive during the afternoon visiting hours."

Ned called Jim and Mark with this information. The others he let sleep because they couldn't do anything until later in the day anyway.

Mark phoned Carol at noon to tell her that he and Jim were at the hospital, and they did get in to see Karen, but she was sleeping peacefully. Dr. White suggested that the family should give her a couple more days of rest before visiting again.

Ned and Ellie, with Granny's assistance, used this down time to finalize Ned and Ellie's wedding plans, which was now only three weeks away.

John called Dora to tell her about Karen. She was saddened by the accident, but was glad to hear that Karen was now conscious and hopefully on the road to recovery. She told John that his veterinarian, Dr. Lawrence, was coming out the next day to look at the injured steer and was hoping that while he was at the barn, he could administer necessary immunizations to the cattle. John knew that the ranch guys could handle bringing the cattle in and assisting the veterinarian, but he felt that he should be there too. He told Carol that he felt that he had to fly back that afternoon to assist the veterinarian the next day. He took Carol into town for lunch before flying back to his ranch. While eating, John asked Carol to please keep him updated on Karen. And, if he was needed, he could be back in a couple of hours.

Before rising from the restaurant booth, John took Carol's hands in his and whispered, "Carol, do you know how much you mean to me?" His eyes sparkled as he spoke, "I'm falling hard for you, lady."

Carol whispered back, "John, I'm happy to hear you say that. And I'm really surprised that you can't hear my heart beating all the way across this table." They both laughingly agreed that they must surely be falling in love.

CHAPTER 15

Ned and the family obeyed the doctor's suggestion to allow a few days to go by before visiting Karen again. Dr. Lawrence contacted them regarding her progress. Jim, however, did not wait. He was there with Karen. He also stayed in contact with Mike. And Mike called Carol every evening with the latest news. Most of the time Karen slept, according to Jim, but he was with her during her wakeful periods. On the third day Mike called Carol and told her that Jim had mentioned that morning that Karen was finally remembering the accident. It slowly started coming back to her. She said her mare was feeling fine when they had gone out riding that Monday morning. They enjoyed a wonderful trot and canter through the woods. They started back towards the barn and were going under a hanging tree branch when they must have disturbed a hornets' nest hanging low in the tree, because all of a sudden hornets were swarming all around them. Everything happened so quickly, she said. She remembered putting her heels into Penny's sides, urging her to get away. That was when Penny must have gotten stung. She started throwing her head around like crazy and biting at her neck and chest. The bit, which was a full cheek snaffle, became entangled in the martingale. This caused the frightened mare to run backwards, falling over into a sitting position. The mare's head slammed

Karen in the face, throwing her off onto a pile of rocks. She said that all this happened in just seconds.

Then Mark went on to tell Carol that Jim told him Karen still had absolutely no recollection of what happened after the fall. She didn't think that she had been stung by the hornets, but she was sure they had gotten Penny. The next thing she remembered was waking up in the ICU, seeing Granny standing beside her bed.

Karen right now really needed to know how Penny fared. It was worrying her pretty badly.

Carol listened to Mark's story and then cried, "Oh, Mark, Penny is fine, and I'm so glad to hear that Karen is doing well too. Granny and I will be visiting her tomorrow afternoon. I'll tell her what happened at the barn that morning."

Before hanging up, she thanked Mark again for keeping the family informed.

The following afternoon, Carol and Granny met Jim at the hospital just a few minutes before visiting hours. They waited patiently in the lobby. Now that Karen was out of the ICU, the waiting was much easier.

The time finally arrived, and the three walked down the hall into Karen's room. It was wonderful seeing her. Even though she was still bandaged and her arm in a cast, she looked so much better than she had four days prior. She was wide-awake now with no IVs attached. Jim, Granny, and Carol all hugged and kissed her and told her how much everyone missed her. Karen was glad to see them too.

After several minutes, Karen excitedly asked Carol about the accident, and especially about Penny. "How did they find me? How and where did they find Penny? Please tell me, Carol, is she okay?" Karen whispered.

Carol replied, "Well, as you know, Karen, I was not at home that morning, but this is the story that I got from Dad, Mike, and Dan."

Carol continued with the story, "Mike was working in the paddock that morning and saw Penny galloping across the field toward the barn. She was snorting and shaking. The bridle and martingale were not only in several pieces, but most of it was dragging on the ground."

Karen listened attentively to Carol telling this story.

"Mike grabbed the loose rein, stopped the mare, and led her into the barn," continued Carol. "He put her in a stall and checked on her for injuries. Dad and Dan, knowing that there must have been an accident, jumped in the jeep and headed out across the field to the woods." Carol nudged Karen and smiled as she added, "Dan claims that the red sweater you were wearing helped them to find you. Dad, using his cell phone, called 911. The police notified the Medivac helicopter. You were still unconscious when they arrived. They flew you to the hospital."

"Wow," Karen sighed, "I don't remember any of that." Then she questioned, "How about Penny, though? Is she really all right, Carol?"

"Yes, she is," Carol answered. "You mustn't worry because other than missing you terribly, we all, Penny included, are just fine!"

Karen smiled at this remark.

Carol, taking Karen's hand continued, "Now it's up to you, lady, to get out of here and come home! Granny, Ellie, and I will wait on you hand and foot," she promised with a laugh. "And Jim, here, promises to carry you home on his back."

They all laughed.

CHAPTER 16

The next morning Dr. White went into Karen's room to assist her from the bed for the first time since the accident. She was surprised when she attempted to stand; her right leg was not responding. Dr. White handed her a cane and explained to her, "Karen, because of your injury, a small amount of bleeding occurred on the left side of your brain, which affects the opposite side of the body, your right leg. You will be using this cane for awhile."

The doctor, realizing that Karen was frightened by this remark, quickly continued, "However, I promise that the numbness in the leg will eventually improve with time and exercise."

"Thank you, Doctor. I was afraid that you were going to suggest that I not ride horses anymore. That would have been the worst news ever."

"Oh, no, you will ride again," he laughed, "but you will have to take it easy for at least three months.

"You know, Karen," the doctor continued, "you've been here six days now, and I think you are ready to go home. What do you think?" he teased.

"Oh, yes," she grinned as she answered, "I am ready right now. It's Saturday. I'm sure that Jim can pick me up today. Can I call him now?" she asked.

"Well, I don't see why not," he said over his shoulder as he walked towards the door. "I'll start the paperwork for your discharge now. Ask your friend to pick you up this afternoon, say about two o'clock."

"Thank you, Dr. White, I truly appreciate you and this hospital for taking such good care of me." She smiled.

"Well, now, you've been a very good patient too," he answered. "But, don't let those hornets get after you or your horse again, ever," he advised as he walked out the door into the hall.

Karen hobbled to the bedside phone and called Jim on his cell phone. "Hi, whatcha doing?" she cheerfully asked.

"Karen, hi. You sound great...you must be feeling better, right?" Jim asked.

"I'm not only feeling better, Jim. Dr. White just announced I can go home *today*," Karen exclaimed.

"Are you serious? Just tell me the time that I should come in. I'll be there with bells on," he laughed.

After talking with Jim, Karen called the Spencers. Ellie answered the phone. Finding out Karen was coming home excited Ellie. She told Karen that she would transfer the call to the barn where she could tell Carol herself.

Carol, hearing the news, shouted to her dad, Mike, and Dan. All were pleased at the news and told her that they all were prepared for Karen's return.

Karen made one more call. It was to Granny. They talked for several minutes. Granny happily exclaimed that she would be at Loafing Hills when Karen arrived that afternoon.

Jim and his friend Mark took Karen to Loafing Hills at 3:30 that afternoon. The gang was anxiously awaiting her. A big sign hung across the porch reading, "Welcome Home, Karen," adorned with many happy face balloons. Karen, with Jim on one side and Mark on the other, was helped out of the car and up into the house. She looked good despite the cast on her left arm, very sore ribs, and her terribly numb right leg, slowing her movements considerably.

Lots of hugs and kisses later, Karen was sitting in the kitchen talking with her friends about her accident and what the doctor had said about things she could do now and things she shouldn't attempt for a while. She told her friends that she was worried because she would be no help at all on the farm, and it might be three months before she could even ride again.

"Now," she asked, "what will you do about Corky and Storm, the two colts that Carol and I are breaking?"

Jim, who was just learning to ride, suggested that he could help, and Mark, a very good rider, offered to take on breaking the colts. They worked out a plan that the guys could get to the farm every day about four in the afternoon, work on the colts for a couple of hours, and then help Mike, Dan, and Ned at the barn. Carol could exercise the other horses during the day. Everyone agreed that this was a good idea; they each thanked Jim and Mark sincerely for offering the much needed farm help.

Ellie spoke up, offering to prepare supper every evening for all of them. It was also decided that Granny would stay weekends at Loafing Hills to help out as much as she could in the house.

Then, they all jokingly told Karen that she could sit on the front porch every day to make sure they were all doing a good job! "We'll call you Captain Karen," Carol added as she gave Karen a hug.

A little later Ellie and Granny assisted Karen to bed. Even though it was still early in the evening, Karen was absolutely worn out. The Spencers stayed up later in the evening talking with Mark and Jim regarding the upcoming three-month farm schedule.

The next morning, Sunday, October 23, Carol awoke early and joined her dad and Ellie at the breakfast table. They discussed the wedding coming up, November the 5th. All the plans were laid, and everything was set. They were all very happy that Karen was home and doing well. This, they felt, would make the wedding happier for the whole family. Carol's granddad would be flying in from England on Thursday, November 3rd. Ellie's sister, Jean, would be arriving from California the next day. Both would be staying at Loafing Hills.

After breakfast, Carol decided to ride her horse Blackjack out for some needed exercise, but first she led Karen's horse, Penny, out of the barn and into the field closest to the house. She knew that Karen planned to sit on the porch that morning and would be very happy to see her horse grazing in the near pasture.

Carol mounted Blackjack and rode the trail towards the woods. She planned to stop by Emerson's grave on the way back home that morning. She knew that the visit would make her feel sad because she dearly loved and missed Emerson greatly. She also knew sitting at his grave for a few minutes under the beautiful old oaks always left her feeling warm, comfortable, and at peace.

The ride through the woods that morning was lovely. The sun was shining; the birds were singing, and the trees were dressed in a rainbow of colors.

Carol rode for an hour, ending at Emerson's grave. She dismounted, exchanged the bridle for a halter and rope, and tied Blackjack to a low tree limb.

She sat quietly at the grave and ran her hand gently over the stone. So many memories surfaced immediately about this wonderful horse: his absolutely brilliant show career, and the years of happiness that he had brought her were insurmountable. He was her friend, her horse, funny, kind, handsome, and strong.

"Oh, Emerson," she sighed, "I miss you so much. I don't believe there will ever be another horse for me."

Tears came to her eyes as she whispered, "You were a fantastic open jumper, Emerson, gallant, trustworthy, and bold. I will never, ever, forget you." She ran her fingers slowly down the letters etched on the marker that read, "I Knew Emerson."

"You know you spoiled me rotten, Emerson," she laughed as she wiped away the tears. "And I'm glad that you enjoyed showing off in the show ring. You always made it look so easy. But hey, guy, you were the greatest!" she said as she slowly stood, replaced the bridle on Blackjack, and climbed aboard. She whispered once more to Emerson as they were leaving the grave site, "Goodbye, friend...and thank you, Emerson, for being such a wonderful part of my life."

Carol rode Blackjack back through the woods and down the hill to home. Hardly a day went by that she didn't think about Emerson. She wasn't sure why, but every time she visited his grave, she always came away feeling better. She decided it must be a sign from Emerson to stay brave, as he always had in his life.

When Carol and Blackjack arrived at the barn, it was lunchtime. Karen and Jim were sitting on the front porch. After taking care of Blackjack, Carol went to the field, caught Penny, and led her up to the house. Jim helped Karen down the steps because she had insisted that she pet and rub her hands over Penny's coat. She wanted to make sure the mare was not injured. All during the last week at the hospital she had worried about this. Even though she had watched Penny from the front porch all morning, she still insisted that she examine the horse herself.

Once she realized that the mare was fine, she felt a lot better. She also had to laugh at herself for being so worried. Carol and Jim, of course, understood.

They went into the house and found that Ellie had prepared a nice lunch of fish and chips for them before she and Granny left to go shopping. There was a message on the phone for Carol. It was John. He told her that he had called her several times during the last week, but couldn't seem to catch anyone at home. He hoped that everything was okay. Carol was disappointed she had not talked with him in a week, but they all had been so busy on the farm and also preparing for Ellie and her dad's wedding the next week. Hardly anyone had been in the house or even been near the barn phone in days. If he had only tried to call later yesterday evening, they had all been home.

Karen told Carol that she had not heard the phone ringing while on the porch that morning, but from this time on she would try to take the calls when Granny and Ellie were not in. Carol decided that she would definitely call John that evening.

During lunch, Mike and Dan came in from the barn and joined them. Mike told Karen that he and Dan had driven the jeep up the hill to where she and Penny had met the hornets. He said that the nest was on the ground, and there were no living hornets around. Just to make sure they didn't return, they burned the limb and the nest. Everyone at the table, including Karen, applauded them.

"Thank you so much, guys," Karen laughed. "Believe me, I've had nightmares about riding Penny under that tree again. I'm still worried that Penny might spook there."

Jim suggested that he ride Penny to the hill that afternoon just to make sure she would be all right in that area.

Carol spoke up, "Jim, I truly appreciate that offer, and if you have no objection, I would like to join you."

Jim answered, "Thanks, Carol, I'd like that. As you know, I'm not the greatest rider in the world and would really like to have you with me."

At three in the afternoon, Carol tacked Penny and Blackjack up for their afternoon ride to the "hornet spot" to make sure all was now well in that location.

Before mounting, they saw Jim's friend, Mark Long, pull his car up to the house. They called to him. He joined them at the barn and told them that he knew that he was a day early, but thought he'd like to start schooling and riding today.

Jim quickly answered, "Hey, if it's okay with Carol, I'd rather stay behind with Karen today anyway. I'll start my riding tomorrow. You and Carol go ahead." He smiled as he headed back to the house.

Carol and Mark rode the horses up the hill. As Mike and Dan had said, no hornets were there. They could see where the fire had been. There were no returning hornets flying around anywhere. Because it was such a beautiful day, they decided to ride on through the woods. They had a good ride. The weather was a bit cooler than it had been earlier in the day when Carol had first ridden, but still was perfect for riding. Carol was impressed with Mark's riding ability.

"Hey, Buddy," she called to him, "I didn't know you were such a seasoned rider. Where did you learn?" she questioned.

"Well, many years ago my mom and dad divorced. I spent my younger years with my mom, visiting my dad occasionally on his cattle ranch in Wyoming. I loved those visits. Then, when I was twelve, I asked my dad at the end of the summer, if I might live with him through the year. My mother really didn't want me to do that, but because my school grades weren't that good, and neither was my pick of friends," he laughed, "she let me go."

"Wow, so you learned to ride on a Wyoming cattle ranch. How neat is that," she smiled.

"Yeah, I got lots of riding in and got along great with my dad. I also did better in school out there too. I eventually went off to a Virginia university, where I met and roomed with my good buddy Jim. But, I still went back in the summers to help Dad."

"Well, Mark," Carol said, "I'm truly impressed with your riding and your good outlook on life that you evidently got from there. Is your dad still in Wyoming?" she asked.

"Yes, and he's still busy with his ranch. I try to get out there whenever I can; however, my construction company keeps me pretty busy. But I call him about once a week. We have gotten to be good friends over the years."

"You are a good and admirable son," she laughed. "Does your mom still live in Virginia?"

"Yes. You'd like her, Carol," he answered. "She's now retired from teaching high school and is doing well."

"It's good to get to know you better, Mark. Thanks for sharing with me. I also need to tell you that I really enjoyed our night out a couple of weeks ago," she continued. "I know that you met Jim Boland in college, but that's about all I know about you."

"Well, now that I'm donating my free time working at Loafing Hills, we'd better get to know a little more about each other, right?" he laughed.

She agreed and then smiling at him, she called out, "Race you back to the barn." She dug her heels into Blackjack's side and galloped away.

Mark, not to be outdone, urged Penny into a full gallop too. They arrived, neck and neck, at the barn.

Carol and Granny helped Ellie prepare supper that evening. They invited Jim and Mark to join them. The roast chicken was delicious, and everyone was in good spirits. They talked and laughed throughout the whole meal and then helped clean the kitchen. Carol, Karen, Jim, and Mark sat back down at the table and continued their jovial talking and laughing until way late in the evening.

Later, Carol helped Karen up the stairs to her bedroom. Then she cried, "Oh, no, I forgot to call John this evening!"

Karen giggled as they parted at the bedroom door, and she called out, "Carol, tomorrow is another day."

Carol smiled back, but still felt guilty that she had forgotten to make the call. *I will absolutely do it tomorrow*, she thought.

CHAPTER 17

Carol awoke at seven in the morning, showered, dressed, and made her bed. She met Karen and Granny in the hallway and helped escort Karen down the stairs. When they got to the kitchen, Ellie was serving breakfast to Ned, Mike, and Dan. Mike, in jest, was nagging Ned regarding an idea that he should hire a cook, so that Ellie would have some free time.

Ned, smiling back, responded, "It's already done, Mike. A new lady named Pearl will be coming in starting next Monday. She will be doing all the cooking, Mondays through Fridays."

"Will she also do the house cleaning?" Carol asked.

"Oh, no," piped up Ellie. I like my own way of cleaning, but I graciously appreciate the cooking help." She laughed.

Carol continued, "Good for you, Ellie; you deserve help." Then turning to her dad, she asked, "Where is this lady from, Dad? Local? Does she like horses? Horse people?"

"Whoa, Carol," her dad answered and laughed. "I called a local agency a couple of weeks ago about hiring a cook. He asked me to come in and interview several. I did that last week. Pearl is a fifty-year-old widow who loves to cook. She has a sixteen-year-old son and an eighteen-year-old daughter. Both love horses and are willing to work here.

"Yah," yelled Mike, "we can always use extra barn help."

The whole family agreed this was a great idea. Ellie would have more free time and Dan and Mike more barn help. Ned would have more time for buying and selling horses. And just maybe, Pearl's daughter would like to exercise horses, which would be a big plus for Carol.

Ned continued to describe Pearl's position. "Pearl will come in at seven in the morning through the weekdays and prepare breakfast. She will stay and serve lunch. After that, she will prepare an evening meal, leaving it in the fridge for us to warm up. The weekend meals will be up to us."

Karen spoke up, "Ned, Granny will be here on the weekends; she and I can take care of the weekend meals."

Ellie added, "And I will also be a helping hand on the weekends. I don't want to be out of business completely," she joked.

Carol spoke up, "This will really be a big help to the farm. Jim and Mark working the two colts, Dad, having the time for buying and selling." She continued, "Pearl's kids, working at the barn, and maybe doing some riding too. I will keep all the sale horses fit," she concluded.

Ned reminded them not to forget the wedding coming up November 5th. "We need to get the cleaning and mowing done for that too." He continued, "A wedding planner will be visiting here on the 4th and then coming in early on the 5th to prepare and set up for the outdoor wedding."

Ellie reminded everyone that Ned's father (Carol's granddad) would be arriving on the 3rd and Jean, Ellie's sister, on the 4th. "We're gonna be one busy bunch that week," she exclaimed.

Soon after breakfast, everyone went off to do their jobs for the day. Carol exercised four show horses and was putting the last one away, when she heard Ellie ring the lunch bell. The whole crew showed up for lunch, except Granny, who had gone home and would be back on the weekend.

It was fun when they all met for meals to hear what each had to say about their day so far. Ned had phoned Ellie a little earlier to tell her that he had just purchased five young, green-broke horses at a Pennsylvania horse sale that morning. She immediately passed this information on to Mike, Dan, Karen, and Carol. They, as usual, were always interested in learning about new horses coming in.

Carol told about the four horses she had ridden that morning. Mike and Dan said that they were now working and would be for the next two days on paddock fencing. Everyone was busy, even Karen. She spent the morning on the front porch cleaning tack. She soaped and oiled three saddles and two bridles, replaced one snaffle-bit, and fixed a broken strap on a martingale.

After lunch, Carol picked up the phone and dialed John's number at New Start Ranch. The answering message said simply, "John and Dora are not available." She then tried John's cell. No answer there either. As Carol left to go riding, Karen called to her saying she had the portable phone with her on the front porch. Ellie was cleaning house today, so Karen said that she'd take all calls.

Carol went back to the barn to ride several more horses while the weather was cooperating. As she left the barn astride one of the show horses, she hoped that Mark and Jim, when they arrived that afternoon, would work with the two three-year-old colts.

At four o'clock, Mark and Jim both pulled in to Loafing Hills, ready to work. Ned had both colts in the barn waiting. Mark groomed Corky, while Jim worked on Storm. After a good cleaning, the guys, with the help of Dan and Ned, saddled and bridled the colts, adding a halter over the bridle for lunging them before riding.

They led Storm and Corky into the schooling ring and exercised them on the lunge line for ten minutes. Dan and Ned, standing at the gate, watched as Mark and Jim climbed aboard their mounts. Both colts acted up a bit at first, but finally settled down and behaved. They walked and trotted quietly around the ring for twenty minutes.

Dismounting, Jim told Mark that he was uncomfortable riding the colt because he, with Karen's supervision, had only been riding for a couple of months. And then, only on well-schooled horses!

Later, Mark mentioned Jim's apprehensive feelings to Ned. It was decided that Mark would work with the colts, and Jim would help Carol keep the show and pleasure horses exercised.

Jim was very glad of this change because he was truly uncomfortable riding the colt. He wasn't so much afraid of getting hurt himself, but he felt that he didn't know enough about horses to be breaking and training one. And, he was worried that he might mess up and ruin the horse for selling.

The rest of the evening Mark and Jim assisted the barn guys cleaning stalls and putting down fresh bedding. When finished with that, Mark helped Dan measure out grain for the barn horses while Jim worked with Ned and Mike throwing hay to the horses outside in the corrals. When Carol returned from her last ride for the day, she took care of her mount, then helped in the barn. It was seven o'clock when they heard the supper bell. They were all hungry and quite ready to quit for the evening.

Karen was waiting for them on the front porch. She had pulled the balloons and the "Welcome Home Karen" sign down from the entranceway. She told them, as they approached the porch, that she had been home two days now. Time for cleanup!

Jim laughed as he hugged Karen and told her, "We sure did miss you at the barn today."

"Yeah," injected Mark, "why weren't you down there throwing hay with us?" They all laughed.

Not to be outdone, Karen returned with, "I've tried to direct you guys ever since you arrived this afternoon, but you didn't do any of the things that I was telling you."

"And what might those things have been?" asked Jim.

"Well, I'm not going to tell you now," she giggled as she returned his hug.

"Uh, oh," called Mark. And looking at Carol, he grinned, "We'd better leave those two alone." Mark took Carol's hand, and smiling, they ran up the steps into the kitchen.

Ellie had prepared homemade pizza. The aroma made their mouths water. Everything else was immediately forgotten as they grabbed their plates and dived into the pizza. Ned brought out a jug of homemade root beer. What a treat, they all declared.

It was ten o'clock at night when the guys left with the promise of being back at four the next afternoon.

Carol, Karen, Ned, and Ellie sat at the table and talked for about an hour about getting ready for the wedding in just two weeks. They all agreed that all that was left to do was cleaning the house which Ellie, Carol, and Karen would all take a part in. Ned said that Mike, Dan, and he would start the final mowing next week.

"Pearl will start fixing the meals for us next Monday," Ellie said, "so that will leave us more time to get things done around the house. After all," she continued, "we will have house guests that weekend. Ned's dad, my sister, and Granny. So, we still have lots to do."

Karen asked Ned and Ellie, "Aren't you two going on a honeymoon?"

Ned answered, "Yes, we are, Karen; we plan to leave the evening after the wedding. We'll fly down to Key West for a week and be back on the thirteenth." He smiled.

"Wow," clapped Karen, "that sounds great. I've never been to Key West, but I've heard it's beautiful."

"If I ever get married," Carol smiled and said as she left the kitchen, "that's where I'm going, too."

"Ladies," Ned spoke, as he rose from his chair, "it's pushing midnight; we've got a big day tomorrow. The five horses I purchased in Pennsylvania will be arriving about noon. I think we'd all better get some sleep."

On the way upstairs Karen asked Carol if she had yet heard from John.

"Nope, not a word," she answered. "Guess he's just too busy to call me!" She sounded a bit agitated.

Karen, giving Carol's arm a squeeze, whispered, "Bet he calls tomorrow!"

The rest of the week Mark and Jim worked at Loafing Hills every day. Jim was riding the show and pleasure horses with Carol, while Mark and Ned worked with the colts, which were progressing admirably. Ned had the two colts ready every afternoon. Mark was doing most of the riding, saying that he was thoroughly enjoying the exercise, and he thought the colts were having a good time too.

Friday evening the gang, obeying the supper bell, came to the kitchen and experienced another tasty meal, courtesy of Ellie. Mark immediately commented, after his first bite, that he hoped Pearl was at least half as good a cook as Ellie.

Ellie had news for Carol. She knew that John and Carol were having problems with missing calls. She told Carol that John had called earlier, but as usual, Carol was not available. Carol felt that she probably should carry her cell phone with her, but when she was riding she did not want to be interrupted by phone calls. Her stance was "In case of an emergency, just ring the supper bell." A person could hear it five miles away. She would definitely come galloping home.

Ellie continued, telling Carol that John's message was that he planned to fly to Maryland the morning of the wedding. He would rent a car and be at Loafing Hills by noon. Carol was glad to hear that he would be at the wedding, but was rather irritated that they had not been able to even talk to each other in over a week. She was beginning to wonder just how seriously they felt about each other.

Then, just minutes later, when Mark asked her if she would like to attend a movie with him, Karen, and Jim that evening, she immediately responded, "Yes!"

Ellie, looking at Carol, didn't blame her. She knew that Carol worked hard on the farm all day, every day. She was too young not to go out with her friends once in a while. She needed time to just be herself...and have fun.

"Goodbye, kids, have a good time," she called as they departed.

John did call later that day; Ellie simply told him that Carol had gone to the theater with some friends.

When Carol awoke on Saturday morning, she lay in bed contemplating her fun excursion with Karen, Jim, and Mark the night before. They had had such a good time. They decided, after the movie, to go to an all-night restaurant for dessert. Oh, she thought to herself, they had each eaten a whole banana split. And boy, it was delicious too!

Later, downstairs, Ellie told Carol that John had called again. Carol answered her, "I will try calling him again today." However, she added, "he doesn't answer his cell, and I can't catch anyone at home. I have not been leaving messages, but I will today."

Ned came in from the barn and joined Ellie and Carol at the table. "Mark and Jim are already here this morning and working in the barn. They told me that they plan to work here all day on the weekends. I invited them up for coffee and some breakfast, but they declined saying that they had already eaten. They truly are a couple of caring young men," he added.

"I'm not surprised they're here, Dad," Carol replied. "They said last night that they planned to be here early, today and tomorrow. They jokingly said they need the exercise, and Ellie's cooking," she laughed. "And you're right, they are both very nice gentlemen."

Ellie, Carol, and Karen went into town Saturday morning, one week before the wedding, to pick up their wedding ensembles. Ellie's wedding gown, off-white silk, accented with pearls, was gorgeous. The veil flowed graciously from a pearl-studded headpiece to just below the shoulders, and Ellie looked beautiful in it. She had lost so much weight in the last couple of months, the gown had needed to be altered three times.

Carol and Karen had ordered matching taffeta gowns in a quiet tone of soft yellow-orange. This would be a delightful accent to the handsome Southern Magnolia trees, which surrounded the gazebo, where the wedding ceremony would take place. All three ladies picked up their gown-matching shoes, before heading home.

When they arrived at Loafing Hills at noon, the men were in the house happily devouring the lunch that Granny and Karen had prepared for them. All five men were busy discussing what they had accomplished that morning, and what more had to be done in the afternoon.

However, Ned suggested that because they had worked so hard that morning, why not all saddle up and go for a nice ride? Mike and Dan, who lived in a small bungalow on the farm, declined the offer, deciding that they would rather go home and enjoy some down time. Ned agreed and said that he, too, would stay home and do some planting in preparation for the wedding. Jim decided that he would stay home with Karen.

Mark looked at Carol and said, "Okay, Carol, it's just you and me!" He grinned. "Let's go!"

Carol, laughing, ran upstairs to change clothes while Mark brought the horses in from the paddock, saddled them, and waited for her.

CHAPTER 18

Carol and Mark rode the trail that took them across Possum Creek, which was the same creek that Carol and Karen had visited several weeks ago. They had allowed the horses to stop and play in the water for a spell. Not today, however, the water was too cold. They quietly crossed the creek and continued through the woods to Loafing Hills' south pasture.

This grassland was set aside for horses not used through the summer months; they were referred to as turnouts and were usually young or injured horses. Barbed wire was stretched over a low fence (called a coop) through the summer. In the fall the barbed wire was removed which allowed riders to enter or exit the pasture by jumping over the coops.

Carol and Mark jumped their horses over the coop into the pasture and continued to the far side of the field. There they enjoyed a scenic view of the valley below the Loafing Hills' border. Looking down they could see a picturesque country town nestled in the hills.

Mark was astounded by this image. He called to Carol, "Wow, this is spectacular."

"Yes," she answered, "it takes my breath away every time I come up here."

Mark suggested that they dismount and enjoy the view for a few minutes, Carol agreed. They sat on the bank, holding the horses' reins and simply stared down at this breathtaking picture.

Mark, sitting next to Carol, asked if she would mind if he held her hand. "I'm not getting fresh," he chided, "it's just too beautiful here, not to be close."

Carol, amused, placed her hand in his. They smiled at each other.

After a few minutes, Mark spoke again. "I think you know, Carol, I like you more than I should. Do I have a chance at all?" he questioned.

"Mark, I like you a lot too," she answered, "and I hate to say this, but I'm really confused right now. I do care for you, but I think I care for John too. I'm not sure how he feels about me. And now, I'm not even sure how I feel about him."

Carol, seeing the look in Mark's eyes, felt like crying. "Please, Mark," she pleaded, "can we just be good friends for now?"

Mark, seeing how upset she was becoming, immediately grinned, stood, and pulled her up. He brought her hand to his face, gently kissed her fingers, and whispered, "I'm sorry, Carol. Yes, of course, we can be good friends. That beats the heck out of enemies," he laughed.

Carol, knowing that he understood, actually felt worse. But they both smiled as they looked at their patient mounts, waiting quietly for them to climb aboard and start the journey home.

All the way back, Carol wondered about her mixed-up feelings about John and Mark. She really liked both of them. She was bewildered, but hopeful that things would work out for the best.

Mark tried his best to be jovial all the way home. He was doing a pretty good job of it too, Carol thought. By the time they rode into the barn, they both were feeling better, even laughing out loud.

Carol was thinking, *Mark is really a wonderful guy. Any other guy would have probably said..."See ya."*

Later that evening, after Mark and Jim had left, Karen was resting in her bedroom. Carol tiptoed to her door and softly called, "Karen, are you awake?"

"Yes," Karen answered. "Come on in, Carol."

Carol confided to Karen what Mark had said to her earlier in the day. Karen listened attentively to Carol's tearful story.

"Oh, my gosh, Carol," she said, "I'm so sorry Mark upset you."

"No, Karen, I am not upset by what Mark said. I'm upset about how I feel. I really like Mark a lot, but I also like John. I'm just so confused right now. I don't know what to think, or what to do about it."

"Well," Karen answered with a smile, "what a predicament. John and Mark, two great looking, super-nice guys, both in love with you. You know, there are many ladies that would enjoy having your problem," she giggled.

"But seriously, Carol," she whispered, "you should not worry about it. You are not wed, or even engaged, to either. If you want my suggestion, I would say date both, have fun, and go places. I truly believe that only time will give you the answer that you're looking for," she concluded as she gave Carol a hug.

"Thank you, Karen," Carol answered, "I really do feel better now that I've talked with you, and I like your advice. Your turning twenty-one really made you smart." Carol laughed.

Still hugging Carol, Karen cried, "No, what made me smart was getting thrown off a hornet-stung horse onto my head!"

Then both girls were laughing and crying at the same time. And then both started singing at the top of their lungs: "Nobody loves me, nobody wants me, I'm going out to the garden, eat some worms!"

Sunday morning after breakfast Carol, walking to the barn with her dad, noticed Mark's car parked in the drive. He was in the barn preparing to clean stalls. Dan was leading the horses out to pasture.

"Mark," she called, "you don't have to work here today; it's Sunday!"

Mark, smiling, just waved back and continued unloading bags of grain from the wheelbarrow. "I was too bored to stay home," he laughed. "How about you getting the two colts ready while I finish here," he called.

They worked with the two colts and then the five green-broke horses that Ned had brought during the last week. Mike and Ned stayed busy most of the day stacking a delivery of hay in the main barn. Joe, the farrier, came in and shod six horses that needed shoes. Everybody was busy. The time seemed to fly by.

That evening Carol walked Mark to his car and thanked him again for his help. He quietly asked if she would mind if he gave her just a little kiss goodnight. She did not know what to say; she just looked at him. "I know," he said, "cat's got your tongue!" He leaned down and planted a kiss right in the middle of her forehead. "Goodnight," he whispered.

She giggled to herself all the way back to the house.

On Monday morning the family met Pearl, the new lady that was taking over the job of cooking. She was very friendly, talking and laughing as she prepared a nice breakfast for all. Ellie was helping her get acquainted with the large kitchen and pantry.

After breakfast Carol, Ned, Mike, and Dan left for the barn and were busy all day with only a short break for lunch. They were all busy at the barn when Mark and Jim came in about four o'clock. Both were warmly welcomed, and they immediately joined the crew in doing various farm tasks for the rest of the evening.

Of course supper was a treat and a time for talk. They decided how and what should be done the remainder of the week. Lots of mowing had to be done in preparation for Saturday's wedding. Dan and Mike volunteered to start mowing the fields the next day. Then on Friday, they would mow the lawns.

The wedding planners would be coming Friday about noon to set up tents and tables. Chairs would be placed facing the gazebo. They would return Saturday morning to finish the preparations.

Everyone at the table picked a task to do for the rest of the week, including caring for the barns and horses. Early Thursday morning, Ned and Carol happily welcomed Ned's parents, Ann and David Spencer, from Delabay, England. It was a wonderful surprise because Ann had not felt well earlier in the month so wasn't sure that she would make the trip, but she was now feeling fine. They were excited to see their son, granddaughter, and, of course, Ellie, the to-be bride. In turn Ned, Carol, and Ellie were thrilled to have them there.

Even though the Spencers exchanged correspondence often via phoning and e-mailing, this was Ann and David's first visit back to the states in several years. It was a real thrill being together once again, talking, laughing, and hugging, in person.

Later Ellie, Karen, and Pearl entertained Ned's parents over coffee while Ned and Carol finished up the outdoor preparations.

The next morning was Friday, one day before the wedding! Everyone was again busy, running in every direction. Each had jobs to do, and they did them well. Even Karen, who was beginning to walk a bit steadier, had fun entertaining their houseguests and assisting Ellie and Pearl in getting ready for the big day!

In the afternoon, Ellie's sister Jean arrived from California. She was greeted by all and was happy seeing everyone and looking forward to the wedding.

Carol had left John two messages at his house during the past week, but so far there had been no response. She wasn't worried because she knew that he would be at the wedding. Ellie, who liked John very much, had asked him to walk her down the aisle.

Mark and Jim volunteered to be ushers. Karen, the official guest greeter, would be sitting at the head of the aisle. Carol would stand at the cabana with the preacher, awaiting the bride and groom's walk down the aisle. Mike and Dan would be available after the ceremony to assist the chef in getting the banquet food on the tables.

Friday afternoon brought the wedding planners with tents, tables, chairs, and miscellaneous decorations.

CHAPTER 19

John Quill called and spoke with Ellie Friday afternoon. He told her that he was flying in. She invited him to join them at supper. In the late afternoon he landed at the small airpark near Loafing Hills and drove a rental car to the farm. When he arrived, a tired, but enthusiastic group met him at the door.

They all enjoyed a delicious supper; and even though everyone was exhausted, the conversation was fun and refreshing.

After supper John asked, "Carol, if you're not too tired, would you like to take a short walk with me?"

She suggested instead that they saddle a couple of horses for a ride. John agreed, and they headed to the barn and saddled up Blackjack and Frosty.

Carol, riding Blackjack, and John on Frosty, rode through the forest up the hill, stopping at Emerson's grave. They dismounted and sat on a handsome wooden bench that thoughtful Mike and Dan had recently built and placed beside the gravestone.

Carol and John spoke softly for a spell, telling each other how sorry they were for not being able to connect phone-wise. John told Carol that he had been so busy on the ranch that by the time he got back to the house each evening he was so tired, he'd just fall into bed, usually missing supper! Carol said that she understood, that she too had been working hard and had been totally worn out every evening.

They decided they would really try to do better from this time on! Before re-mounting, Carol rose from the bench and placed her hand on Emerson's headstone. She didn't say anything vocally, but John guessed she was telling Emerson how much she still missed him. He didn't know that her thoughts included missing John too! But, he must have felt it in his heart because he gently pulled her into his arms and tenderly kissed her. For a moment she didn't respond, but then placing her arms over his shoulders, she returned his kiss.

She looked into his deep brown sparkling eyes, felt the strength and warmth of his body against hers, and thought quietly, *I think I'm in love with this guy.*

He, gazing back into her dazzling-blue smiling eyes and loving the feel of her softness in his arms sighed, "Carol, you know I love you."

She gently pulled away saying, "John, I think that we're very much attracted to each other, but we don't truly know each other well. I'm hoping that we can see each other more and get to know each other better. Don't you agree?"

"You're right," John whispered, "when I get back home, I'll call you every evening, and I'll spend more time here at Loafing Hills with you. And, hopefully, you will occasionally allow me to fly you to New Start."

Carol smiled up at him. "John, I do appreciate what you are saying. However, I realize that you are heavily engaged in running your ranch, and I am incredibly busy here too, so why don't we plan to definitely see each other at least twice a month and then stay in touch daily, even if it's via telephones?"

"Carol, you're right," he answered. "As much as I'd love to see you every day, your idea would most likely work the best for us." He laughed, and continued, "When we get back to your house, let's once again check over that old calendar of yours and pick some coming dates, okay?"

Carol and John rode back to the barn and put the horses away. Once in the house, they immediately looked at Carol's calendar, picking out two "dates" in November and two for December. They decided that immediately after the wedding on Saturday, they would sit down and choose what they planned to do on those dates and where they would take place.

It was ten p.m., time for bed. Everyone was in very good spirits, but also tired. They knew the next day was going to be very active.

That night bedrooms would have to be shared. Karen and Carol were in Karen's room; Granny, Ellie, and Jean were in Carol's room. Ned's folks were in one of the guest rooms. John and Ned took the twin beds in the second guest room. The house was full!

As everyone ascended the stairs, Ellie called out, "There are several small tasks to do before the wedding planners arrive at nine tomorrow morning, and Pearl will be here with breakfast at 7:30 a.m. So please, let's get to bed. Nighty night all, sleep tight," she called as she threw each a kiss.

John escorted Carol to Karen's room and hugged her goodnight at the door and then went to the downstairs guest room where he and Ned jokingly fought over which bunk bed they'd get. The chaos finally settled down, and the house became, at last, comfortably silent.

CHAPTER 20

Saturday morning brought a beautiful sunny day, sixty degrees, with a promise of seventy by the afternoon.

Everyone was excited and cheerful at the breakfast table and eagerly looking forward to the wedding. All the little tasks outdoors were quickly completed. Carol and John led the barn-kept horses out to pastures, while Mike and Dan took care of the horses kept in stalls. Ned was doing last-minute lawn trimming, while Ellie, Pearl, Granny, and Karen took care of the house and entertained the houseguests.

At precisely nine a.m., the wedding planners pulled into the drive. They unloaded dishes, flatware, and flower arrangements and set all the tables. The four-piece band arrived and set up in the table area. The food for the banquet would be arriving at one o'clock.

Everyone did a magnificent job; the place looked absolutely spectacular. The decorators adorned the gazebo facing the chairs with a glorious array of red, white, and gold carnations. The giant trees in their fall splendor of yellow, orange, and brown surrounded the area. The intense sun glowing through the trees added spotlights to this awesome scene. It was breathtaking.

The wedding ceremony at two o'clock was impressive. Everything went like clockwork. Karen in her lovely gown greeted the guests. Mark and Jim, looking very handsome, led each guest to a seat. Carol, looking gorgeous in her fall-colored gown, stood in the gazebo doorway with her good-looking tux-attired dad.

The band played the wedding march as beautiful Ellie, escorted by handsome Mr. Quill, walked elegantly up the aisle to the gazebo. Carol and John stepped quietly aside. Ned took Ellie's hand and together they faced Reverend Thomas Clark. The Reverend, a tall, distinguished gentleman with smoky-gray hair and smiling hazel eyes was from the town church, where the Spencers were devout members. He was also a dear friend of the family.

After the vows were spoken and Reverend Clark pronounced them husband and wife, Ned kissed Ellie and then both turned and hugged Carol. She and John watched the new Mr. and Mrs. Spencer walk back down the aisle through throngs of happy, congratulating friends. Carol couldn't have felt more contented. She looked up at John and smiled. He took her hand, squeezed it gently, and whispered, "Someday, Carol... that will be us!"

Carol was too surprised to answer.

Mike and Dan assisted the waiters in setting up the buffet of shrimp, steak, vegetables, and salad. Mark and Jim helped serve at the outdoor bar.

The band was fabulous, playing stimulating "top 40" music on a stage that had been erected by Ned and Dan for the occasion. All the guests were enjoying themselves while dancing the afternoon away.

The outdoor lights were turned on at five o'clock, and the band took a break. The wedding cake was brought out and placed on a table. It was a beautiful five-tier white cake, decorated with pink and yellow flowers.

Everyone gathered around and applauded when they saw the unusual decoration on top. It was a miniature bride and groom holding hands. Standing behind them, a young girl was sitting on a chocolate horse. A tag on the horse read, "Emerson."

Carol, holding John's hand, was so taken that tears came to her eyes, but she assured John and the guests that they were tears of happiness for her dad and Ellie.

At 7:30, the bride and groom climbed into Ned's Corvette, waved goodbye to their guests, and headed for the BWI airport. They were flying out for a week's stay in beautiful Key West. The wedding day was over, and it was, all agreed, a spectacular success.

At eleven o'clock everything was cleaned, cleared, and gone! Mark, Jim, Dan, and Mike left. The family and houseguests went to the house to relax. It had been a very long, but exciting, day for all. Ned's parents would be leaving in the morning for Georgia to visit some old neighbor friends. Ellie's sister, Jean, had plans to visit a girlfriend in Washington, DC for several days. Granny would leave for her home Sunday evening. John planned to fly home Sunday afternoon. That would leave Carol and Karen to hold down the fort by themselves for a week. Mark and Jim volunteered to come in every day the following week until Ned and Ellie returned.

Carol and John were tired. They decided to wait until morning to plan their upcoming dates for November and December.

John woke up early Sunday morning. The house was so quiet he figured everyone was still asleep. However, smelling the delightful aroma of coffee brewing, he followed his nose and joined Karen sitting quietly in the kitchen, cup in hand.

"Good morning," he called.

Seeing him, she answered, "Hi, John," and then offered him a cup of the fragrant brew. They sat and talked for about half an hour before John rinsed his cup and placed it in the drainer. The house was still eerily quiet; he bade Karen goodbye and left to help Dan and Mike in the barn.

Next to arrive downstairs was Carol. She joined Karen who was now on her third cup of coffee. Karen complained she had not slept well and had finally given up and gotten out of bed at five a.m. She also told Carol that John was not only up, but already had had his coffee and was now working in the barn.

Carol, looking at a tired Karen, cup in hand, spoke. "Well, Miss Karen, if you keep on drinking that coffee, you'll be so wired you won't be able to take a nap today, much less sleep tonight!"

"I know," Karen answered as she carried her empty cup to the sink, rinsed it, and announced. "I'm done!"

During the next hour John came back from the barn. He found everyone awake and downstairs. They all looked perky from a good night's rest. Ned's parents, Ann and David Spencer, were the first to leave. They planned to drive their rental car to their old neighborhood in Baser, Georgia, where they would stay with friends for several days. Then they would drive to Atlanta and fly from there back to their home in England. As they left that morning, there were lots of hugs, kisses, and promises to come back and also invitations for everyone to visit them in England.

Jean was driving her rental car to Washington, DC to stay with an old college buddy for a couple of days before taking that long flight back to San Diego. She, too, invited them all to visit in her western home.

Later in the afternoon, Granny would be driving her trusty old Pontiac back to her beloved retirement village.

John, planning to leave in the evening before dark, approached Carol asking her to please get her calendar, so they could settle on those important future dates.

Carol obliged. After careful consideration, they picked the weekends, November 12-13 and 26-27. In December they chose 10-11 and 24-25. They were both excited with the idea and the dates.

Carol walked John to his car Sunday evening. She was sad to see him go, but she knew that he had an important meeting Monday morning with several realtors. John had additional property in New Bern that was for sale, and many developers were interested.

At the car door, John put his arms around her and whispered, "Being in love with you, Carol, is the most beautiful thing in my life."

Carol put her arms around him too, answering, "John, you are the nicest, and I must say, the most handsome guy I know."

Seeing Dan and Mike waving goodbye to him from the barn, John waved back to them and then leaned down and kissed Carol's lips, very lightly, and whispered, "This is just a peck so Dan and Mike won't tease you."

They both laughed as he got into the car and closed the door.

He let the window down. "Now don't forget," he said, "I'll fly in early on the 12th to pick you up. That's only one week away now, so be ready."

She threw kisses at him as he drove away. *I don't care if I get teased or not,* she thought to herself as she walked back to the house.

Karen and Granny both had huge smiles on their faces when she walked through the door. Seeing their faces, Carol asked, "What?"

"What do you mean, what?" Karen giggled.

"What are you and Granny up to?" Carol asked again, grinning.

"Oh, nothing at all." Karen smiled. "Granny and I were just looking out the window and a song came to us both at the exact same time."

"Yeah, okay, now I guess I'm supposed to ask, what song?" Carol said, "I'll bite."

"Love is a many splendored thing...." Karen and Granny both began to sing loudly and very much off-key! Then, all three began to laugh.

"Ouch," Carol retorted. Then seriously she said, "I still don't know how I feel about John. I know I like him heaps, but I'm not sure about love. I always thought that when you fall in love, your head would spin and you'd be floating on air. Am I nuts?"

"No, Carol, you are not nuts, a little crazy maybe, but not nuts!" Karen stated.

Granny added. "Carol, give it time; you'll know when and if it happens."

Carol spent the rest of the day at the barn helping Dan and Mike. Of course they immediately hit her with, "We saw all that a-smoochin' goin' on up there in that there car. Next thing we know, there'll be another rip-snortin' weddin' right here at Loafing Hills," they teased.

"Okay, guys," Carol laughed, "you can quit that any time now. If you don't, I'm going back to the house and let you two mugs do all the work down here today by yourselves!"

That ended it. Both guys, grinning, went off to do their jobs, and Carol went on to do her stuff with the colts.

All afternoon she wondered about herself. *Am I in love with John?* she mused. Then she thought, *Wait a minute, if I am in love with John, why am I right now thinking about Mark?*

Monday, Dan and Mike worked at the barn while Carol exercised several horses. Pearl came to the house early and prepared the meals for the day. She left meatloaf for supper. Carol was happy to see Mark and Jim come in at four. She brought out the colts, Storm and Corky, to be schooled. She and Mark worked with them for about an hour while Jim brought the barn horses in, put grain in their buckets, and filled the hayracks with timothy hay.

They were finished by six o'clock. The group then headed to the house for supper. Karen warmed up the meatloaf, took baked potatoes from the oven, and warmed creamed carrots. Carol, Mark, Jim, Mike, and Dan all helped Karen carry plates of food to the table. They were tired, but talked and laughed as the hungry crew wolfed down the appetizing meal. When finished, Jim and Mark volunteered to clean the kitchen while Dan and Mike carried the trash out before Jim and Mark headed home. Carol, deeply appreciating the outside help from Jim and Mark, thanked them profusely once again.

Karen had talked with Doctor White earlier. He had suggested that she start taking short walks every day to help strengthen her legs. Jim affectionately assisted her in this new venture. They decided because it was dark outside, they would walk on the farm's long driveway thus preventing walking on uneven ground.

The temperature had dropped considerably after nightfall so everyone donned jackets. Carol and Mark decided to sit on the front porch because the moon was full, and the night appeared to be full of glittering diamonds. It was a beautiful sight.

After some small talk and a little kidding around between Carol and Mark, he suddenly got very quiet. Carol asked him if something was wrong.

Mark turned and looked at Carol. The moonlight fell across her lovely face and accented her shining hair. He could feel his heart beating. He finally spoke. "Carol, I know at Ned and Ellie's wedding you and

John spent the whole day together, and I can't say I blame you. He seems to be very nice, and he's a good-looking dude too. But, I really need to know...do I have any chance at all with you?"

"Mark," she began, "believe me, I do want to be your friend, but I need to be honest. I really do not know how I feel about him or how I feel about you. It's crazy I know, but that's how I feel."

"Wow," he exclaimed. "I'm so glad I asked. Sounds like I have a teeny, tiny chance. And Carol, I'm gonna take it!"

Carol smiled at him and said, "Mark, I also have to tell you that John and I worked out a plan to see each other more than we have in the past. We will be together every other weekend, either here or at his ranch."

"That's okay, Carol," he laughed out loud. "That leaves every other weekend for me! And now that Jim and I agreed to continue our help here, we will be coming in every day at four. So I'll get to see you more than John does, yeah!" he clapped his hands, grinning.

Carol had to laugh. *What a character*, she thought, but she couldn't help liking him.

Looking him in the eye, she smiled and said, "You know what, Mark? I'm gonna be one busy lady with you two guys around."

He readily agreed! Then added with a chuckle, "And, may the best dude win!"

Well, she thought to herself, *I guess I can like anyone I want to. And as Karen and Granny said, I'm not married, engaged, or even going steady!*

Jim and Karen finished their walk and slowly climbed the porch steps. Seeing Carol and Mark on the porch, they joined them. Carol immediately asked Karen if she enjoyed the walk and if she thought it helped.

Karen stated, "I'm satisfied that I followed Doctor White's directions and, yes, I did enjoy it, and I'm sure it helped even though I'm exhausted. But I plan to continue walking every day," she continued, "until I finally have the strength to walk to the barn and once again climb up on Penny's back."

They applauded their approval.

CHAPTER 21

The following Saturday, November 12, John flew in from New Bern, arriving at Loafing Hills just minutes after Ellie and Ned returned from their awesome week in Key West. The couple brought back many endearing mementoes, gifts, and stories for all. Everyone was glad to have them home again and listened intently to their wonderful tales of their southern trip. John seemed especially interested because he told them he loved to travel and had high hopes that someday he would be able to visit the home of Hemingway and see other scenic sights of Key West.

It was Carol and John's first weekend date at Loafing Hills. However, Carol spent Saturday morning with Pearl's daughter, eighteen-year-old Joanne. Carol understood the teenager had taken riding lessons the previous year, so observing her riding on one of the schooled horses, Carol happily discovered Joanne's equitation to be excellent. John, of course, was helping out at the barn while Carol was busy with the teen.

Carol and John were hoping that surely by evening they would have time to go someplace and do something!

It didn't work out that way. Ned and Ellie needed a day's recoup from the trip; Jim and Mark didn't come in on weekends, so it was up to Mike, Dan, John, and Carol to get all the necessary daily tasks done on the farm. Later in the evening, John and Carol took the two colts in training for a very pleasant ride.

Immediately after supper, Carol helped Karen do her daily walk. When they returned, Carol and John were too tired to go out, so they invited Karen to join them in the large, comfortable family room. There the three sipped soft drinks, munched on a big bowl of popcorn, and watched a grand old John Wayne movie on TV.

At ten o'clock everyone was tired and began to saunter off to bed. John walked Carol to her room. At the door she apologized for this disappointing date. He smiled and told her that he wasn't at all unhappy about the date. He was truly content just being with her. He tenderly took her face in his hands and gently kissed her before parting.

How cool is that, thought Carol, as she prepared for bed. *But tomorrow we will do something besides work on the farm! I don't know what yet, but I'll sleep on it tonight*, she told herself as she slid beneath the covers, *and I'll surprise John with it tomorrow morning.*

Sunday morning everyone was up by eight-thirty helping get breakfast onto the table. Ellie scrambled eggs, Carol fried bacon, Karen poured orange juice, John buttered toast, and Ned and Granny set the table. It was a busy kitchen, sometimes too busy for Mike and Dan who sometimes preferred to just grab something from their cottage and eat on the way to the barn.

In the kitchen, all were sitting and enjoying the delicious breakfast when Dan came to the house and stuck his head in the door.

"Come on in, Dan," Ellie called.

As soon as he entered the kitchen, they all could see by the expression on his face that something was wrong.

Dan looked distressed as he told Ned, "Sky Cloud is down in his stall. Mike used the barn phone and called Dr. Harper. He's on his way here," he shouted over his shoulder as he started back to the stud barn. Ned, Carol, and John immediately jumped up from the table and ran quickly across the lawn to the stallion barn.

Carol was frightened as she ran. She kept thinking over and over... *Oh, please, not like Emerson!*

Dan, Mike, and Ned reached the stall first and found Sky Cloud lying on the stall floor, grunting. They needed to get him up and outside. The men helped the horse to his feet. John felt his hooves for possible founder (heat in the hooves). They felt cool.

Carol looked in the stall and immediately noticed that he had not touched his grain this morning.

"He's definitely got a bellyache," Ned said as he and Dan attempted to walk him, keeping him moving. They knew that a colicky horse might twist a gut if allowed to lie down and roll, which could result in death.

Within minutes Dr. Harper, the veterinarian, came in. He took one quick look at Sky Cloud and knew the horse was in trouble. He pulled out a hypodermic needle with twenty cc's of banamine and injected into the horse's neck. This would ease the pain, which would allow the doctor to insert a medical tube through the horse's nose down into his stomach. Sky Cloud was not happy with this procedure, stomping his feet and swinging his head around.

Next the doctor mixed oil and water together and poured it into the tube. This would flow through the stomach and intestines, hopefully washing any obstructions out.

Sky Cloud began to settle down after the procedure although he still seemed uncomfortable. Carol removed his grain bucket from his stall, but did leave him a bit of timothy hay. No one seemed to be able to answer the question of why the horse had become ill. Dan remembered that yesterday a county truck had sprayed the bushes on the side of the road for insects. Maybe the wind had carried it over the fence into Sky Cloud's pasture. The doctor thought that could have happened; and if there were horses in other pastures bordering that same road, they should surely be watched too. Mike answered that Sky Cloud's pasture was the only one on that road, but he would still check all the other turned-out horses just to be certain that it hadn't gotten blown further than they thought.

John told Ned that he would walk the horse until he started feeling better and would keep an eye on him for the rest of the day. The doctor agreed and suggested that someone keep an eye on the horse for the rest of the weekend. John agreed that he would take care of that. He knew that Ned, Mike, and Dan had lots to do checking the other horses for illness and taking care of the farm.

Carol stayed at the barn while John walked Sky Cloud. She cleaned the horse's stall and filled his bucket with fresh water.

I can't believe this, she thought to herself. *I'm really happy that Sky Cloud's okay, but there goes another big weekend!*

It was Sunday evening, and John was leaving to fly home. Carol, almost in tears, walked him to his car, apologizing again for the weekend.

John answered her, "You know, Carol, you don't get it," he smiled. "I don't care that we didn't go out dancing or didn't sit in a movie theater or didn't even get to watch the seagulls at Ocean City. I've got you by my side. And that's what matters; that's all that matters to me." He gently pulled her to him.

She faced him and smiled back replying, "Well, I would have liked that dance with you, or that movie, and I would have loved the gulls at Ocean City. But John," she continued, "I loved having you here, and you were a wonderful help with Sky Cloud. I don't know what we'd have done without your help."

He pulled her into his arms and they kissed, this time completely oblivious of anyone, anywhere that may have been watching!

"I will be back here to pick you up on November 26th," he whispered in her ear. "This time I'll fly you back to New Start, and we'll decide what we want to do from there. Maybe another cruise down the Neuse River? Or, if you prefer, we could go into town and just goof around? But we will find something fun to do. And I think, Carol," he added, "It will be good for you to get away from the farm for a couple of days too."

She readily agreed and told him that she was going to speak to Joanne to see if she would be willing to help out at the farm during that weekend.

After John drove off, Carol was feeling a little guilty. She loved her home and farm, but for years she had been so busy showing Emerson that she just never realized how much work was going on at the farm while she was gone. Of course, without Karen's help now, it was a real handful for her dad, Dan, Mike, and herself to take care of. *Maybe if Joanne can help*, she thought, *I wouldn't have to feel so guilty about our planned visit on the 26th and 27th. And, I'm so looking forward to that!*

On Monday morning, Carol sat at the table with her dad, Ellie, Karen, and Granny. Pearl poured each a cup of coffee. Carol asked Pearl if she thought that Joanne might be willing to help out at the farm on weekends.

Pearl answered, "I know Joanne would love to help at the barns as long as she gets to ride some," she laughed. "And Billy, only sixteen, would like to help out with the farm work too, mainly because he likes hanging around with Dan and Mike."

"That's great," Carol laughed. "I know that the guys like Billy too, so that will work out well for all of them," she happily exclaimed.

Ned, sipping his coffee added, "Pearl, I don't expect the kids to work here for nothing. I can't pay a lot for their help, but I will pay them both a little something along with meals.

"Oh, pooh," said Pearl, "you pay them nothing! Billy will learn about farming and will have less idle time on the weekends, and Joanne will get to ride horses. I know that's all she'll want. Besides," she added, "Ellie needs a rest, so I'll be doing the cooking on the weekends from now on too! I know the kids will be getting three healthy meals right here on Saturdays and Sundays. What more could I ask?"

Everyone agreed and laughed heartily at her declaration. The family was happy that Pearl was willing to come in every weekday morning to prepare meals for the day, and now she had agreed to cover the weekends too.

"Marvelous," cried Ellie. "I'll be glad to give up the kitchen to you, Pearl. Bless you," she said. "And I will now be the leader of the house cleaning," she laughed.

Karen spoke up quickly, "I will help anywhere I can, the kitchen or the cleaning."

Carol said that she would help too. Ned also agreed and volunteered to help whenever possible. Pearl, seeing the folks responding so positively said that she, Ellie, and Karen could surely take care of the house, while Ned and Carol did the farm stuff. Dan, Mike, Joanne, and Billy would help them outside.

"Good start for Monday," Ned laughed, as he put on his jacket to go check on Sky Cloud. Dan had told him that morning that he was okay. "But, I'll feel better looking in on him myself," he said as he left the house.

Carol went with Ned, informing him that before John had left that morning, they had looked at all the stabled horses and the turnouts. They all looked okay.

"Great," Ned answered. "I think it was just one of those freak things that happen once in a while. Hopefully, it will not happen again."

Carol and Ned exercised eight horses each and came back into the house at two o'clock for a late lunch. Pearl, true to her word, had baked a huge yummy pizza pie. It was sliced equally and enjoyed tremendously by the hungry lunch gang.

Later in the day Mark and Jim came in and helped at the barn. The first thing Mark did was ask Carol how her weekend date had gone. He tried to make the question sound casual, but it came out rather strained. Glancing at him, she could tell he was a little upset. She told him about Saturday being so busy they ended up just watching TV. Then she told him about what happened to Sky Cloud on Sunday, again leaving them too tired to do anything!

Mark tried his best to look disappointed when he said, "Oh, too bad, Carol."

She had to laugh because she could see that he was pleased, not about the sick horse, but about her lackluster date. She swatted him with a bridle and told him that he should be ashamed of himself.

"What did I do?" he questioned.

"You're being mean," she said. "I'll tell you this. Our next date will not be here. We're going to his New Start ranch. So, I don't think we'll be too tired on that date."

"Too tired for what?" he laughingly questioned as he pushed his lips out at her in a kissing mode.

"None of your business, Mark." She pushed him aside as she said, "Let's get started with the colts, okay?"

The rest of the evening they worked peacefully side-by-side, very comfortable with each other. First, they worked both colts on the lunge line and then mounted and took them out for a trail ride. They enjoyed working together and were looking forward to showing the colts in the spring.

Jim finished working in the barn and went up to the house to assist Karen with her daily walk. She was getting much better now, walking faster and becoming much stronger.

When Carol and Mark ambled to the house that evening, he shyly said to her, "Carol, I really do feel sorry about your bad weekend. Would you let me take you out this evening for supper?"

Carol immediately said, "Wait a minute, Mark. I didn't say it was a bad weekend! It was pleasant even if we didn't get off the farm."

"Bad choice of words," Mark whispered. "I felt that you were a little disappointed, that's all."

She had to agree with that remark. Turning to face him was a mistake. He looked really distressed.

"Okay, where are we going for this supper?" Carol asked, now watching him perk up with a bright smile. *Egad*, she laughed to herself, *this guy's face is an open book! And I'm the receptive reader!*

"I know a real neat place in town," Mark answered. "Serves the best seafood in Maryland."

Carol, trying not to encourage him too much said, "That sounds great, Mark. Let's ask Karen and Jim to join us."

Carol got the feeling that Mark was not thrilled about asking folks to join them, but he didn't argue. He even smiled warmly and nodded in agreement.

Karen and Jim both liked the idea of the supper and readily accepted the invitation.

The evening was wonderful: lobster bisque followed by crab imperial. It was quite delicious, and the company was great fun. The four were so much alike they enjoyed each other's company immensely.

After the meal they felt that it was still early enough to go to the movie theater right next door to the restaurant. The movie playing was an old James Bond thriller. None had seen it before so that was what they did. It was a very unplanned evening they decided, but much fun and enjoyed by all.

Tuesday morning, Ellie told Carol that John had called as promised. He had also tried her cell phone, but had gotten no answer. Carol felt awful. She had not had her phone with her all that evening. She immediately tried calling him first at his house and then on his cell. There was no answer at either. She left messages at both.

John did not answer her message until Thursday evening. He apologized saying that he had business out of town and couldn't seem to find a good time. He didn't want to call her when he was running from place to place during the real estate business deal he was working so hard on. They spoke for a good twenty minutes about lots of things and said goodbye with promises of future calls. However, both decided that the phone calls were not so important that they would be upset or irritated if they could not reach each other. They would call when they could and be thinking about what they would like to do on their next weekend together.

The rest of the week went quickly by. The stallion, Sky Cloud, was now back in good health, and Carol and Mark spent most of their time schooling and exercising the horses. Mark and Jim came in every afternoon and were a great help.

Loafing Hills was always active on the weekends. There were Granny, Pearl, Joanne, and Billy there for the two days, plus the permanent farm group. This sometimes made for a rather hectic picture: busy folks heading off in various directions, some working in the house, others at the barns or in the fields.

That was also the time of the week when interested horse buyers would arrive to look at the ready-to-sell stock. Many looked, some rode the hunters and the jumpers; others more interested in the younger and greener horses would be taken to the second barn and shown the stock there. People interested in the breeding program for their mare would go to the stud barn where the handsome farm stallion, Sky Cloud, would be led out for the visitors. This horse loved prancing around and showing off. He did himself proud for visitors.

It was truly exhausting work on the farm, but people that made up the Loafing Hills crew were patient, tolerant, and high spirited. They always made the weekends enjoyable and exhilarating for everyone. If a job became too much for one, others would immediately assist.

On the weekdays, Mark and Jim would show up to lend a helping hand. Jim would help at the barn and then go with Karen for her exercise walks. Mark schooled the colts with Carol, and then the two would ride the horses that needed exercising.

Later the four would come to the house for supper or sometimes drive into town for a burger and fries, maybe stopping at Jesse's ice cream parlor to enjoy one of her delicious hot fudge sundaes.

Carol spoke with John twice as the weekend date approached. They spoke about many things that were happening at Loafing Hills and at New Start. Both places were busy. Carol was busy with the horses, John with his cattle and selling parcels of land in New Bern. However, they both were anxiously awaiting their upcoming date of November 26th and 27th. John would fly into the small Maryland airport on the morning of the 26th, and Carol would meet him at the airport.

It was Friday, the day before John would be flying in, when Karen went to Carol and said, "Carol, I know that this weekend is yours and John's time to be together, and I know you've been looking forward to it for two weeks.

But, Carol, I must ask a very special favor of you," she continued. "Jim and I very much want you and Mark to join us this weekend at a very special place for a very special weekend."

"Karen," cried Carol, "how in the world can I do that? I'm packed and ready to go with John to New Start for the weekend."

"I know, Carol, I know," Karen answered. "If this was not most important to me, I would never ask this of you. You are my favorite person in the whole world, and Mark is Jim's very best friend. We really want you two to be with us this weekend. And, Carol, I really hate to ask you to do this, but please believe me when I tell you this is really important to Jim and me," Karen concluded.

Carol, seeing the look on Karen's face now, almost in tears, realized that this had be something extremely special to her.

Carol loved Karen like a sister and knew that she would never ask her to give up her weekend with John unless it was terribly important.

Carol, taking Karen's hands to calm her, told her that she would call John to see if it would be at all possible to postpone their date to the following weekend.

John did not answer his cell phone so she called his housekeeper, Dora. She explained to her as best she could why they should delay the date. Dora, always understanding, told her that she would get the message to John as soon as possible.

An hour later Dora returned Carol's call. She said, "John is in a meeting and sounded a little upset by the change of plans, but he knows that it has to be something pressing for you to change the date so late. He will call you Saturday, and he said to tell you that he is very much looking forward to seeing you the next weekend."

Carol asked Dora to please ask John to please call her via cell phone.

Carol ran to tell Karen that she could go with her and Jim for the weekend. Karen was absolutely ecstatic. She hugged Carol and danced her around the room.

"Whoa, Karen," Carol laughed. "How about telling me now, where are we going? And what am I supposed to wear and take with me?" she inquired.

"This is Jim's plan," Karen answered. "We are driving to the Baltimore Harbor tomorrow morning where we will board the Boland's yacht, the *Sea Princess*. We will sail to Sunray Island, off the Carolina coastline, and stay the weekend in a beautiful beach house owned by Jim's family."

"Wow," Carol cried, "that sounds great. What's the occasion?" she asked.

"I don't know," Karen answered. "I think Jim just wanted us to be together for a weekend of fun, and he really truly wanted you and Mark to share it with us."

Carol thought later that this was strange. Jim knew that she and John had planned this weekend at New Start. She thought maybe it was Jim's idea to get her and Mark together and away from horses for some leisure time.

Later in the day she questioned Mark about this trip. Mark replied that Jim had just asked him that day to go also. He did say, however, that he thought it was a great idea and was looking forward to the weekend. Then he reached over and placed a kiss on Carol's forehead and uttered, "I won't know how to act with you without a horse looking on!" he laughed.

She had to smile at his remark, but added, "Well, I just want you to know that you are a good friend, Mark, and for this weekend, that's what we'll be...good friends!"

Not to let it go at that, Mark asked, "Are you and John good friends too?" he quizzed.

"Yes, Mark, John and I are, at this time, good friends too," she smiled.

He quickly leaned down and kissed her lightly on her lips and called out as he walked away. "You know, Carol...that's what good friends do, *They Kiss!"*

Carol called back, "You're impossible, Mark." But he noticed she had a smile on her face.

CHAPTER 22

The four arrived at the Baltimore harbor early Saturday morning and were greatly impressed with the Boland's yacht, the *Sea Princess.* Jim was quite a boatman and handled the yacht with practiced ease. Jim Boland and his parents were all expert sailors, venturing often from Maryland to their island getaway. Jim expertly piloted the boat out of the harbor, passing under the Baltimore bridge and into the open Atlantic Ocean. Everyone was very comfortable aboard and loved the seating arrangements, allowing them a stunning view of the ocean and surrounding areas. Later, as they strolled through the galley and bedrooms on the boat, they were quite impressed with the order and efficient layout of the vessel.

Once well underway, Jim opened the basket that he had brought aboard. He laid out bread, cheese, crackers, and wine. Carol and Karen had brought a basket also, containing sandwiches, soft drinks, and brownies. Mark, not to be outdone, brought forth a huge box of donuts——all flavors, shapes, and sizes.

"Well," Jim laughed, "we sure ain't gonna starve; that's for sure!"

They had left before breakfast so everyone was hungry. The four helped themselves, eating and drinking, except Jim. He would not drink the wine while at sea. "The captain's gotta have his head on straight," he announced, "not only to steer the boat, but to be able to locate the island." He laughed.

They all agreed. In fact, Mark placed the bottle out of sight and stated, "This is for later."

The trip to the island was smooth sailing, sunshine, and fun. In just five hours they arrived at Sunray Island. The weather was magnificent, in the mid seventies.

Jim carefully berthed at the dock. There were a few other boats docked there also as several families shared the docking area. The owners' homes were scattered close by. Mark and Jim helped Karen and Carol exit the boat; Jim climbed back aboard to collect his paperwork. Mark, who had been on the island many times over the years with Jim and the Bolands, led the girls across the lawn to the house just a short walk away and ushered them inside, returning to the boat with a dolly to transport the luggage to the house.

From the living room, the girls walked out onto a large screened porch facing the ocean.

"What a gorgeous scene," Carol said. "It looks like a calendar picture."

"Yes," agreed Karen. "I don't think it's real," she laughed.

When the guys returned, Jim showed them the house. It was not a colossal mansion, but a good-sized, very comfortable, three-bedroom cape cod. A large living room, bath, kitchen, and study, also used as a bedroom, were found on the first floor. The decorations in the home were breathtaking. The colors were the shades of the sea, accented with seashells, sand sculptures, and white netting. The striking white-stone fireplace in the living room ran the length and height of the room. Jim said the fireplace was the only heat needed in the winter months. Upstairs were three nice-sized bedrooms and a large bath. Jim placed Karen's suitcase in the downstairs study because he didn't want her to have to use the stairs.

In the Boland's lovely beach house there was an air of tranquility. This, in just minutes, made everyone feel comfortably at home.

The four were not hungry when they arrived on the island, as they had been feasting all the way on cheese, crackers, sandwiches, and donuts. Jim suggested they take the old Plymouth out of the garage for an island excursion. They all agreed and hopped into the old car. Jim drove and pointed out different points of interest, such as the best swimming spots, fishing areas, walking trails, bird-watching locations, and fast-food spots. Then he also showed them the no-no areas: the swamps and gator canals.

Driving through downtown Sunray, he pointed to a classy looking restaurant sitting atop a hill overlooking the ocean. "There," he told them, "is where we're heading tonight for a very special treat." He had already made the reservations for seven o'clock. "It's the best restaurant on the island, Everlee's Seashore Inn. Best shrimp and lobster you've ever tasted, best margaritas made, and a great band for dancing the night away."

Karen quickly suggested that they had better head back to the house. "It's already two o'clock," she said, "I don't know about the rest of you guys, but I gotta take a nap if we're goin' drinkin' and dancin' tonight." She laughed.

Everyone agreed so they headed back for a nap. On their way, they asked Jim what they were expected to wear at Everlee's Seashore Inn.

"Something a little on the dressy side," he answered. "Suit and tie for the guys, ladies, something feminine."

Carol and Karen looked at each other and both smiled. Jim had asked Karen before the trip for her and Carol to please include a dress-up outfit. Now they were glad they had. They answered, "We brought dresses that will absolutely knock your socks off!"

When they reached the house, Carol walked Karen to the studio bedroom on the first floor. As she was leaving Karen at the door, she said, "I'm glad that you and I went shopping a couple of weeks ago, Karen, and bought those two dresses."

"Oh, me too," Karen answered. "They'll be perfect for tonight."

"As you know, I bought mine for the weekend date with John," Carol continued, "but I'm happy that I can wear it tonight." She squeezed Karen's hand as she left her and proceeded upstairs to her room.

Mark heard Carol in the hall and asked if she needed anything before retiring. She asked him if he would be kind enough to wake her at five-thirty. Throwing her a kiss, as he headed towards his room, he assured her that he would wake her. She closed the door to her room, slipped off her clothes, pulled on her bed shirt, and crawled under the light spread. *Very comfortable*, she thought. She fell asleep almost immediately.

Later Mark knocked on Carol's door at five-thirty on the dot. She called a thank you to him, put on her robe, and headed for the bathroom to shower. However, Mark was headed for the same room. They met at the bathroom door.

"My, my," he called to her. "Looks like we'll have to share the shower."

"That's okay, Mark. I'll wait for you to finish," she smiled.

"No, I'm a gentleman." He bowed. "You first." But then he quickly added, "Would you want me to come in and talk to you while you shower?"

With that, Carol shut the door in his face.

"Hey, can't blame a guy for trying," he called through the door.

At six forty-five, all were ready to go. Jim wore a dark brown suit with a tan and gold tie. Mark wore a deep gray suit with a tie of dark-gray and light-gray stripes. Both guys looked quite spiffy!

The girls, however, stole the show; Karen was a knockout in a gold rayon dress with sparkling bead accents and low gold pumps. Carol looked spectacular in a black bare-shoulder velvet top and black velvet skirt accented with mirrored sequins, finishing off with one-inch black pumps. Both ladies wore drop earrings matching their ensembles.

The guys enthusiastically showed their admiration for both beautiful ladies with whistling, clapping, and shouting. The ladies, not to be outdone, did a few noisy catcalls for the guys too. Each tried to outdo the other. It ended in a draw, all laughing heartily. They drove off to Everlee's Seashore Inn.

The restaurant was surprisingly impressive. Subdued colors shaded the room using hidden ceiling lights; this was enhanced by circles of white wall candles. In the room were several tables covered in white linen, and at the center of each table sat a lovely sandstone mermaid sculpture, each artistically unique in pose.

At the core of the room was a large dance floor adjacent to the stage for the band. The inn was positively awesome, leaving guests almost spellbound with its beauty. The well-groomed four saw that the room was almost full with very impeccably dressed patrons. They nodded approval to each other, knowing they fit in perfectly. They looked their very best.

Their host led them to a table bordering the dance floor and introduced them to their waiter, Sam. Mark and Jim gentlemanly seated the ladies. While Sam handed each a menu, he informed them that the band would begin playing at nine.

Jim stated, reading the menu, "I have to tell you that the food here is the most delicious I've ever tasted. Everything is absolutely the best."

Mark agreed that John was right. "I know that to be a fact," he said. "I've been here a couple of times with Jim and his family."

Carol, after considering their recommendations, decided that because they all had lobster not long ago at the seafood restaurant in Maryland, she'd go instead with another seafood, baked flounder, in a spicy spinach sauce. Karen seconded that order for herself. Jim and Mark decided they too would order the flounder, but theirs was served in butter and lemon sauce. They were not disappointed. The meal was absolutely a delight. They all agreed: Best flounder dinner ever!

When they finished dining, it was eight-thirty. They planned to dance that evening, so they ordered a round of drinks while watching the handsome band being set up.

Their waiter showed up at their table with a pie box and four plates, which he set gingerly in front of Karen.

"What's this?" she cried.

Jim whispered to her, "Bet they noticed you limping earlier, Karen. I think they're just trying to give you a nice dessert."

"How thoughtful," she answered as she smiled at Sam.

"Open it, Karen. Let's see what they gave you!" Jim directed.

Karen lifted the lid off the box. There was no pie inside. There was, however, a small black velvet box sitting in the center.

They told her to pick it up and open it. She was so surprised she wasn't sure what to do. She reached in the box and tentatively picked up the small velvet container and carefully opened it. She couldn't believe her eyes. There sat a gorgeous ring: one center diamond, with four smaller stones surrounding it.

At this point, Jim took the ring from the box, knelt down on one knee beside Karen, and spoke, "Karen, you know I've loved you since we were kids in high school. I missed you after we graduated. But, lucky for me, four years later I found you again. I don't want to lose you again, ever. I love you, Karen. Will you marry me, please?"

The table held total silence. Karen was stunned speechless. She looked at Jim with tears welling in her eyes and spoke softly. "Jim, I do love you too, and *yes*, I will marry you!" The table came alive with hugs, kisses, and congratulations from her very best friends.

What an evening, thought Carol. She was just ready to declare this thought to her friends when she saw her dad, Ellie, and Granny walking towards them. Several steps to the rear were Jim's parents, Ron and Donna Boland. "What a shock," she shouted. She and Karen both stood in utter surprise.

Again, there were lots more hugs, kisses, and congratulations from, and to, everyone. Chairs were pulled to the table to seat the five extra guests.

Ned explained to Carol, Karen, and Mark that Jim had set this whole weekend up. He said they had left Baltimore harbor with the Bolands, using a borrowed cabin cruiser, just one hour after Jim and his party departed Baltimore. They were all staying at the Sunray Island Motel and planned to head back the next day around noon.

"We wouldn't have missed this night for anything in the world," piped Granny as she hugged Karen, Jim, Carol, and Mark.

"Now you know why, Carol," Jim explained, "I had to ask you to miss your date this weekend. It would not have been the same without you. You and Mark had to be with us on this very special night."

At that moment the band began to play *Stand By Me*, which Jim had asked them to play. It was Karen's very favorite song. Everyone in the inn applauded. It was a happy, happy event, with everyone dancing 'til closing at two a.m.

Ned, holding his drink high, announced to everyone, "What a beautiful proposal, and what a wonderful, happy engagement dinner dance for two very, very nice people. We love you both. Here's to Karen and Jim...*Salute*...!"

Later Karen and Carol sat in the cottage's kitchen, sipping coffee while Jim and Mark, in the living room, started a fire in the fireplace.

"Tell me, Karen," Carol asked, "were you honestly surprised?"

"Yes, absolutely," said Karen. "I knew that it was important that you and Mark be with us, but honestly, Carol, I truly thought Jim wanted you and Mark, our very dearest friends, to join us this weekend because we love you both."

Carol clapped her hands, saying, "Good for Jim. He really did pull this off. I can't believe that Granny, Dad, and Ellie never uttered a word. And now I also know why, when I told Ellie that I was upset about breaking John's date, she said simply to go on with Karen and Jim this weekend and see John next week, which is really weird because she loves John and usually takes his side in everything."

"Well, anyway," said Karen, "it was a most beautiful surprise. I will never ever forget it."

"You are so right, Karen," Carol said as she stood and hugged her dear friend. "I'm so happy for you and Jim! And I must thank you for letting Mark and me be a part of such a wonderful weekend!"

They walked into the living room. The fire was burning brightly and felt good. The four lazily watched the morning sun fill the sky with stunning colors, mirroring its images onto the water. They talked and laughed about the proposal party. It was beautiful and fun.

They all agreed that it was truly a grand and memorable event.

It was dawn, all four were totally worn out. They went to their respective bedrooms to get some sleep.

Carol woke up at about noon and found Karen also awake downstairs. The guys were outside preparing for the trip back to Baltimore. When they returned, the four decided to take a walk along the coast to a fast-food restaurant about two miles down the shoreline. Karen limped along, laughing, with her left hand waving high in the air, catching the glitter of the sun on her beautiful new diamond ring. They all laughed at her antics.

It was an interesting stroll. They found all kinds of odd objects washed up on the shore including a seaweed-wrapped bottle. The brown bottle contained a note. It read simply, "*This is your lucky day!*"

"Must be somebody's idea of a joke," Mark said, laughing.

"I don't think so," answered Karen, "I think *Jim* was supposed to find that *yesterday*!" She laughed.

Jim took it further by looking skyward, hugging Karen, and shouting: "T'was a message from heaven to Karen and me!"

They all happily agreed.

They were not very hungry when they finally arrived at the restaurant, so they shared shakes and fries while they wandered back to the cottage.

Before boarding the boat at two o'clock for the trip back to Baltimore, Carol looked at her cell phone. There were two messages from John, both from last evening. *He must have called while the band was playing,* she thought, *and I did not hear the calls.* She tried immediately to call him and, again, no answer.

As Jim cautiously pulled the yacht away from the pier, the group called out, "Thank you and farewell to beautiful Sunray Island!"

The day was calm with a cool breeze coming in from the south, which made for a refreshing trip. About two hours out of Baltimore, however, the night air prompted them to don their jackets.

Mark whispered to Carol as they sailed under the Baltimore bridge, "Thank you, Carol, for coming today. It wouldn't have been fun without you. Do you think John will be mad at you for going with us?"

Then before she could answer him, he added in a whisper, "I really hope he's too mad to ever see you again...then, just maybe, I'd have a chance!" he smiled.

"Mark, you are so awful." She smiled as she answered, "I must tell you, though, this has been a most enjoyable weekend, and Mark you are a wonderful friend. But, yes," she added, "I do hope that John is *not* angry with me!"

After pulling into the harbor, they tied up the craft and stepped ashore. It was seven o'clock, and they were all hungry. Knowing that it was a two-hour drive to Loafing Hills, they visited a neat little harbor restaurant where they leisurely ate a delicious supper.

They did not reach Loafing Hills until after midnight. Even though they had been sitting most of the day, they were all exhausted. After a quick thank you and goodnight to Jim and Mark, Karen and Carol wearily climbed the steps to bed.

Monday morning Pearl rang the bell for breakfast at eight a.m. Ellie, Ned, Mike, and Dan were at the kitchen table when Carol and Karen came dragging down the stairs. Ellie and Ned had arrived home about four-thirty in the afternoon the day before, dropped Granny off at her place, and had gotten home in time to have a good night's sleep.

The family welcomed the girls home and told Karen they were very happy for her and Jim. They all knew that it had been an exciting weekend, but very wearing. Carol and Karen agreed. Carol told the story of the note in the bottle. Karen added with a smile, "I'm keeping that note under my pillow forever!"

After breakfast, Ned, Carol, Mike, and Dan all went to the barn. Karen and Ellie helped Pearl in the kitchen. Joanne and Billy would be coming in after school today to help; Jim and Mark should be coming in about four o'clock too.

There was a lot of work to do on the farm all week. Everyone was very busy.

Carol kept thinking about her coming weekend date at New Start with John. She hoped that he would call in the evening; if not, she definitely would call him.

Right after supper on Monday evening, John finally called. Carol was pleased to hear that he was not angry with her at all; in fact, he was very pleased to hear about Jim and Karen's engagement.

Tuesday through Friday was also an extra busy time at Loafing Hills. Ned had purchased three green-broke Quarter Horse geldings the week before, and he planned to have them ready for sale on Sunday. Carol, Mark, and Joanne were active all week readying the geldings to show prospective buyers.

CHAPTER 23

John arrived at Loafing Hills Farm early Saturday morning. Ned enthusiastically invited him into the kitchen and offered him coffee and a chair at the table. He joined Ellie and Ned. Pearl was fixing breakfast and telling John that this was number-one breakfast. The rest of the family and crew would share breakfast number two at eight in the morning.

"Whoa," John responded, "you cook two breakfast meals every day?"

"Oh, no," she laughed, "only one on Mondays through Fridays. But on the weekends it's hard to get everyone together at one time."

Ned told John, "This family is growing. On the weekends, besides Ellie, Pearl, and myself, are Carol, Karen, Granny, Joanne, Billy, Mike, Dan, and sometimes Jim and Mark. But it's great to have everyone sit down together to talk about the weekend plans before they begin. Ellie, Pearl, and I arise a little early, eat a small breakfast at seven, and then have coffee with the main group at eight."

John, smiling, said, "It's quite a job running this farm, Ned; you must surely love it."

Ned, glancing at Ellie, spoke, "I do love it, John, but to be honest, I'm getting a little too old to run all the time. I'm beginning to think about retiring."

Ellie laughed. "Oh, John, don't pay any attention to that statement. Now I wholeheartedly agree, Ned should think about retiring, but I don't believe for a minute he, or Carol, would give up Loafing Hills."

Ned answered with a smile, "Well, I'll still think about it. We'll see!"

Carol and Karen came into the kitchen. John stood and pulled two chairs up to the table, seating Carol and Karen comfortably between Ned and himself. He took Carol's hand and gently kissed her fingertips. While still holding her hand, he told Karen how pleased he was in learning about the engagement. Smiling, she raised her left hand so he could see her lovely ring.

John exclaimed, "What a gorgeous ring!"

Carol and Karen both told John about the marvelous surprise dinner-dance and weekend at Sunray Island that Jim had so artistically organized. "It was incredible," Karen added.

Carol, shaking her head, declared, "It was absolutely *awesome!*"

After the early breakfast, John and Carol took her luggage to the rental car. They said goodbye to the folks sitting at the table being served the second breakfast of the morning. On their way out of the house, they met Jim and Mark coming in. They stopped for a minute to say "Hi" to each other. Carol told them, with a smile, to hurry or they might not get breakfast.

Carol tried not to notice the depressed look on Mark's face when he saw that she was going off with John. *He's just like an open book*, she said to herself. Even John noticed Mark's sad gaze.

The weather had turned very cold, but the flight to New Start was pleasant. Upon landing, they found it a bit warmer as they transferred the luggage to John's Buick. They noticed, however, that dark clouds were forming; showers were on the way.

It was good to be at New Start Ranch again and to see Dora again. Dora was also happy to see Carol, making her feel very much welcome and at home. Little Piggy, the Pekinese, danced on his hind feet welcoming her too. Carol hugged Dora while handing her an African Violet for her garden, and to Piggy she gave a hug along with a milk-bone doggy treat.

John, carrying Carol's luggage, led her upstairs to the same guest room she had had the last time she had visited New Start. She was very pleased because she loved the charming room; she was especially entranced by the scenic view it offered, waving green pasturelands surrounded by majestic oak and hickory trees.

Carol changed out of her travel jeans and stepped into a light mauve pantsuit. She also unpacked and slid on a comfortable, but stylish, pair of sandals. Looking in the mirror she said to herself, "I have no idea what John's planned for this weekend. Hope he finds me presentable."

When she came down the stairs, John's brown eyes sparkled as he whispered, "Carol, you are so beautiful." That was all he had to say. Carol felt goosebumps!

"Is there anything that you especially want to do this weekend?" he quietly asked.

"No, John, maybe a movie?" she answered.

"Well, let me tell you what I had in mind," he said. "If it doesn't sound good to you, please tell me; we'll do a movie instead. But, if you like dinner theaters," he continued, "the classical play *Showboat* is now playing close by at a new dinner theater. It's had great reviews, good actors, actresses, and scrumptious food. How's that sound to you for this evening?" he asked.

Carol was delighted. She had never seen the play and was excited about attending.

When they arrived, Carol found the lobby of the dinner theater gorgeous. In the center of the ceiling hung a spectacular crystal chandelier. Several large gold vases were placed around the perimeter of the room on bright burgundy carpet. Each vase exhibited beautiful flowers of every shade. To top it all off, the personnel were all decked out in formal attire.

The theater itself was a vision to behold. Luxurious seating was offered on the main floor. Several balconies sat majestically above the floor, adorned with lovely art sculptures.

Carol and John both thoroughly enjoyed a delicious dinner and the fantastic classical play *Showboat*. It was a beautiful and successful evening.

They cozily spent the later evening hours cuddled together in the big, soft suede chair in the TV room. They enjoyed watching together and talked easily with each other, agreeing that they were very much alike.

The next morning they had planned a boating trip, but it was too cold and too wet outside so they decided instead to go into town for an early afternoon movie, which they thoroughly enjoyed.

Arriving back at New Start, Carol packed in preparation for the flight home. John, feeling the two days had gone by so quickly, asked, "You know what, Carol, I didn't see you enough this weekend. How about if I stay with you at Loafing Hills for a couple of days and fly back Wednesday?"

"Oh, my gosh," Carol exclaimed, "I would love that."

"I know everyone at Loafing Hills is so busy, I could surely lend a helping hand for a day or two," John volunteered.

Carol walked to him, placed her arms around his neck, and kissed him. She surprised herself, but was glad she had done it. He was surprised and glad too. He pulled her to him and gently kissed her again, saying, "Carol, I love you. I really do."

Carol, without blinking, answered, "John, I love you too, for sure," and she meant it. She was so glad that she finally, for the first time, admitted it to herself and to John.

At five o'clock they told Dora and Piggy goodbye at the door and drove across the ranch to his plane. The flight back was a little scary because it was dark outside, and the rain and fog followed them all the way back to Maryland. John, being a good pilot, closely followed the flight plan and was very attentive to the task.

About an hour later they landed safely, transferred luggage to the rental car, and arrived at Loafing Hills a few minutes after seven.

Ned and the family were glad to hear that John had volunteered to help out for a couple of days on the farm. They also noticed that John and Carol were close all evening. Holding hands, they left, carrying a flashlight, to go to the stud barn to see how Sky Cloud was doing. John knew that the horse had recuperated, but had not seen him since his illness. He was happy that the stallion was looking so good.

While they were gone, the family talked about the two lovebirds.

Karen said, "Yaaaa, those two are definitely in love!"

Monday morning Carol and John sat at the table with Ned, Ellie, and Karen.

Pearl, always making up songs and jokes while she worked, didn't disappoint the early morning folks. Carrying a tray, she came dancing across the kitchen floor, wearing a bright red apron over her large blue sack-dress. She bounced so hard, her gray bun sitting atop her head bobbed up and down wildly as she belted out her new song:

"The fun has just begun,
with breakfast number one.
Then out of the blue will come
breakfast number two.
The first one's the light one,
for quiet folks with pull.
The second one's the full one,
for those who shoot the bull!"

Ned chuckled and said, "Pearl, the barn guys are going to love your new song, but I'm not at all sure about your kids!" He grinned.

"Oh, they know I'm kidding and always making up silly things. They'll love it," she laughed.

John turned to Pearl and remarked, "I'm sure glad I was here to hear your original music this morning, Pearl." He smiled.

"We all love to hear your songs, Pearl," said Karen. "And I think it's a great way to start a day. See I can rhyme too," she laughed.

Everyone agreed that Pearl really knew how to start a day. She was fun and always managed to put everyone in a good mood.

When things finally settled down at the table, everyone sipped coffee while Ned told Carol and John about the weekend sales. "It was fantastic. Good folks buying good horses," he said. "It was a very profitable weekend despite the weather."

Karen excitedly described some of the visitors to Carol and John. Three adults with several kids from a local pony club came in. The kids rode two of the well-broke horses, Big Red and Buttercup. They loved them both. Joanne was great all day long. She patiently helped the kids and kept a careful eye on them as they rode in the indoor arena. Both horses were sold within an hour.

Ned agreed with Karen. "We thought that it would be a washout because of the dreary weather," Ned said, "but it didn't seem to bother anyone. All three of the horses that I recently purchased were sold. That's five horses sold on Saturday, and one on Sunday.

"We also sold one of the colts, Storm." He smiled at Carol, knowing she had worked hard on both colts, and now one was already sold, to her delight.

"All through the day," Ned continued, "we had many folks, owning well-bred mares, who came in to look at Sky Cloud. Dan logged in seven prospect mares to be bred to Sky Cloud in the coming breeding season."

Ellie smiled broadly at Ned and agreed that it had indeed been a great weekend.

"That's grand," Carol and John said with satisfaction.

"Maybe we should often pray for rain," laughed Karen.

Pearl broke these thoughts by expressing her desire to sing for breakfast number two. All five departed the table at the same time, laughing.

Even though they had sold six horses, the work did not seem much lessened. There were still several horses that had to be exercised every day, and one remaining colt had to be worked too. Two of the barn-kept horses were show prospects so they needed daily training. John and Carol worked all day on these tasks. Joanne came in at three o'clock after college class and helped too. Later in the afternoon John planned to ride one of the show horse potentials, and Carol would ride the remaining colt, Corky. They planned to exercise these two horses by riding the trails through the woods and across the farm.

Carol and John, standing in the barn tacking up their mounts, heard someone calling Carol's name. It was Mark. He had the gelding, Frosty, in tow because Mike had told him that Carol was getting ready to trail ride, and he wanted to join her.

He was surprised to see John standing in the aisle, tacking up a horse. Mark looked perplexed. Carol and John, seeing the anxious look on his face, asked him to join them.

They rode out across the pasture, explaining to Mark why John was at Loafing Hills that day and the next. Both Carol and John attempted to bring Mark into the conversation, but he felt uncomfortable with John.

He finally asked, "It's very cold out here today. Where are we riding to?"

Carol answered him, saying John wanted to ride up to Emerson's grave. After that Mark did not say another word. At the grave, they dismounted. Carol, as usual, ran her hand over the gravestone. John, feeling her sorrow, stood quietly at her side with one arm over her shoulder. Mark stood back holding his horse. He was not enjoying this outing.

It was still very cold when they arrived back at the barn. They untacked the horses and walked them for several minutes. They had had a good workout and needed a cooling down time before going back to their stalls.

Ellie called to Mark from the house, saying he had a phone call. Carol and John cleaned the saddles and bridles and then straightened up the tack room before going up to the house. On their way, Carol noticed Mark's car was gone. She knew that Mark was upset, but didn't think that he would have left without a goodbye!

Karen and Jim met Carol and John at the door telling them that the phone call to Mark was from his mother. She told him that a hospital in Wyoming called her, saying that Neal Long, Mark's father, had a heart attack that morning and was in the intensive care unit.

Mark was distraught and left immediately. Jim said that he was sure Mark would try to catch a flight to Wyoming that evening.

This bad news put everyone on the farm in a quiet mood. Even Pearl seemed subdued. Later, after obtaining the name of the hospital, Carol called to see if she could find out anything more about him. The hospital's answer was, "He is in the intensive care unit and doing as well as can be expected."

When Carol told the family this, Karen piped up with, "No news is good news."

Carol told her she hoped that was right. Jim added, "We'll just have to wait to hear from Mark. He promised that he would call as soon as he could."

It was bedtime, and there still was no word from Mark. Carol and John were tired from a long day of schooling, training, and riding horses. They were watching the late news on TV and trying hard to keep their eyes open. Jim had left earlier and promised to call if he heard anything from Mark. Ned, Ellie, and Karen had gone to bed; Carol was feeling sad for Mark. She knew that he was upset because John was there, and now he was worried about his dad too.

John reached over to Carol, took her hand in his, and whispered, "Carol, I know that Mark was upset today, and I know that he doesn't care for me. The reason is very obvious. I'm sure you know that Mark is in love with you."

"John," Carol replied, "you're right. I've known it for a while, but I've told him over and over again that I love him too...*as a friend!*"

"Well, I'm sure he was hoping you'd change your mind," John said, "and, of course, I'm praying that you won't! True love is precious, Carol, and that's how I feel about you," he said as he looked into her eyes.

Carol reached up and stroked John's face and whispered, "John, I am in love with you, and I think I've known it for a long time, but was afraid to admit it even to myself."

"Why would you be afraid of me?" he asked seriously.

"I'm not afraid of you. I guess I was afraid of love. I've been out of the dating game for several years," she said. "Too busy breaking, training, and showing Emerson to get involved with anyone."

"Afraid of love," he repeated. "I like that because I also was afraid of love. Then one day I saw you at a horseshow. I was hooked at first sight. Carol, honey," he said, "I'm so glad we both woke up!" They smiled at each other.

He gently took her into his arms and kissed her. She laid her head on his shoulder; the TV blared away. They both fell asleep, peacefully wrapped in each other's arms.

CHAPTER 24

Tuesday, there was still no word from Mark. After Pearl served breakfast number one, Carol and John went down to the barn to plan for the day. While there, John asked Carol to accompany him to the stud barn again to see Sky Cloud.

"Hey, what's all this interest in Sky Cloud, John?" she asked.

"I just wanted to check the facility: how big the stalls are, is there a paddock for each horse, how big an exercise area is there for each horse. I'm just being nosey, honey," he answered.

Carol tagged along with John. He seemed genuinely interested in the stud barn. *How strange*, thought Carol. *But, after all, he's a man, and it's hard to read them sometimes!*

Ned had left earlier that morning to attend a horse sale in Ohio. He was interested in some colts he had seen advertised in a horse magazine.

John gave a helping hand to Dan throwing hay down from the loft. He later helped Mike clean stalls.

Mike told John, "Be sure to leave at least three stalls for Billy to clean this afternoon. Billy would feel offended if we had nothing to do when he comes in after school today." Mike laughed.

Of course, John had to tell Mike how very sorry he was for not allowing him to clean all the stalls by himself. They both laughed as they gladly hung their pitchforks up on the peg rack.

In the mid afternoon, Carol and John exercised Blackjack and Penny. Neither horse had been ridden for awhile. It was cold and the wind was blowing, so a good canter across the fields was invigorating for both the riders and the horses.

Shortly after supper, John had to start home. Everyone wished him a safe flight as Carol escorted him from the house. At the car, John held Carol in his arms for a long time before finally kissing her goodbye. Carol didn't care this time if the whole world was watching!

When she returned to the house, she showered and fell exhausted into bed. It had been a full, physically and mentally draining, four days.

It was Wednesday morning. There was still no word from Mark. Jim had not heard anything either. John had called before Carol went to the barn. It was good to hear he had a good flight home. His strong voice and deep laugh sent chills down her neck. Oh, how she loved this man! She had to laughingly agree with Karen...she was no longer in *like* with John; she was definitely in *love* with John!

Later, as Carol schooled the horses, she was missing John. And to be honest she missed Mark too, but mostly because he was always there in the afternoon to help, and she was worried about not hearing from him.

Ned arrived home with two very good-looking, green-broke colts. Carol was admiring the colts when they heard the dinner bell ring.

That's funny, Carol thought, *it's not lunch time yet*. She told her dad she would run to the house to see why Ellie was ringing the bell. Ellie met her at the door and told her that Mark wanted to talk to her on the phone. He was holding for her.

"Mark," Carol cried, "where are you?"

"I'm at my mother's house in Virginia. I need to talk to you, Carol, today. It's very important," he begged. "I can pick you up in one hour. Will you be ready?"

"Ready for what?" she asked.

"We need to go someplace quiet," he said. "How about coffee at that little restaurant in Westminster that we went to a couple of times?" he suggested.

"Okay, Mark. Shall I ask Karen to join us?"

"No, I haven't talked to her or Jim yet. I really want to see you first."

"All right, Mark, I'll be ready when you get here."

Carol did not tell anyone except Ellie about Mark's picking her up. She was glad that Karen was napping in preparation for a shopping trip with Jim later that evening.

True to his word, Mark pulled up to the front of the house in one hour. Before he could get out of the car, Carol quickly opened the passenger door and got in. She couldn't help but notice Mark's disoriented demeanor.

"Mark, are you okay?" she asked.

"No, but thanks for noticing," he laughed.

"We're only about twenty minutes away from Westminster," he said. "Let's wait 'til we get there before we talk."

Carol was a little concerned about the way he was acting, but she sat quietly in the seat until they arrived at the restaurant. She got out and waited for him at the door while he parked.

As soon as they were seated and the waitress took their coffee order, Carol couldn't contain herself any longer and blurted out, "Mark, we were all so worried about you. How is your dad?"

"I've got a long story to tell you, Carol," he spoke softly; "please bear with me. I flew to Wyoming late Monday night and got to the hospital about two Tuesday morning. They let me go into the ICU to see Dad. He recognized me and told me that he wasn't going to make it. I tried to calm him, but he kept shushing me.

"'I have to tell you this,' he said. 'The ranch is yours, Mark. Call Mr. Johnson, my attorney. He will give you all the details.' I tried to tell him he would be okay. He should rest.

"Carol, he looked at me, shook his head no, closed his eyes. He was gone! I bawled like a baby."

Carol, shocked at this news and seeing Mark's distress, moved her chair closer to him. She held his hand and laid her other hand on his shoulder. She felt such sorrow for him; tears flowed down her cheeks as she told him how sorry she was.

"Thanks, Carol, I really need and appreciate your strength right now. Would you be willing to fly back to Wyoming with me for the funeral? I'm also going to ask Jim, Karen, and my mom."

"Of course, I will," she whispered, as she blotted her tears. "I can't speak for your mom, Mark, but I'm sure Karen and Jim will go too."

When they arrived back at Loafing Hills, Mark and Carol went to the house. Karen was waiting for Jim to pick her up. She, like Carol, was surprised and delighted to see Mark. As she hugged him, she questioned him about his dad. Mark asked her to please wait for Jim to arrive, as he wanted to speak to them at the same time. Ned and Ellie, also glad to see Mark, realized that they too should wait to question him.

When Jim arrived, they sat at the kitchen table. Ned poured a glass of cider for everyone, and Ellie placed a large platter of cheese and crackers on the table.

All sat quietly while Mark explained his visit to the hospital and his father's demise. He talked about his father's last wishes and his meeting with Mr. Johnson, his attorney. The ranch and all its belongings, including three hundred head of cattle, had been totally turned over to Mark. He explained his immediate plans to close his construction business. He also talked with his mother the day before. She agreed to sell her home in Virginia and move with him to his Wyoming ranch.

"Now, here is where you guys come in, I hope," he spoke softly. "Jim, you are my very best friend in this world," he said as he looked at Jim. "I will really need a partner on the ranch. I know I'm asking a lot," he sighed. "To do this, you would have to give up your coaching job at the high school and leave this area."

Seeing the look of disbelief on his friends' faces, he quickly added, "Please hear me out. It would be a fifty-fifty deal. We would build a second house on the property, for my partner and, of course, his wife, Karen!"

He smiled at Karen and said, "Karen, I know you will be well soon, and I want you to know, if you come, Penny comes too. And, of course, once there, you can buy all the horses you want. And, Karen," he added, "please know, we expect Granny to be there with you, also."

Everyone stared intently at Mark, unsure how to react. Looking at Carol, he sighed. "I hope that you will come visit often, Carol. As you are well aware, I would love to have you there permanently," he smiled. "But after seeing you and John together, I know that's not possible. He loves you, Carol, and I think you love him too," he concluded and smiled at his friends. They were still so surprised at his plans; they were unable to find words to answer him.

Mark, realizing the shock he had thrust upon them, quietly whispered, "I know, folks, this is a lot to lay on you at one time. I don't want answers right now, but please seriously think about it. I'm hoping that you will attend the funeral this Saturday, and maybe you will give me your answers shortly after."

They decided that Karen, Jim, and Carol would fly out Friday evening with Mark, stay for the funeral, and fly home Saturday evening or Sunday. Ned and Ellie could not make it to the funeral, but sincerely passed their heartfelt condolences to Mark. They all hugged Mark as he said goodbye before driving to his mother's home in Virginia.

After he left, the four sat at the table. They were feeling, with tears, Mark's pain at the death of his father, and then there was the surprise of his unexpected proposal! It was a sad, yet exciting turn of events, which left them feeling rather overwhelmed.

They decided that they would each think seriously about what Mark was offering them. It sounded good, but it would be quite a move on their part. Karen, in tears, told Carol that it would be very hard for her to leave Loafing Hills. Carol, trying to see the bright side, offered Karen encouraging thoughts about life on the cattle ranch.

"Karen, if you and Jim do decide to go, I promise I will come see you at least twice a year, maybe more, and I want you to visit Maryland every chance that you get."

Karen still looked scared at pulling up roots from this farm that she loved so dearly.

Seeing this, Jim suggested they sleep on it that night and later do some serious thinking about Mark's proposal. "We shouldn't make any quick decisions," he ventured. "Let's at least take a look at that Wyoming ranch this weekend. Then, we'll ask ourselves if we are we ready to leave Loafing Hills, Maryland."

Carol jumped in with, "Jim, Karen, please don't feel guilty about leaving us here. I love Karen, and you too, Jim, but this may be that once in a lifetime opportunity for you both. I know that none of us here at Loafing Hills would ever want to stand in your way of becoming part owners in a cattle business. Please consider it seriously.

"If it would make you and Jim happy, Karen, then it will make us happy too. And you both know that we will all still get to see each other often, and thank God for e-mail!" she laughed.

Before going to bed, Carol phoned John. He did not answer. She left him a message to please call her as soon as possible.

Jim left shortly afterwards. Carol and Karen talked for a few minutes before retiring. It had been a long, difficult day for them all.

John called Carol the next morning before she left for the barn. She explained about Mark's father's death and told him about Mark's partnership proposal to Jim and Karen. Carol was pleasantly surprised at how John reacted to this news. He was very sympathetic to Mark regarding his dad's death, but happy to hear about Mark's generous offer to Jim and Karen. He went on to tell Carol that he certainly understood her genuine support of her friend by attending the funeral. He even asked if she needed him to go with her. She thanked him for being so caring, but told him that she would be fine. The five would be traveling together: she, Karen, Jim, Mark, and his mother. John understood and told Carol to stay safe and call him when she returned. He also asked her for the funeral information so he could send a card of sympathy to Mark and his mother.

Before hanging up, he whispered softly, "Carol, I'm so looking forward to hearing from you and seeing you soon. I love you so much, sweetheart."

Carol answered, "I will call you the minute we return. And, John, I love and miss you too."

Hanging up the phone, she realized that she was tantalized by John's voice and his meaningful words. She felt absolutely dizzy for the rest of the morning...she was sure she was walking on a cloud!

Saturday morning Mark and his mom, Edna, drove to Loafing Hills and picked up Carol, Karen, and Jim. They flew from the Baltimore Washington International airport to Temple, Wyoming. There they rented a car and drove across ten miles of scenic prairie to Neal Long's ranch. The sign at the gate read simply, "Long River Ranch."

It had been several months since Mark had visited his dad's ranch, but things looked pretty much the same. The main house, painted a pale yellow, sported a large white porch surrounding the entire dwelling. The effect was quite welcoming and comfortable. In the open fields stood an occasional water pumping windmill, catching the steady breeze from the north. The barn, a huge red wooden structure, looked sound and promising. Several paddocks and cattle runs were connected to the barn.

Close behind the barn sat a log cabin, which housed the six ranch hands. All six came out to welcome Mark and his guests. Mark had previously met with these guys, and all had agreed to stay with the ranch.

The funeral was set for three o'clock. They all went into the large house, changed their clothes, and set out for the funeral home several miles away. The ranch crew followed closely behind.

The funeral parlor was elegant with attractive baskets of flowers encircling the room. Neighbors and townspeople filled the parlor. During the service, the choir from Mr. Long's church sang lovely hymns, and several good friends of Mr. Long's offered sincere and warm eulogies for their friend and neighbor.

After the service as Carol was leaving, she noticed a basket of beautiful white blooming hydrangeas at the door. The card was signed, "Sincerely, John Quill."

Immediately after the service, Mr. Long was buried just two blocks away in the church graveyard. It was in a beautiful area, and the burial was handled with elegance.

Then the minister announced that all were cordially invited back to the church for dinner.

Again everything was handled with superior style and fine grace: good food, good friends, and as Mark said to everyone, "No crying. This is exactly what my dad would have wanted his leaving this earth to be!"

Everyone answered with, "Amen."

At six o'clock Carol, Karen, and Jim had to leave Mark and his mom at the church hall. The dining room was still full with Mr. Long's good friends. Mark and his mom planned to stay until all the guests had left. Then one of the ranch crew would take the two of them back to the ranch where they planned to stay for a couple more days.

Carol, Karen, and Jim had to catch the ten o'clock flight that evening back to Baltimore.

Mark told them as he hugged each goodbye, "Thank you so much for your support today. You are my best friends in this whole world, and I love you dearly."

Looking at Carol, he whispered, "And, I love you too, my dear *friend*. And you tell John he's one lucky dude!" He smiled.

They each hugged him back and told him they loved him too. Mark, walking them to the door, said, "While you're at the house today picking up your suitcases, please take a few minutes to check out the ranch before heading home."

Shaking Jim's hand, he added, "Jim, pick out a spot where you might want to build your house...and don't forget," he winked at Karen, "build it big enough for Granny too!"

They all smiled as they left Mark at the church door.

They did as Mark suggested and took a quick tour of the ranch. They all agreed it was a great place. Everything was neat and clean. The whiteface cattle, all three hundred head, were way out on the grassy range. The main house reminded Carol and Karen of Loafing Hills. The house was large, with three good-sized bedrooms and two baths upstairs. Downstairs were a huge living room, dining room, bath, and kitchen. There were many skylights and windows, letting in plenty of light throughout the whole house.

As they were leaving the ranch, Jim and Karen picked out a beautiful place for a house. They knew that they needed to make that important decision soon.

Carol told them both, "I think that decision is a very simple one; it's a great opportunity for you both. You'd be absolutely nuts not to accept Mark's offer."

Turning to Jim, she continued, "He is your best buddy, Jim. He loves you and Karen and wants to give you half of his ranch. You should be squealing with joy!" She laughed.

Karen turned to Carol and asked, "How should I feel, Carol? I love Jim and I would go anywhere he'd want me to, but it's so hard to just pull up roots and leave you, your dad, Ellie, and Loafing Hills."

She continued, "It's the only home I've ever really known." Tears were streaming down Karen's cheeks. Carol, seeing her friend's distress, felt tears coming into her own eyes.

Jim, saddened by this scene, pulled the car to the side of the road. "I can't drive with you two crying," he choked out.

Carol, looking at Karen, grinned through her tears and said, "Karen, we are a mess."

Karen, looking back at Carol, started grinning too; tears were flowing. Now they were both laughing out loud, and Jim joined them. It was a ridiculous sight for anyone passing by them in their car, seeing three people on the side of the road, laughing like idiots with tears flying everywhere.

When they all calmed down a bit, they blamed it on today's happenings. Flying in, attending the funeral, picking out a spot on the ranch to maybe build a house, and trying to decide what they wanted to do about Mark's proposal. It was too much. They made a pact not to talk about it anymore until tomorrow at noon; then they would make their decision.

Karen, still being silly, started singing out, very loudly, her and Carol's favorite *Feel Sorry For Yourself Jingle*: "Nobody loves me, nobody wants me, I'm goin' to the garden to eat some worms."

Carol joined her, "Great big gooey ones, little itsy bitsy ones, I'm goin' to the garden to eat some worms."

Jim was surprised at this outburst, but laughed heartily telling them they were both nuts!

The flight home was smooth and uneventful; all three were quiet and subdued on their drive back to Loafing Hills. However, seeing the farm before them brought on more tears by both girls, but smiles also. Jim, totally confused, said with a grin, he was sure glad to get them out of the car.

The first thing Carol did after greeting her dad and Ellie was to call John. He was there and happy to hear from her. She told him about the funeral and talked about Jim and Karen's planning to make the big decision the next day at noon.

"Please tell them I wish them luck, and I'm sure they will make the best decision," he replied.

John went on to tell Carol how much he loved her and how deeply he was missing her. She answered, "I love you and miss you so much too. If possible," she asked, "could you fly in next weekend?"

John answered, "I will. I'm really busy on the ranch right now, but I will fly in and spend the day. Maybe you will fly back with me for a day or two. If you can, you will have to spend most of the daytime with Dora. But I promise we will have the evenings together. I need you with me," he concluded.

She was feeling the same as John. She needed to be with him too.

The plan was he would fly into Maryland early Saturday morning. That evening, they would fly back to New Start. He would bring her back to Maryland the following Wednesday.

She would have liked to stay longer, she told him, even though Joanne and Billy were a big help now on the farm. Without Mark coming in and Karen still not riding, Carol was needed mainly to exercise their many horses.

"It is kind of scary too," she added, "Ned and Ellie are talking again about retiring!"

"Oh, don't worry about it, honey," he answered; "we'll talk to them about their plans when I get there Saturday." They whispered their love for each other before hanging up.

The next day Carol had exercised one of the stall horses and was turning him out in the paddock when Dan, calling her from the barn, told her that she was wanted in the house.

She jogged to the house, noticing that Jim's car was in the driveway. Going in, she found Ellie, her dad, Karen, and Jim sitting at the table. She quickly joined them.

Jim told them that their decision had been made. "However, there is a different set of circumstances," he added.

Everyone listened intently. "Karen and I," Jim continued, "have decided that we will *try* Mark's deal for three months. We will go to the ranch and live in the main house with Mark and Edna."

Seeing the rather surprised look on Carol's, Ned's, and Ellie's face, he quickly added, "This, believe it or not, was Mark's idea. He wants us to be sure that we would be happy on the ranch. If after three months we want to stay, then we'll talk about the partnership and building the house and bringing Granny in. If we decide this is not what we want, then we will part, still best friends."

Even though everyone realized that this was a good idea, it was still hard to say so. Carol and Karen looked at each other with tears welling in their eyes. Ellie quickly handed Kleenex to each.

"I know," said Carol to Karen, after wiping her tears, "that you should do this. It's a great opportunity for both of you, but I'm really glad to hear that you will try the three-month arrangement first."

Ned and Ellie both agreed with Carol's statement. Ned added, "It's very wise of Mark to offer a trial run on this business deal. That way if things don't work out, no one gets hurt. And it will be a lesson well learned."

Ellie furthered Ned's statement, "You know, we love you both, and if for any reason your deal does not work out, we and Loafing Hills will always be here for you."

Carol, standing up, held her water glass high and whispered, "You know it's too early for the hard stuff," she laughed, "but we toast you both with sweet water from Loafing Hills. Here's for much happiness and success in your new adventure."

They all stood, touching their glasses together, "Cheers."

Carol immediately ran to the phone to tell John the news. Dora answered and called John to the phone. He was glad to hear the news, especially regarding the business trial period. "Great idea," he acknowledged. "And an even greater idea is that I'll see you early next Saturday morning." He laughed.

On Monday afternoon when Joanne came in to help ride the horses, she was excited to learn about Karen and Jim's plans. She and Karen had become very friendly over the past weeks. Karen believed her to be a true equestrian, as she remembered how wonderfully Joanne had handled the kids who were riding horses at the Loafing Hills horse sale. Joanne also liked Jim and Mark a lot too, having exercised horses with them several times.

Karen promised Joanne that if things worked out in Wyoming, she would invite her often to visit at the ranch.

The rest of the week was very busy, schooling, training, and exercising the many horses. Joanne and Jim helped in the afternoons. Even Karen, now feeling much stronger, came to the barn too and took over the tack room, keeping the tack, saddles, bridles, and equipment clean and orderly.

Jim and Karen were leaving in three weeks for Wyoming. They were busy packing their clothes in boxes, ready for Mark to pick them up. In two weeks Mark was planning to rent a U-Haul truck in Virginia to pick up his mom's furniture. He told Jim and Karen if they could have their things packed and ready to go in two weeks, he would, after leaving Virginia, stop at Loafing Hills, pick up their boxes, and then drive on to Wyoming.

This plan was good for Jim because he wanted to give the school, where he was the sports director, a two-weeks' notice before leaving.

This would also allow Karen and Jim to spend Christmas at Loafing Hills, which they and the family truly wanted. The two would fly out a couple of days after the holiday.

CHAPTER 25

John flew in to Maryland Saturday morning, got his rental, and drove to Loafing Hills. Carol met him at the door. They embraced and kissed before wandering into the kitchen where Pearl was serving breakfast number two.

John apologized to her for missing the first breakfast, saying with a smile, "Air traffic was tight this morning."

Only Mike, Dan, and Pearl's kids, Joanne and Billy, were at the table. Carol and John shared coffee and honey buns while talking and kidding with Joanne and Billy. Mike and Dan got into it too, jokingly telling Billy that John really wanted to clean the stalls that day, and he bet that he would be glad to pay Billy to let him. This started a lot of wisecracks which were thrown back and forth from each to the other, until Pearl finally got tired of it all and told them all with a hearty laugh, "Get out!"

Carol and John strolled to the barn behind Dan, Mike, and Billy. Joanne stayed to talk with Karen before heading to the barn.

It was cold out; sweaters, jackets, and gloves were definitely a must! Everyone got to work quickly in the barn, mainly to stay warm.

John and Carol first schooled the two new colts and then Corky.

A little later Karen came to the barn with Joanne; both began cleaning the horses in the stalls as soon as they finished their grain. After several had been brushed to perfection, Karen suggested that Joanne go ahead and start riding while she finished grooming the remaining few. Joanne saddled and bridled the first horse, climbed aboard, and exercised him in the outside schooling ring.

As Karen finished grooming a horse, she would saddle and bridle each one and then clip the horse to the hitching post in the aisle way. It succeeded like clockwork. Horses were groomed and tacked and then stood patiently in the aisle waiting for the rider to mount. Each was then taken to the ring for a good workout. They had a good system going, and the girls were ecstatic; ten horses were cleaned and exercised in one morning. Carol and John were truly impressed; even Dan and Mike applauded.

John and Carol decided before lunch that they would take a quick ride to visit Emerson. She climbed on Blackjack, and John on Penny. After warming the horses up a bit, they cantered up the hill. It was bitter cold up there, but Carol and John both dismounted and walked to the gravestone. Carol once again touched the stone and whispered a few caring words to her old friend. John, too, standing quietly by the stone, murmured sincere words to Emerson and quietly thanked him for bringing Carol and him together. Hand in hand, the two walked back down the hill leading the horses, neither speaking, both lost in thought.

When they reached the woods, they stopped. John pulled Carol into his arms and gently kissed her. Speaking softly, they exchanged their heartfelt feelings of love for each other; then they slowly mounted the horses and headed back to the barn.

When they arrived at the house, lunch was on the table. Ned laughed, saying that the aroma of Pearl's fried chicken was magnetic, and this hungry crowd was absolutely captivated!

Everyone ate heartily and shared stories of happenings at the barn that morning. Carol praised Karen and Joanne for the hard work they had put in.

When lunch was finished, all thanked Pearl graciously for the tasty meal before heading back to the barn. Carol and John, wanting to talk with Ned and Ellie, stayed at the table.

John, turning toward Ned, asked, "I understand that you are serious about retiring, Ned. Any plans yet?"

Ned answered, "No, nothing definite. I'm just getting too old to work this hard every day." He smiled. "I'd like to have some time to travel a little and maybe see my folks in England and maybe do a little Pacific Ocean cruising."

Carol and John laughed and agreed, "A great idea!"

Ned went on to say, "I haven't mentioned this to you yet, Carol, but I've been seriously thinking about giving you this house and building a smaller place here at Loafing Hills, for Ellie and me."

Carol, in total shock, looked at her dad and said hesitantly, "I didn't know how serious you were when you talked about giving up the farm."

"No, Carol," her dad smiled, "I would never give up the farm. I know how much it means to you. Someday, in the near future though, you will be running it. And if I may give you some advice, Carol," he offered, "it would be to start downsizing now. Keep the very best stock and sell off the rest."

Carol, still amazed at her dad's words, asked him when and how she should begin the downsizing that he suggested.

Ned answered, "Very carefully pick out the best stock to keep, Carol; then have a big sale here at Loafing Hills in the early spring. Everyone here will help you."

"How about Mike and Dan?" she asked. "They've been here for years. Would they stay?"

"You will need them for at least a year," Ned said, "and I'm sure they will stay with you until you won't need them anymore, honey."

John added, "Good guys like those two will never have a hard time finding work with farm stock, Carol."

"And I'll see to that," Ned added. "And I promise I will find them work when and where they're needed."

Carol was floored. She couldn't believe what she was hearing. John, seeing she was becoming upset, asked Ned to let her think about this for a while. After all, it was quite a surprise.

Ned came to Carol and hugged her. "Please don't fret, Carol. I love you and I promise I will always be here for you."

Carol, upset, excused herself from the table and headed for the bathroom. She knew she was going to cry.

At the table, John told Ned and Ellie that he would talk to Carol to assure her that everything would be okay.

Ned asked John, "Please explain to her that I, her dad, will financially take care of everything until she is well on her way in the business. And even after she is running the business, I'll still be there for her."

Ellie was looking very upset too.

John said, "Please don't worry. I will talk to Carol, and I am sure that she will be just fine."

John waited for Carol at the bathroom door for a few minutes before knocking lightly. When she came out, she was smiling.

"I'm sorry," she said. "That was a lot to digest in just a few minutes."

John took her hand as they walked back to the kitchen. Ned and Ellie, both still sitting at the table, looked distressed too, thought John.

"I'm so sorry, Dad," Carol cried. "I was being so ungrateful."

"No, Carol," Ned and Ellie both answered. "We're the ones that are sorry. We were anxious to get this plan out to you, and we didn't prepare the news very well," said Ned.

Carol and John walked slowly back to the barn still talking about Ned's surprise announcement. John helped Carol see the good side of the arrangement. "You will be head of the farm," he exclaimed and then added, "They will all have to call you *boss lady*." He laughed.

This brought a smile to Carol's face. "Oh, please, I hope nobody calls me that," she laughed. "I'd rather just be Carol."

"Honest, honey, it's no big deal," he said, "and I promise you I will be there for you too. You won't be alone."

Carol looked into John's face and saw honest sincerity. She felt so much better once she realized that he would be her strength and would stand by her side.

They worked together exercising the remaining horses until they knew that it was time to head to New Start. They said goodbye to Karen and Joanne, working in the tack room, and then to Billy finishing up the cleaning of stalls. They also waved to Mike and Dan, busy outside unloading grain from a truck.

John laughingly called to them, "Don't you boys work too hard now!"

They, of course, had some colorful advice to yell back to him too. They were all laughing as they parted.

At the house, Carol hugged her dad, Ellie, and Pearl before heading out. John shook Ned's hand, hugged Ellie and Pearl, and then picked up Carol's suitcase as they walked out the door. The drive to the airport was quick, and the flight to New Start pleasant and uneventful.

When they arrived at the house, Dora was standing in the doorway; Piggy was excitedly dancing around on hind legs, anxiously begging to be picked up. Carol happily obliged him. Dora was content to have John home and delighted to see Carol again.

Dora had prepared a delicious supper for them. Carol and John were both very hungry; they didn't have to be begged to eat! Dora had lots of news for John regarding the land parcels that he'd sold and the many calls from folks interested in the ones still for sale. She also told him about Dr. Lawrence's visit to see several of the steers. The barn guys called him because the steers had runny noses and eyes. Dr. Lawrence's conclusion was colds. He decided to give them and the whole herd antibiotic shots. He said that he would be back to check them again next Thursday.

Shortly after supper, Carol and John, both worn out from all the work at Loafing Hills, said goodnight to Dora and retired for the evening.

Sunday, John escorted Carol around the ranch; she was riding the Quarter Horse, Cazual Dan, and John was riding the Morgan horse,

Big Jake. Carol found it fun using the western tack. It was a first for Carol using a bosal on a horse, which is a bitless bridle. Both horses were trained to neck rein, meaning when the rein was laid against the horse's neck, the horse turned away from the pressure. This was a great assistance when using only one hand while riding, and it was quite necessary for western riding, leaving one hand free for roping.

On Monday and Tuesday, Carol and Dora chatted and had a good visit. Carol also rode out both mornings to check the cattle. Each day, John would get back to the house in the evening. After supper, they would sit and talk and watch TV. John's land-selling business was going quite well. He discussed it openly with Carol regarding the deals made. They were very comfortable with each other.

Wednesday morning, Carol and John said their goodbyes to Dora and, of course, Piggy, as they left to fly back to Maryland. John would have to return Wednesday night to New Start for some imperative business deals.

Carol was simply entranced by John. She found him irresistible, and he loved her deeply too. He absolutely worshiped her.

They landed in Maryland and decided to drive to Westminster for lunch. Carol had faint misgivings, for this was where Mark had just recently told her about his father's death, and of the plans for the Wyoming ranch.

She was so glad to be sitting beside John, and the remembrance of that day with Mark's sorrow didn't disturb her as she had feared.

The weather outside was cold, but the restaurant's country theme was warm and cozy. Small candles and a lovely vase of flowers sat invitingly on each table. The background music from the jukebox added a soothing ambience. John and Carol sat, staring into each other's eyes, held hands, and smiled as the waitress approached them to take their order. She smilingly excused herself for interrupting them.

They, caught up in the moment, laughed with her while they placed their order for coffee, BLTs, and tomato soup. Both agreed it was their very favorite lunch.

The waitress, when in the kitchen, told the chef to do it up pretty. It was for two people totally in love, and he did. He placed a red candy heart on each sandwich and adorned the plate with a gorgeous pink rose.

After savoring their lunches and leaving a generous tip, they, as the waitress told the chef, simply floated out the door!

Arriving at Loafing Hills, they walked to the house, still holding hands. Jim was there; he and Karen were glad to see them. They sat and talked some more about the Wyoming ranch deal. John agreed with them that it sounded like a wonderful opportunity. Carol told them about Ned's offer to her. They, actually beaming, were really happy for her too.

John, knowing that he couldn't stay long, asked Carol if she would take a ride with him up the hill to visit Emerson before he had to leave.

Carol, always ready for that trip, answered, "Of course, I'll go with you."

They left Karen and Jim, went to the barn, saddled up Blackjack and Penny, and rode across the pasture through the woods and up the hill.

Arriving at the gravesite, they dismounted and strolled to the headstone. Carol, holding John's hand, placed their hands together on the stone. She said a short prayer, again thanking the horse for the wonderful show years he had given her.

John very quietly said to Emerson, "Again, Emerson, I am so very sorry that your life ended so soon, but I must thank you from the bottom of my heart for helping me find Carol. I love her and I want her to marry me."

He turned to Carol, held out a small black box, sank to one knee and whispered, "Carol, I love you so very much. Will you please marry me?"

Carol was so surprised, her mouth dropped open, and she stared at John. Her eyes were wide; she stared first at the ring and then at John.

"Good grief, Carol," John said, looking at her shocked face. "You're scaring me," he said. "I was sure you knew I loved you."

"Yes, John, I do know you love me, and I love you too. It's just that you surprised me!" Then she quickly added, with happy tears in her eyes, "Of course, John...I would be honored to be your wife!"

He placed the glittering diamond ring on her finger, pulled her into his arms, and kissed her long and lovingly. She returned the kiss and then held her left hand up to gaze unbelievably at the dazzling ring. "Wow," she shouted, "we're engaged!"

She couldn't wait to get back to the house. Carol knew that Ned and Ellie would be working in his office.

She, holding John's hand, burst into the room. Ellie and Ned, sitting at the desk, rose quickly to their feet.

Carol, lifting her left hand high, sang out, "Notice anything different about me?" She smiled.

Ned and Ellie were both surprised, but seeing the ring on Carol's finger, they smiled happily and offered hugs and congratulations to the couple.

Karen and Jim, hearing the commotion, came quickly to the office door. Carol and John smiled at their dear friends as she held her hand up high so that they could see the ring.

Karen and Jim, excited about the happy news, took Carol's and John's hands in theirs while hugging and kissing them; then they danced them around the room for several minutes.

The two couples, followed by Ned and Ellie, ran to the kitchen to tell Pearl and then out to the barn, yelling for Joanne, Billy, Mike, and Dan. Everyone was happy and offered sincere good wishes to the excited couple.

Later as John was preparing to leave for the airport, he told Carol, "I really intended to propose to you and present the ring at Christmas, but I simply couldn't wait that long. It was killing me."

"I'm so glad that you asked me when and where you did. John, it couldn't have been a better time, or a more appropriate place." She laughed.

John agreed with Carol and asked, "Why don't we set the wedding date so we can announce it at Christmas?"

"Good idea," she answered and placed the calendar on the table in front of them. They both studied it at length. The decision was made.

CHAPTER 26

The week before Christmas everyone was busy taking care of the farm, the horses, and doing lots of Christmas shopping and wrapping. The tree was up and beautifully decorated. Attractive wreaths were hung in windows and at the doors.

On Christmas Eve, sparkling white snow began to fall. By evening it had covered the Maryland landscape in dazzling splendor. The cedars and pines, bowing gracefully in the wind, wore dazzling white gowns.

The loose horses, those who chose to leave the loafing sheds, were painted in white crystal coats. Penny, Karen's bright red chestnut mare, standing directly under the paddock lights, appeared absolutely magical. She wore a white luminous covering sprinkled over her brilliant red coat. The whole picture was surreal...like in a dream.

On Christmas day, the whole family was housed at Loafing Hills, including Karen, Granny, John, and Jim. Ned volunteered to take the four-wheel-drive truck to Pearl's house to fetch her and the kids. Mike and Dan would be at the house later. They were outdoors now, using the two tractors with snow blades, plowing the long driveway. John and Jim were busy most of the morning too, shoveling snow around the house, sidewalks, and stairs.

The ladies were all working in the kitchen. The meal included turkey, ham, sweet potatoes, sauerkraut, peas, string beans, and tossed salad. Carol and Karen had baked several pies the day before, and Granny had stayed busy making strawberry ice cream. All should be ready by three o'clock.

The fragrant aroma of the yuletide feast wafting through the house teased everyone. The anticipation was immense.

Ned delivered Pearl, Joanne, and Billy, and the guys finally got the driveways, walkways, and steps shoveled. It was three o'clock. No one had to be called to the table twice!

The meal was a great success; everyone enjoyed the food and conversation. Pearl said she enjoyed it most because, she laughed, "I did not even go into the kitchen all day!"

At the end of the meal, Ned stood and told everyone that John and Carol had an announcement to make.

John stood and thanked the Spencer family for a delightful meal. He continued, saying, "Carol and I would like to announce our wedding date. We have picked the first day of spring, March 20, and we would love to have it here at Loafing Hills."

Everyone smiled and applauded.

John, still standing, said, "I understand that Jim and Karen have an announcement to make today too."

Jim stood up, smiled at John and Carol, congratulating them again and then said, "Karen and I also have a surprise for you. We also picked our wedding date. Guess what? It's the 20th of March. The first day of spring! And at Loafing Hills." He laughed.

Everyone looked surprised.

Ned stood up, smiling and said, "Ellie and I would love to host the double wedding here. After all, folks," he said, "this is a planned event by both couples. They decided this themselves. *What else could best friends do?*"

Everyone at the table jumped up and cheered. There was lots of hand shaking, kisses, and hugs. Everyone agreed; it was a great Christmas dinner and two wonderful surprise announcements, all equaling a fantastic holiday.

Three days later, Carol visited Karen in her room while she was doing some last-minute packing to take on the plane with her.

"Karen, I hope that you and Jim will be happy in Wyoming. If not," she added, "please know that there will always be a place for you and Jim right here."

Karen answered, I know that, Carol, thank you. I also know that two men could not get along with each other better than Jim and Mark. I'm sure they will work together well, as Jim says, like two peas in a pod!"

"I feel the same, Karen. If it works out that you two do stay in Wyoming, please don't forget that you have to visit here often and you must be back here on March 14th, to prepare for our big day."

And she quietly added. "Please don't forget me!"

"Carol," Karen answered, "I promise you, Jim and I will be here on the 14th, one week before the 20th." Then she cried, hugging Carol, "We are closer than sisters; I could never forget you."

Carol, attempting to control her emotions, asked Karen what she was planning to do about Granny.

"Granny will be flying out to the ranch next month," Karen answered, "and Joanne is planning on going with her."

"Yes," Carol answered, "I knew that Joanne was going. She told me two weeks ago. I think she really likes Mark too. They really got along great while he was here. But I hadn't heard about Granny."

"She was slow making up her mind," Karen said, "but she now says she and Joanne will be flying out in January."

Karen asked Carol if she would be all right without Joanne's help. Carol answered, "Yes, Joanne has already found a replacement for herself. She will be coming in next week to talk to us about it."

Karen turned and whispered to Carol, "It's been three months since my accident, and I'd really love to take a short ride on Penny before leaving today. Would you go with me?"

Carol answered, "You know I would. Come on, let's go; we don't have a lot of time before John and I gotta drive you guys to the airport."

Laughing, they both left the room, skipped down the stairs, and out the porch door. Karen was doing great. Both legs seemed to be working well again, and her balance was finally back. They placed Karen's last suitcase in the car and went on to the barn. Carol brought Penny and Blackjack into the barn aisle, helped Karen saddle and bridle her mare, and then held her while Karen carefully mounted her. She, sitting high on Penny's back, was thrilled at the feeling of finally getting to ride again.

The girls walked and trotted their horses out across the pasture and through the woods. Instead of following the north trail that ended at the bluff that overlooked a small town, Karen asked to go south instead, which would take them to Emerson's grave.

"You know, Carol," Karen said, "that's where I was heading when Penny and I got attacked by the hornets. I hope I can get there this time." She laughed.

When they arrived at the grave, they both dismounted. Karen said quietly, "You know, Carol, I loved that horse too. He was beautiful, strong, gallant, and funny." She added, "I loved the time we finally realized that he *would not stand anyone using a whip on him!* He truly balked. Then, using no whip, Emerson would do absolutely anything you asked him to do."

"I know," Carol answered, as she placed her hands on his gravestone. "He was my hero. I miss him so, and I don't think I will ever find another Emerson."

"Yes, you will," Karen answered. "Someday, you will."

They remounted and started back to the barn. It was almost time for them to leave for the airport. On the way back, Karen talked about getting Penny to Wyoming. They agreed that when Karen and Jim returned to Loafing Hills for the wedding, they would make arrangements to have the mare transported to the ranch.

When the girls returned to the house, the first thing Karen did was shout to everyone, "Yeah, I made it; look, no stings, and Penny, too, is alive and well." She bowed at their laughter, congratulations, and applause.

It was three o'clock. The flight was scheduled for six o'clock. The car was packed. They decided to leave because they needed to be at the airport at least one hour before departure time; this would give them time to go through customs and get something to eat in the terminal.

Before leaving, Karen and Jim received lots of well wishes and hugs from Ned, Ellie, and the whole farm family.

The hour trip to BWI gave them time to assure each other that they would e-mail every day and phone at least once a week. Then, if Karen and Jim decided to live in Wyoming, they would make future visiting plans while at Loafing Hills in March.

Carol and John let Karen and Jim out at the airport entrance, found a parking spot, and then came back to meet them at the restaurant.

As they enjoyed a light meal at the terminal, Karen began to feel more and more depressed. She repeated several times, looking at Carol, "I'm so afraid that I'll never see you after we move to the ranch. It will be so hard." She continued, "We grew up together, Carol; I was with you through good times and bad times. I was with you when you bought, trained, showed, and lost Emerson."

Now tears were streaming down her face. She looked at her friends and apologized for how ridiculous she was acting, but couldn't seem to control herself. Jim, holding her hands, didn't quite know what to do to help her either.

John quickly promised her, "Karen, I will put Carol in my airplane and fly us both out to see you two in Wyoming every chance we get." Finally, at that remark, both Karen and Carol smiled.

Jim thanked John for being so understanding and added, "It kinda gets to me too. If it weren't for Carol taking Karen out on her birthday this past year, Karen and I might never had gotten together again. So you see, I owe, love, and will miss Carol too."

As they parted to board the plane, they called heartrending goodbyes to each other.

Carol stood at the window and waved until she saw the plane lift off the runway and disappear into the evening sky.

CHAPTER 27

On the way back to Loafing Hills from the airport, Carol noticed that John was unusually quiet.

"I'm sorry, John; did Karen and I embarrass you? If we did, we didn't mean to let our feelings get so unhinged!"

"No, Carol, you didn't embarrass me at all. Actually, I know that you are a very caring person, and I'm thankful that you are. I was just mulling something over in my mind tonight and would like to run it by you to see what you think."

"What, John? Don't leave me in the dark," she smiled.

"I know you will be running Loafing Hills soon, and I want to help you. But being so far away from you, in North Carolina, troubles me. I was wondering, if I were to sell New Start, leave North Carolina, and ship my cattle to Maryland, how would you feel about that?" he asked.

She reached up and gently touched his face, saying, "John, you know once we select the choice horses we want to keep, we will have plenty of room and pasture land for the cattle. Oh, please," she exclaimed, "let's make Loafing Hills our home."

John answered, "I think we have the right idea, Carol. As soon as we get back, let's run this idea by Ned and Ellie to see how they feel about it." John added, "The sale of New Start will help us get going; then we can work out an amenable financial agreement with Ned and Ellie."

On the way back to Loafing Hills, Carol felt more relaxed than she had felt in weeks.

When they returned to the farm, Ned and Ellie were in the TV room engrossed in a movie on TV, which had just started. Carol and John joined them, deciding to wait until morning to discuss their idea.

After a good night's sleep, they joined Ned and Ellie for breakfast at seven in the morning. Pearl, still in her bathrobe and being her funny self, had them all laughing within minutes, telling them a story about the horses that had been loose earlier that morning. She said she looked out the window at the barn to see if Dan and Mike were coming to the early breakfast. She didn't see them, but she did see a horse's hindquarters sticking out the rear door of the barn: rump, back legs, and swishing tail. And, peering out of the front door of the barn, appeared a horse's head, shoulders, and two front legs!

"I thought," she giggled, "now, that's one long horse. Then I saw Billy and Dan run both horses out of the barn.

My guess is Billy, cleaning stalls, left the barn doors open, forgetting the horses loose in the paddock. But, I tell you, I sure wish I had a camera for that one."

Everyone laughingly agreed. Minutes later the barn crew joined them and was ribbed unmercifully about the long horse in the barn.

Finally breakfast was over and everyone left for the barn except Ned, Ellie, John, and Carol. Pearl, cleaning up, was not happy about having only one breakfast to serve that morning because, she told Carol, "I'm sorta depressed about Karen leaving, and I know I'll be real depressed when Joanne goes too. I need to stay busy." She laughed.

John asked Pearl, "If Joanne decides to stay in Wyoming, would you and Billy want to join them there?"

Pearl, not wanting to hurt anyone's feelings, simply said she didn't know yet how she would feel or what she might do.

John had quietly mentioned to Ned that he and Carol would like to talk to him and Ellie that morning for a few minutes. Ned and Ellie immediately agreed. They thanked Pearl for a delicious breakfast and headed for Ned's office. Carol stayed a few minutes to talk with Pearl.

"Please don't worry," Carol said. "We love you, Pearl, and we want what is best for you. If you decide to stay here, great; if you decide to head to Wyoming, we'd understand." She continued, "John and I are now talking about living here instead of at New Start, which means we will be bringing his cattle here. Dad and Ellie, as you know, are planning to build a house here too. So, as you can see, we are open to any and all changes. Please do what you feel is best for you."

Carol could see by Pearl's demeanor that she understood. With a "Pearl smile," she hugged and thanked Carol.Pearl told her, "Carol, I love this family, and I know that I need to decide what to do if Mark's ranch deal works out. Mark and Edna both told me that Joanne, Billy, and I would be warmly welcomed to join them there."

After she and Pearl talked, both were feeling much better. She left then to join the family in Ned's office.

When John and Carol told the Spencers their idea and asked how they would feel about it, they were both surprised and very pleased at their reaction.

Ned, smiling from ear to ear excitedly told them, "That's the best news I've had in a long time. I wasn't worried about you managing the farm, Carol. I knew you could do it, but if you and John decided to take up residency in New Bern, I don't know exactly what we would have done."

John, pleased to see that Ned and Ellie were happy with the idea, spoke. "Ned, I'm so glad that you are content with this plan, and now I think we need to obtain an attorney to help us with the financial end of the agreement."

"Already done that, John," Ned said, "the house and farm are Carol's. I've already seen to that. Spelled out very specifically in our wills. So, what the two of you do here is strictly up to you two. Ellie and I plan to take one acre on the south side of the Loafing Hills' entrance and build a small house for us."

Ned could see that Carol and John were flabbergasted. He quickly continued, "I have to tell you two, your idea is wonderful for us. We would love to do some traveling before we get too old to enjoy it. So, this news today sets Ellie and me free," he laughed.

Ned, still seeing disbelief on John's and Carol's faces, went on to explain the will. "Ellie has no children and agrees that when it's our time to leave this world, and the last one goes, the whole thing will go to Carol."

John and Carol were astounded. She had not known about the will.

Ned continued, "After selling New Start, John, you two may want to make some changes here on the farm and then invest the rest. That way, upon retiring, you both should be able to do so quite comfortably."

Carol and John, still surprised, looked at each other and agreed. What a great plan.

They profusely thanked Ned and Ellie before leaving. Hand in hand they walked down to the barn. Billy was cleaning stalls. They waved to him and then went into the barn to talk with Dan and Mike. One was feeding grain; the other was forking timothy into the hayracks. John called to them. They stopped working and joined John and Carol.

They discussed the farm plan with them. Dan and Mike were both greatly relieved to learn that they would be staying at Loafing Hills, the new Horse *and Cattle* farm.

On their way back to the house, John said to Carol, "Well, now all that has to be done is to convince Dora to come to Maryland." John continued, "How about you flying back with me tomorrow to help me persuade her? We could stay for a few days before coming back to Maryland."

Carol, looking slightly perplexed, replied, "I have to be back in two days, John; the rider replacing Joanne is coming in after school that day. I need to find out about her riding ability and her horse experience."

They decided to fly to New Start early the next morning, stay the day, and then head back to Loafing Hills the following morning.

Neither could stop talking about the wonders of their ownership of Loafing Hills and John's selling New Start and various other properties in New Bern. Carol dreamily said, "Now we know what floating on cloud nine feels like."

John reached down, picked her up in his arms, and held her high.

She giggled so hard they both fell over backwards onto the ground. They had on thick jackets so were not hurt; in fact, they rolled around on the ground for several minutes until he stopped her, held her face in his hands, and kissed her.

"Someone may be watching," he whispered.

"I hope so," she laughed.

Before heading to the airport, Carol e-mailed Karen to tell her about the happenings at Loafing Hills and questioned her about the activities at Mark's Long River Ranch. She also told her about John selling New Start and coming to Loafing Hills. In closing, she told Karen that Pearl was not happy with Joanne leaving Maryland. She added, "So, please, if it's okay with you and Jim, let Pearl and Billy join you there. She signed, lots of love and kisses to all, Carol.

Carol and John left Loafing Hills at noon and arrived at New Start in the early afternoon.

Dora met them at the door with smiles, kisses, and hugs. She was really excited and happy about their wedding plans.

John told her that they had something they wanted to discuss with her. John and Carol both felt a little hesitant because they understood that she was dedicated to her church work, which always kept her busy.

John finally stated, "After the marriage, Dora, would you be willing to leave New Start Ranch permanently and join Carol and me at Loafing Hills?"

She answered his question with a question of her own. "Is there a church nearby that I could join?"

"Yes," Carol answered. "There is a beautiful universal church close by. We love the church, and I think you'll love it too. And, Dora, I know they will love you."

"Well, if you two are going to live at Loafing Hills permanently, then I'm going too," she said.

John was amazed and glad. He had been braced for some serious questions, and there were none!

He looked at Carol and said, "And I made you fly back here with me to help convince her." He laughed.

Dora said, "Well, John, you should know that if you move, I move too! And besides," she added, "I love Carol also, and I can't wait to start our new life in Maryland."

John, Carol, and Dora sat up late talking about the upcoming wedding, meeting Carol's family, selling New Start, moving from North Carolina, transferring the cattle, settling in at Loafing Hills, and even about joining the church. John explained they should be ready to move in three months after the wedding and after he and Carol had returned from their honeymoon.

John and Carol arrived back at Loafing Hills early the next morning just in time for an early breakfast.

The family and barn crew were, once again, all sitting together at the kitchen table at the same time. Pearl, in her usual jovial persona, joked with them about asking for only one breakfast again this morning. "My goodness," she sputtered, "now what am I gonna do the rest of the morning?"

This opened up the group to fun. The first was Mike, who suggested that she fix the throttle on the lawnmower. Dan, not to be outdone, asked that she tack a loose shoe back on Corky. Ned said the tractor needed a tire repaired. Then they all joined in with, the two new colts need riding, and the barn stalls need to be cleaned. They told her that there were several downed trees in the woods needing to be dragged out, and the manure needed moving.

Pearl had heard enough. She yelled, "Okay, you characters, if you want lunch today, you'd better just hush up now!" Of course she laughed louder and heartier than they.

When breakfast was finished, they put on their jackets, exited through the kitchen door, and laughed all the way to the barn. Pearl was, after all, Pearl, and they all loved her.

After working with the horses for a while, Carol went back to the house to see if Karen had responded to the e-mail she had sent her. She was glad to read the returned message:

> Hi, Carol. First of all, Jim and I were so happy to hear about you and John planning to settle at Loafing Hills. That's the best idea ever! I know that makes you happy too. Carol, please know that if Pearl and Billy want to join us here, we would welcome them with open arms. I'm sure that with Dora on the farm with you guys, you can spare Pearl. I, like you, want her to be happy too.
>
> We are slowly getting settled here, and it really is a beautiful place. Jim and I went riding across the plains yesterday using western tack. That's a first for me and wow...it was fun! I can't wait to get Penny out here. She'll love it too. Jim and Mark and I send our love to all the folks at Loafing Hills, and especially to your dad and Ellie; we miss them and we love them. I love you most. And, I miss you *lots!*
>
> Love, Karen.

She took the message to the barn so that John could read it. But only Billy was in the barn. "Where is everybody?" Carol asked.

"I don't know, Carol," he answered. "I think they went down to the stud barn."

"Thanks, Billy," she called as she headed down the hill, wondering why her dad, Dan, Mike, and John were down there.

When she went into the barn, she could see the men all standing in the barn aisle talking. As she neared them, they stopped talking. "What's up?" she asked, perplexed at their strange demeanor.

"Oh, nothing," Ned answered, "just talking about John's cattle."

"You're gonna keep some of them in the stud barn?" she questioned.

"No, honey," John answered, "we were just looking around the farm."

With that said, they all began walking back up to the main barns. Carol, shrugging off the strangeness, handed Karen's e-mail to John. He grinned as he read it. "Looks like she's really taken in with their home, home on the range," he laughed. "If they stay," he added, "let's hope she and Jim will be happy cowpokes out there on the plains, watching the buffalo roam and the deer and the antelope play!"

John always seemed to know how to make Carol smile. Holding hands and gazing lovingly at each other, they strolled back to the barn. They knew that there was still work to be done at the barn, but they were so taken up with each other that they had a hard time getting back into the "working in the barn" modes.

CHAPTER 28

The next two months were busy ones at Loafing Hills. Carol, John, and Ned picked out the horses that the farm needed to keep, which included seven horses presently in training to hunt or show, four well-bred brood mares, and of course Carol's horse, Blackjack; Karen's mare, Penny; and the farm stallion, Sky Cloud. That left twelve to be sold, all well-schooled animals very much ready for the hunt field or the show ring.

The new girl, Gloria, taking Joanne's place was, to Carol's satisfaction, highly qualified to work and train the horses and was a great help at the sales barn. Also assisting with the sales were John, Ned, Mike, Dan, and Carol. The farm was more than pleased with the results; high quality horses were going to good, caring equestrians, and the total sale of the twelve horses proved to be quite satisfactory financially.

John was kept extra busy those two months. Even though he had a realtor handling the sale of New Start, he, while helping Carol run the farm, moved Dora, himself, and little Piggy out of New Start and into Loafing Hills, plus bringing in over a hundred head of cattle onto the south pasture of Loafing Hills. It was a very busy time for all.

March was nearing. Carol received a phone call from Karen and Jim, telling her that they had finally made their decision. They would stay at Long River Ranch. Carol was not surprised. Just a couple of weeks prior, she and John had flown there and stayed for two days during the week. They could easily see that it was a dream occupation for both Mark and Jim.

Granny and Joanne had flown in earlier and felt warmly welcomed by Mark and Edna. Pearl and Billy, it was decided, would go to Wyoming as soon as he graduated in June. The house was full, but everyone got along well together. They were working on Jim and Karen's new house. It would be finished soon.

"Please tell me, Carol, that you understand this move here and it's okay with you. I never want to lose your friendship. Please don't forget me," Karen pleaded.

Carol answered immediately, "Of course, I understand, Karen. I'm really pleased that you and Jim are happy there. And, you and I will *always, always be,"* she emphasized, "the closest of friends.

"But I must tell you, Karen, you missed February foaling this year at Loafing Hills. There were three fillies and one colt born. Thoroughbreds. All healthy, all good looking, and they should sell well next year as yearlings."

Karen answered that she was sorry she had missed the new babies. "But I have some news for you too," Karen continued, "Joanne has only been at the ranch for a short while, and she and Mark, who is only seven years older than her, are now *dating!* How's that for a surprise?"

Carol, grinning, answered, "I think that's great, Karen. I'm so glad to hear it. I'm especially happy to know that Mark has someone special in his life. Joanne is a wonderful young lady, and Mark is a truly nice guy."

Carol went on to tell Karen more Loafing Hills' happenings. Ned and Ellie were still living at the main house with Carol. John was also there most of the time.

The contractors had started building Ned and Ellie's house near the front gate of the property. They had decided to build a log cabin: a living room with fireplace, an office, a large kitchen with dining area, two bedrooms, two baths, and a big deck on the back of the house. It was a great place to sit and enjoy the country scenery.

Before ending the call, she told Karen about herself and Gloria staying busy daily exercising horses, and Mike, Dan, and Billy, busy learning about the new cattle, plus building the heavy-duty cattle stanchions needed to hold the cattle for veterinarian inspections.

Carol ended the call with... "I love you, Karen."

CHAPTER 29

The first day of March, John got word from his realtor that New Start had sold. Everything looked good, the realtor said. March 10th was the settlement date. John would need to fly back and take care of the settlement and several other miscellaneous tasks. He would be gone for approximately one week.

Carol, hearing the dates, reminded John that he was getting married on the 20th. The invitations had been mailed out in February. John promised her that he would be back in plenty of time.

The two couples decided that the double wedding would be held in the town church. Reverend Thomas Clark, Ned and Ellie's pastor, would officiate. Mark would be their best man; six of Carol's girlfriends would be the bridesmaids in attendance. Little Kayleigh, the four-year-old daughter of Betty Matthews, a good family friend, would be the flower girl. There were three ushers: John's North Carolina friend, Earl Garrison, Mike, and Dan. The wedding reception would be held in the enormous church hall. The same band that played at Ned and Ellie's wedding would perform. A wedding planner would do the food, and Ellie called in a professional designer to do the wedding decorations in the church hall.

Carol and Karen had decided that they would wear the exact same dresses to be married in, so several weeks prior to the wedding, Carol visiting a bridal shop in Westminster, found a beautiful dress that she absolutely loved. She took pictures of it and e-mailed them to Karen.

"Yes, yes," Karen e-mailed back. "I love it. Please order the same one for me." This was easy as both girls wore the same size.

All the guys had their orders in for dark blue tuxedoes, except John and Jim who would wear black.

All of the folks from the Wyoming ranch arrived at Loafing Hills ten days prior to the wedding. They doubled in rooms at the main house.

John returned to Loafing Hills on the fifteenth, right into the welcoming arms of Carol and family.

John's mom and stepdad came to Maryland three days early and stayed at a nearby hotel. Carol's grandmother and grandfather arrived from England two days early and also stayed at a local hotel. They visited the main house during the day and went to the hotel in the evenings.

Karen stage whispered, "Too much noise and confusion for them!" Laughing, they agreed.

It was wonderful having everyone together again. Pearl, Ellie, Dora, and Edna prepared delicious meals for everyone. Little Piggy running through the house was everyone's best friend and seemed to fit right in at Loafing Hills. The whole house was full of much confusion, but at the same time, it was great fun.

It was good to see Mark and Joanne together. They liked the same things and seemed to be very much alike.

The day before the wedding John brought into Loafing Hills two horses. Dan took them both to the lower barn. Nobody paid much attention as there was so much to do getting ready for the wedding.

John, Jim, Carol, and Karen talked at great length about their upcoming honeymoon trip to Key West. Of course, Ellie and Ned had told them all the good things to do and see while they were there.

Karen finally got to try on her wedding dress. It fit perfectly. Both girls looked beautiful. They just had a few minutes to admire themselves before changing. They didn't want any of their guests to see them yet, especially John and Jim! Everything was ready for the next day's *big* occasion.

March 20th held a big breakfast for all and then light work at the barn for a couple of hours.

The wedding was planned for three o'clock. The ushers left for the church earlier to seat the guests.

The wedding party dressed at the house and left at two-thirty. John and Jim left just minutes later. Carol and Karen dressed and waited as patiently as they could for Edna, their official driver of the morning. At twenty minutes of three they left with Edna.

At the church, people began arriving at two o'clock; the courteous ushers escorted them promptly to seats.

The weather could not have been more fantastic. It was the perfect first day of spring. The morning was cool, but quite clear. The sun was shining brilliantly through the dazzling purple ash trees surrounding the church.

In the car Carol said, "Karen, here we go. We are right now...single young ladies. One hour from now we'll be...ole married women." She laughed.

"I know," Karen laughed, "I can't wait!"

The church was beautiful with vases of glorious spring flowers placed at the altar. Each row of church pews was adorned with white bows accented with pink and yellow carnations.

The church was completely filled with seated, smiling guests.

Reverend Thomas Clark followed by John, Jim, the ushers, and Mark, came in and stood quietly at the altar.

A couple of minutes later, Dan and Mike, sitting at the back of the church, stood and carefully rolled a white carpet down the aisle.

Mrs. Evelyn Hudson, a professional singer and good friend of the Spencers, sang a lovely rendition of *You Light Up My Life*, accompanied by the church organ. As the touching song concluded, the organ struck up *The Wedding March*. This exciting music announced the entrants of the wedding party. The smiling guests stood as Kayleigh, the tiny flower girl, appeared in the doorway. She was wearing a lovely light gold, floor-length organdy dress. Her long blond hair, pulled back from her angelic face, fell into ringlets tied with a strand of gold satin ribbon. As she moved daintily down the aisle, she tossed handfuls of pink rose petals, proudly aware of her importance and responsibility.

She was followed by the six bridesmaids, all bedecked in stunning gowns of lime-green silk and carrying clusters of colorful spring flowers.

Carol and Karen were escorted by Ned, with Carol at his right and Karen at his left. As they gracefully entered the church proper, they were a sight to behold.

Ned, distinguished and quite handsome, wore a black tuxedo with a pink carnation at his lapel.

The ladies wore matching white satin gowns with empire waists, softly gathered at the back. Their veils, mists of lace, fell gently from seed-pearl tiaras, creating a picture of simple elegance. In their hands each held bouquets of spring flowers tied with flowing lime-green ribbons.

The two grooms to be, standing at the church altar, looked spectacularly handsome, wearing black tuxedos with white carnations at the lapels. John stood at the right of the altar and Jim at the left.

The four ushers, in dark blue tuxedos, stood two at John's side and two at Jim's side.

Seeing their brides approaching brought joyful smiles to the faces of the grooms.

When at the altar, Reverend Clark, looking quite distinguished, asked who was giving the brides away. Ned answered, "I will," as he stepped forward.

He went to Carol first, took her hand, and walked her to John. Returning, he took Karen's hand and led her to Jim. The couples then knelt at the altar for prayer.

While the couples knelt, Mrs. Hudson sang sweetly and lovingly, the song, *True Love.*

At its conclusion, the couples stood and faced Reverend Clark. A hush fell over the congregation as he explained the double wedding to the guests.

He turned to Carol and John. The vows were received and acknowledged. Turning to Karen and Jim, the service was repeated. At its conclusion, the brides and grooms kissed and faced the congregation.

"Ladies and gentlemen," the reverend spoke, "it is my duty and my pleasure to now introduce to you Mr. and Mrs. John Quill and Mr. and Mrs. James Boland."

The organ began playing a joyous march, and the smiling newlyweds walked down the aisle followed by the wedding party and the guests. Everyone continued to the hall for the wedding reception.

Ellie's wedding planners had done themselves proud. The hall was gorgeously decorated with balloons, streamers, flowers, and confetti everywhere. The guests, when entering, were escorted by the handsome ushers, who placed them at beautifully decorated tables. At the center of each table stood a miniature golden horse statue surrounded by an elegant flowered horseshoe.

After the photographer finished taking pictures, the newlyweds and the wedding party proceeded into the reception hall.

As they stepped through the doorway, the band began playing *I Love You Truly*. Ned, walking to Carol, danced a few steps with her, and then led her to John. Karen followed, dancing with Ned for a few minutes, ending the dance with Jim.

The guests were happy for the newlyweds, evidenced by their excitement, smiling faces, and cheerful support.

Later, while everyone was enjoying a salmon and roast beef dinner, Mark stood and said a few words about his best buddy, Jim, and, of course, heartily wished both couples much luck and happiness.

John's friend, Earl Garrison, was the next to stand. He spoke about his college friend and how impressed he had been when meeting Carol for the first time. He too wished the new couples a life of success and pleasure.

Ned stood next. He had some good words for both of the couples. Then, raising his wine glass high, he said, "Our toast here today is to two fine couples; may they always have good fortune, healthy lives, contentment, and," he paused... "give Ellie, Edna, Granny, and me lots of grandbabies! He laughed as the room laughed with him, raised their glasses high, shouting, "amen."

After dinner, the wedding cake was brought in. The two couples, when seeing the cake, were pleasantly surprised. It was tastefully decorated with many colorful flowers on the sides. At the very top stood five horses. The two outside ones were bays, and on their backs sat two gentlemen in tuxedoes. The inner horses were a black with a lady rider, dressed in white, and a chestnut with a lady rider also dressed in white. At the very center stood a bay with a garland of flowers and a tag around its neck. The name on the tag read "Emerson."

Of course, most of the guests recognized that the outer horses and riders were John and Jim, and the inner black horse represented Carol's Blackjack and the chestnut, Karen's Penny. The middle horse, of course, was the one and only Emerson.

The wedding bouquet thrown by Carol was happily caught by Joanne, the *departed* rider from Loafing Hills. Karen's bouquet was caught by Gloria, the *new rider* at Loafing Hills. Carol and Karen laughingly declared that it had *not* been a fix!

However, Carol and Karen both joyfully agreed that the close relationship that had developed between Joanne and Mark was quite noticeable and most satisfying.

The wedding, the dinner, and the dance were beautiful affairs; Ellie's management of it all was impeccable. The two newlyweds sincerely thanked Ellie and Ned, the wonderful wedding ensemble, and, of course, their guests for support and attendance. They were, the couple declared, the most magnificent collection of family and friends ever!

CHAPTER 30

Because the house on the farm was slightly crowded, the newlyweds opted to spend their wedding night at the lovely Hilton Hotel, in Frederick, Maryland.

When arriving at the hotel, they were given a bottle of champagne by the management. After changing clothes, they met in Carol and John's room to sample it together. It had been a tremulous day. They needed some quiet time.

Carol and Karen, like sisters, knew each other well. John and Jim, realizing how much alike they were, got along great also. The four sat, drank, talked, and laughed late into the evening. Around midnight, Karen and Jim left for their own room.

The four met for breakfast the next morning at ten o'clock. Their first night, the couples agreed, had been very special, and now they were really looking forward to their Key West honeymoons.

They returned to Loafing Hills at noon to pick up their suitcases. They would be flying out of BWI at four that evening. They decided, before leaving, to saddle up for a quick ride. Of course, they ended up at Emerson's grave. Karen, very gallantly, stood at the gravestone and introduced Emerson to Mr. and Mrs. John Quill and Mr. and Mrs. James Boland.

There were a few minutes of quiet meditation before mounting and riding back to the house.

Once back in the house they had to put up with lots of teasing from the household. First from Mark and Ned, but especially from Pearl. She told the guys that she had mixed up a special drink of syrup and lemon juice for them to drink before they left.

"Why?" John asked.

"It keeps you strong," she answered, "you know...for those long, long nights," she grinned.

Carol burst into laughter. She said, "Okay, Miss Pearl. Bye, we're getting out of here right now while the gettin's good!"

The two couples said thank you to all and goodbye to those leaving the next day. Karen and Jim offered a special thanks to Mark and Joanne who offered to transport Penny to Wyoming.

They arrived at BWI, checked their baggage, picked up their tickets, and enjoyed an early supper before boarding.

CHAPTER 31

The flight was comfortable and arrived in Miami at seven p.m.

The two couples had decided to fly to Miami, spend the night there, and then in the morning rent a car and drive to the Keys. That way they would get to see a bit of Florida and have the use of the rental for the week. At the end of the week, they would drive back to Miami. From there they planned to fly to Wyoming. John and Carol would visit with Jim, Karen, and the folks there for a couple of days before heading home.

They enjoyed the evening in Miami, did some sightseeing, and relaxed over a good supper downtown.

Early the next morning they headed south down US 1, (also called Oversea Highway), across the bridge into Key West.

Wow, what a beautiful place, they excitedly declared. Everything was green and flowers were everywhere. They finally found their way to their hotel just off Duval Street on the south shore. It was a beautiful six-story oceanfront hotel; the outside walls were festooned with colorful flowers and ivy. The balconies overlooked brilliant snow-white sandy beaches descending into sparkling emerald-green water. The breaking whitecaps added a striking accent to the panorama.

They were surprised and pleased by this awesome scene and impressed when they entered their rooms. Both suites were decorated exactly alike, casually elegant. Both had luxurious bedding, small comfortable sofas, and tables with chairs. Off the bedrooms were large marble bathrooms. On the balconies sat marble tables and comfortable cushioned bamboo chairs. On each table sat an olla of gorgeous flowers.

They had stopped for breakfast before leaving Miami and were ready for lunch. After unpacking, they met and ate in the fabulous dining hall. They all agreed that the food was delicious.

After lunch, they strolled barefoot along the shoreline. The weather couldn't have been nicer, so they decided to put on their sandals and tour Duval Street. They browsed through several shops and picked up a few souvenirs along the way. They noted and laughed at a sign they passed that read, "If you're in Key West and you're looking for something and can't find it....Well, then, it ain't lost!"

John said, "If I had seen that sign anywhere else, I wouldn't have gotten it, but here, I got it!" They all agreed and laughed with him.

Awhile later, they stopped at a quaint little shop for a shrimp platter. It was fresh and yummy. Afterwards they wandered down Whitehead Street and then over to Duval, returning to the hotel.

Karen and Jim sat with John and Carol on their balcony, sipping margaritas while witnessing the unbelievable Key West sunset. It was absolutely phenomenal: rose, lavender, pink, and yellow.

John told Jim that with the wedding, flying to Miami, and running to Key West, this felt like the first real night of their honeymoon. Jim laughingly agreed.

John got up, led Carol out into the hall, turned around, scooped her up, and carried her back through the door. "Hello, Mrs. Quill," he whispered, "I am so in love with you."

She smilingly answered, "Mr. Quill, I love you too, and I'm happy and proud to be Mrs. John Quill."

Jim and Karen, catching on, smiled and stood up and hugged. Jim picked Karen up and carried her out the door and down the hall to their room. They called out to each other all the way, "Goodnight, Mr. and Mrs. Quill."

"Goodnight, Mr. and Mrs. Boland."

The plan for day two at Key West was boarding a catamaran and sailing out to the reefs to do some reef snorkeling. John and Jim were first to jump in. Carol and Karen were a little hesitant at first, but after seeing the fun that the guys were having, they too climbed down into the water.

It was a great adventure and quite beautiful below on the reefs. It was so quiet and peaceful down below and the water was crystal clear. They could easily see the fish swimming around them, and they soon realized that the fish were bold enough to approach them, hoping for, and expecting, a handout.

They stayed at the reefs most of the day, swimming and lying on the boat deck in the warm sun. The breeze carried a pleasant ocean fragrance, making it a most delightful and exciting day's journey.

That evening they visited a bar on Southrard Street. They sat at a table and sipped their drinks as the entertainment came on stage. The groups of professional sun worshipers put on a spectacular show dance presentation. Each carried, and tossed, lit torches. It was an unusual and riveting performance. After the dancing on the stage ended, the bar's band began playing. They played all top forty music and were very good. The two couples danced the night away.

The next two days they took guided tours of the island. Even though Key West is a small island (only two miles by four miles), it is a most interesting place. Their guide led them through many homes and gardens and then on to famous bars, several museums, and art galleries. And, they even visited a chicken farm, which was a story in itself.

Of course, they stopped at several places to purchase items to take home with them. Carol bought a real gold coin, brought up from a sunken Spanish ship at the bottom of the ocean. She and John also bought Key West items for the folks at home. Karen and Jim found many novelty articles for Granny, Edna, Joanne, and Mark.

They found a really neat Latin American restaurant where they ate before heading back. After finishing a scrumptious plate of delicious chicken quesadillas, they began their stroll back to the hotel. They wanted to make sure they got back in time to sit on the balcony, sip margaritas, and watch the glorious sunset. They all readily agreed one could never tire of the astonishing sunsets in the Keys. They decided the sunsets there were, absolutely and totally, mind-boggling!

On day five, they spent the whole day riding the trolley cars from one end of the island to the other, debarking at many points of interest, and then catching another trolley car to continue. There was so much adventure and history associated with the island and lots of interesting stories of Indians, pirates, and the Civil War. Even more fascinating, and sometimes humorous, were legends regarding the early settlers on the island.

They even stopped at one point and waded in the water with the dolphins.

They ended the day with a sunset dinner cruise aboard a luxurious sailboat. It was a most romantic evening. The weather was warm, and the sky's colors were phenomenal as they sailed into the sunset. They agreed that this was even more exhilarating and sensuous than margaritas on sky-lit balconies!

Walking home after sailing all evening, they were still in wonderment about this island. All around them sprouted brilliant green plants and waving multicolor flowers. The night's fragrance was a stir of ocean, flowers, and fresh air, making chills run up and down their backs. And, it was not from cold! The couples huddled together, dearly loving the closeness of the night.

On their sixth day in Key West, they spent the day relaxing under an umbrella close to the shore. The waiters from the hotel maintained a steady flow of refreshments to the guests lolling on the beach.

In the evening, they strolled to one of their favorite restaurants on Simonton Street and enjoyed good food, jazz music, and lots of dancing.

When they left at one a.m., it began to sprinkle, but in no time the heavens opened up with sheets of rain. Water ran down their heads, their faces, and their bodies. All four were completely drenched!

"Wow," Jim shouted in the rain, "this is the first rain since setting foot on the island, and it's a good one."

"It's warm," answered Karen, "and feels *goood!*"

They were almost running when they decided that they were really enjoying the rain. John grabbed Carol and started dancing, twirling, and splashing down the middle of the street, pulling Jim and Karen along with them. Two other soaked couples joined them, all shouting, singing, and laughing.

What a night, they thought later in the hotel. "It's a wonder we didn't get arrested," Carol said.

"It was too wet for the cops," John laughed.

It was the seventh day in Key West. They would be heading back to Miami the next morning. The weather was once again sunny and warm; there was no rain in sight.

They went out on the beach and played volleyball most of the morning. They determined that they were absolutely terrible at it, except Jim who was, after all, a high school athletic director. But, as they continually kidded him, he wasn't much better than they!

After mulling over what they would do on their last day, it was decided that they should visit the Ernest Hemingway House on Whitehead Street. On their way they passed the bar that Hemingway used to spend a lot of time in. They went in and had a noon drink.

"Jeez," said John, "one can feel the history in here."

The others agreed and whispered, "You could even imagine Mr. Hemingway sitting right there at the bar next to you."

After leaving the bar, they walked to the corner of Whitehead Street and Truman Avenue. They went through the beautiful old historical house and read about Hemingway's many books, such as *For Whom The Bell Tolls, The Garden of Eden*, and his Pulitzer Prize book, *The Old Man and the Sea*. They also learned that Ernest Hemingway took his own life in Idaho in 1961. It was a very informative tour covering a great man's life.

Leaving the house, they wandered back up Whitehead Street and found a charming little piazza on the corner. They ordered a late lunch and island wine. As they sat at the quaint little table sipping their drinks, they could not believe the comfort they felt at this tiny area in Key West.

In the background a phonograph softly played old, old songs: *My Foolish Heart, Smoke Gets in Your Eyes, Misty, Sentimental Journey,* and other tender, romantic songs. This spell was accented by a soft ocean breeze sending whispers of warmth over them, mingling with the sweet aroma of island jasmine. It was absolutely hypnotic.

They spent the whole afternoon just sitting there, simply transfixed by the scene, the music, and each other's company.

They all decided, without question, that this very small spot in Key West was their very favorite place, and its memory would stay with them forever.

CHAPTER 32

They checked out of the beautiful Key West hotel shortly after breakfast, saying goodbye to many new acquaintances and exchanging several e-mail addresses.

They arrived at the Miami air terminal and boarded the one o'clock flight to Wyoming. The trip was so comfortable that they slept most of the way. Before boarding, Jim had called Mark to tell him they were on their way and they would take a shuttle van to the ranch. Mark, however, insisted that he would be there to pick them up.

Upon landing, Mark and Joanne were there waiting for them. It was good to see them both. The couples talked non-stop most of the way home about the Keys and what a great time they'd had there. Then Mark told them about the weekly grind on the ranch. They'd had a cattle roundup during the week, had run some of the herd into the corral, and had done some branding and some medical maintenance.

What Mark didn't tell them was that they'd had a great building crew come in while Karen and Jim were away, and they got their house up almost to the point of moving in.

When the group arrived at Long River Ranch, the first thing they saw was the new modular house. Karen started screaming, crying, laughing, and jumping up and down. Jim was just as thrilled. He couldn't believe what they had accomplished in just one week. Carol and John were also very happy for them. As they walked through the house, Mark told them that he had just been kidding about the cattle roundup.

Mark, grinning from ear to ear, said, "I just needed to make you think that I was too busy with the cattle to do anything else. But, as a matter of fact, I want you to know, I helped build your house, so now you are really indebted to me!" He laughed as he playfully poked Jim in the belly.

Even before investigating the new house, Karen and Carol ran to the barn to see Karen's beloved Penny. The girls were pleased to find the mare relaxed and looking quite content.

They then hurried on to the new house; it looked great now and would be gorgeous when finished. They would do a walk through later.

Heading back to the main house, they were met by Granny and Edna, whom, of course, they had just seen one week before at the wedding. But the two ladies ran up to them, hugging and kissing them as though they hadn't seen each other in months.

"Oh, Carol, John, I hope you can stay for a spell," Granny cried. "I truly love it here, I really do, but it's so spacious, we need your company here."

Carol laughed and said, "Yes, Granny, we can stay, but just for a couple of days. You remember how much work we have to do at Loafing Hills." She smiled.

Granny, returning the smile, told Carol, "Karen is going to teach me to ride a horse, and then I'm going to go with them when they round up the cattle. After all, "she continued, "who out there on that wide open range is going to do the cooking for them?"

"That's a big job, Granny," John said, also smiling.

"I know," chuckled Granny, "but when Pearl gets out here next summer, I'm gonna teach her how to ride too; then we'll be asharin' that cookin' out yonder," she said in her best imitation of a western drawl.

They agreed with a loud, "Yippy-yi-yo-ki-yay!"

It was great seeing the gang again, and they had a delightful supper supplied by Edna and Granny. Edna, strictly a city lady, was finally feeling at home, but it had taken some doing she admitted.

The sunset in Wyoming was almost as beautiful as the one in the Keys. The stillness and seeing the waving grass on the prairie was a delight.

On their last visit at the ranch, Mark, Jim, and Karen had taken Carol and John for a horseback ride across the prairie to see the cattle. It was truly, as Carol said, "The wide open spaces." The mountains appeared to be rather close, but according to Mark they were a good hundred miles away.

This time, Mark invited Carol and Jim to take a ride across the ranch in his jeep, so after a good night's sleep and a tasty breakfast, the whole gang piled into Mark's jeep. It was a bouncy ride across the range; everyone had to hold on tight to the sides of the jeep or onto the seats, but even though it was rough, it was a fun trip.

They crossed some deep ravines and saw a variety of cactus plants and flowers before coming on to the grasslands. Several miles further they came to a swiftly moving river and the herd of cattle. The herd stood grazing peacefully at the river's edge. Seeing the far away mountains in the background, the river, and the cattle, made this a beautiful picture. It was so lovely, Mark stopped the jeep and the passengers stepped out. They basked in the sheer beauty and tranquility of this prairie scene.

Carol whispered, "And I thought Maryland was beautiful." She smiled. "But, don't get me wrong now," she continued. "I love Maryland, but seeing this place, I now know where those gorgeous western calendar scenes come from!"

Back at the ranch house, Mark, Carol, John, Karen, and Jim strolled over again to the new house under construction. It was smaller than the main house, but plenty big enough for two to six people to live comfortably in.

The construction crew was already there and busy. Mr. Kent, the supervisor, told Karen and Jim that the house would be ready to live in, in about two weeks. "You can start painting the rooms now if you want," he concluded as he handed them a paint sample brochure.

Karen and Carol had a great time going though the brochure picking out colors, while the guys went to the unfinished basement to check out the furnace, electrical system, and the plumbing.

Realizing that they needed to get out of the crew's work area, they left and walked to the large fenced-in corral where the cattle were brought into from the grasslands for their physical examinations and needed injections.

Mark commented, "I'm glad that my dad took such good care of this place; it's run efficiently and is well organized. The guys working here are great," he continued. "The four share a cabin on the grounds, and they are pleasant folks to work with."

Later that afternoon, Joanne asked Carol if she could speak to her alone. "Of course," Carol responded. "How about taking a walk with me to the barn down by the corrals," she suggested. "I've never seen the inside of that old barn."

"Okay," Joanne answered, and the two strolled down the lane together.

As they sat on bales of hay in the old barn, Joanne asked Carol, "I know that you are aware that Mark and I are seeing each other now, and I need to know how you feel about it."

"Joanne," Carol answered, "I think it's great. You know, Joanne, ever since you came to Loafing Hills to ride, I thought highly of you. And Mark is a wonderful guy too. I couldn't be happier for you both." She smiled.

Joanne, looking relieved, sighed and said, "I'm so glad, Carol, because I knew that Mark, when in Maryland, was madly in love with you. And I feel that he still may be a little, but maybe not as much now, I hope."

She smiled. Looking at Carol, she continued, "I just want you to know that I fell in love with Mark at Loafing Hills, but never said anything about it then because I knew the way he felt about you. But

I want you to know that I do love him dearly and hope that eventually he will love me too." She sighed.

Carol responded, "Joanne, I think you're wrong. I saw the way Mark was looking at you today. He is in love with you, right now," she laughed.

Joanne, feeling much better after talking with Carol, walked back to the house with a happy smile on her face. Carol, too, felt better because Joanne would be good for Mark, and he for her. They both, Carol felt, deserved happiness. *I just hope*, she thought to herself, *they will be as happy together as John and I are.*

The rest of the day the friends sat on the large front porch of the main house talking. Karen and Jim decided that they would fly back to Loafing Hills with Carol and John the next morning. From there the four would fly to New Start to look at fifty head of cattle that John had not taken to Loafing Hills. Jim wanted to see, and possibly purchase, them for the ranch.

CHAPTER 33

The next morning, after Karen took a handful of carrots to Penny, the four said goodbye with hugs, kisses, and promises to return. After looking at the cattle, John would be flying Karen and Jim back to Wyoming in just a few days. Carol and John promised another visit in June, bringing Pearl and graduated Billy to Long River Ranch to stay for the summer and maybe to live there all year round, depending on Billy's getting into a college there.

The four had a nice flight back to BWI and arrived at Loafing Hills in time for one of Pearl's late lunches. Carol and John were happy to be home again. The four sat at the table with Ned, Ellie, Mike, Dan, Gloria, and Pearl, and excitedly told them about their thrilling stay at beautiful Key West, followed by their two fun-filled days in Wyoming.

After lunch, Carol and John decided to saddle up and take a ride. Karen and Jim opted to pack up several items they wanted to take back to the ranch. When finished packing, they placed a leash on little Piggy and took him for a stroll around the farm. This was exciting for the little dog because Dora always took him out on a leash several times a day, but not far out of the yard. It was an adventure for him to visit the barn and see the horses up close.

Carol and John rode out across the pasture to the lovely setting that overlooked the small town nestled below the pastureland. Next they located the cattle and found them grazing peacefully. On the way back they stopped by Emerson's grave. Dismounting, they walked to the stone. John held the horses while Carol spoke softly to Emerson.

"I want you to know that I still miss you so much, Emerson, but I also need to tell you, that because of you, I've found John. I love John with all my heart. It was sad when you died, Emerson, maybe even fate, for it was you that brought us together." Tears dropped from her eyes.

John, taking Carol's hand, softly added, "I missed you, Emerson, when I sold you, but as it turns out, it was the best decision I ever made, and I truly believe that you gave your life to bring Carol and me together. I love Carol very much, and I make this promise to you now, I will take good care of her forever." Silently they mounted and quietly rode back to the barn.

After supper that evening, they were all pretty tired, but decided to settle down in the TV room to watch an old Michelle Pfeiffer/Al Pacino movie. They enjoyed the drama and made it though to the end, but had to literally drag themselves to bed.

After a good night's rest, they all felt invigorated the next morning and were looking forward to their trip to New Start. The owners had not yet moved in and were not concerned that John still had some of his cattle there. He had taken most of the herd to Loafing Hills. The fifty cattle left at New Start were of interest to Jim and Mark. Jim was on a mission to look at the cattle, buy some, or all, and have them transported to the ranch.

They left Loafing Hills after breakfast and drove to the small airport. John checked out his plane and called in his flight plan.

The flight was calm and relaxing. This was the first time that Karen had flown in a small plane. She called excitedly over the engine noises, "Wow. This is great; you can see houses and cars and trees. And, there's Sugarloaf Mountain. I thought flying in a little plane would be really scary," she said, "but it's not at all; it's beautiful." They winged south, on to New Bern.

John called the maintenance crew from the plane and was cleared for a landing. They glided in and stopped smoothly. A couple of the crew came out of the barn and assisted the ladies down from the plane. John had advised the new owners of New Start that this crew was the best. They readily agreed and elected to keep them all on the ranch. They planned to ship cattle from their old ranch in Georgia to New Start.

The crew brought four saddled and bridled horses from the barn for the four to ride out to check the remaining cattle.

Karen and Jim had no problem with western riding. They felt like old pros and swung right up onto the big Morgan and Quarter horse. Carol and John mounted two horses both owned by the barn crew.

The cattle were not far from the barn and looked strong and healthy. The four rode as close to the peacefully grazing herd as they dared, for they did not wish to disturb them.

Jim liked what he saw, and John made him a very lucrative deal.

Back at the barn, John spoke with the barn crew, asking about transporting the herd to Wyoming. They agreed, and with the new owner's permission they were glad to comply.

John called on his cell phone and received permission. Turning to Jim, he said simply. "Done deal!"

To celebrate the sale, they visited a quaint little restaurant in town. They enjoyed a delightful supper and toasted their "Done Deal" with Burgundy Chablis.

Jim held his glass up saying, "Here's a toast to two great people, Carol and John Quill." Smiling at them, he continued, "Karen and I want you to know that we have enjoyed the last three weeks with you two immensely. You are truly great friends."

John acknowledged and immediately added, "Carol and I have appreciated and enjoyed the company that you two offered us also. You both will be our best friends forever." Then he smiled and added, "Even in a pouring rainstorm!"

That broke them up with a good laugh.

Later in the afternoon, they decided that they had better head back to Loafing Hills. The plan was to fly Karen and Jim back to Wyoming the next day.

As they climbed aboard John's plane, they called goodbye to the barn crew and a rather sad farewell to New Start Ranch.

CHAPTER 34

The weather was quite cold, but calm, allowing for a nice flight back to Maryland.

When they arrived at Loafing Hills, it was five o'clock. Walking towards the front door of the house, they were almost run down by Ned. He excitedly called to them, "John, your mare is showing strong signs of foaling."

"Foaling?" Carol cried. "John, I didn't even know you had a mare in foal."

"Yes," John answered. "She's not due for a couple of weeks, but I guess she's a little early."

Turning to Karen and Jim, John said, "Is it okay with you two to stay a little longer here than planned? I'd like to be here for the birth of this foal."

Jim and Karen both nodded yes. "I'll call Mark," Jim answered, "to let him know what's going on."

The four went to the barn to check out the mare.

"She's waxing," John said after examining her, "which is a good sign of preparing to deliver."

Ned had placed a foaling belt on the mare, a surcingle stretched around her girth line. Most foaling mares do not lie down in the later months of pregnancy, so when the mare does go down, the probability is she's preparing to foal. The transmitter attached to the surcingle sets off a signal to the barn and the house, making people aware of the situation. A mare is not like a cow, which can take hours to birth; a mare gives birth quickly and can be in trouble if she does not. John was not willing to take any chances. He opted to sleep in the barn. Carol said that she would too.

Then Karen and Jim said simply, "You sleep down here; we will also."

Neither Carol, Karen, nor Jim questioned John at all. If he felt it was so important to stay with the mare, then they would also. They went up to the house and brought down four cots, blankets, and pillows.

That night Carol asked John the story on the mare. She remembered him bringing in two horses to Loafing Hills right before the wedding, but knew nothing more about either one and had not even seen them.

John's answer was that he had purchased them about a year ago, and they both were very special to him.

During their first stay in the barn, the mare simply nibbled on hay throughout most of the night. In the morning she seemed comfortable and at ease. The four decided to go to the house for breakfast. They would easily hear a signal in the kitchen.

Pearl, as always, did herself proud with creamed chip beef piled high on warm biscuits accompanied with sliced tomatoes. Fresh coffee and fruit juice were also offered. This was breakfast number one; only Ellie joined them. All at the table were rather subdued.

Then Ned came in from the barn and told them of a strange happening at the main barn early that morning. Dan and Mike arrived at the barn at four a.m. and found one of the barn horses, "Gingerman," had gotten loose in the barn during the night and had caught his halter on a stall door hook. He ended up pulling the whole door loose, and it fell around his neck. He backed up, dragging the whole thing down the aisle. By the time Mike and Dan found him he was not hurt, but soaking wet and trembling from head to tail, eyeballs rolling. He was even scared of Mike who tried to approach him. Gingerman snorted and backed up even more, pulling the door with him until he finally was against a wall and couldn't move. Dan grabbed some shears, climbed up the doorframe still hanging around the horse's neck, and quickly cut through the rope, freeing the hook from his halter. The door fell away. The horse, still frightened, raced down the aisle and out of the barn down the driveway.

It was not yet light out so Dan jumped in the pickup truck and Mike followed on foot with a bucket of grain. Dan's idea was to get ahead of the horse and block the driveway entrance with the truck to keep the horse from running off the property and onto the road.

Ned related that the guys said the horse had gotten out of the barn about four a.m., and they were still looking for him at daylight. When they finally did find him, he was in a field, peacefully nibbling grass. Mike, carrying the bucket of grain, walked right up to him and snapped a lead shank to his halter. Of course, Ned added, all the folks at Loafing Hills know that halters are *never* left on horses while in their stalls.

Later Gloria came into the kitchen in tears and admitted that she was responsible. She had been in a hurry the day before and had neglected to take the halter off Gingerman before putting him in his stall for the night.

Pearl, smiling at Gloria, announced, "A lesson well experienced is a lesson well learned."

The folks sitting at the table laughingly agreed that their night in the second barn was not so bad after all!

CHAPTER 35

The second night in the barn, the four were sitting on the cots sipping coffee. The mare was not eating and seemed rather restless.

After watching her for about an hour, they decided to try to get some sleep. They were just getting comfortable when the mare started circling in the stall.

A few minutes later, she cumbersomely lay down. John was the first one up, going quietly to the stall door.

Carol, rising from the cot whispered, "I think this is it," as she went into the stall and unhitched the mare's surcingle. She didn't want the bell to wake the folks in the house.

The mare was definitely in labor, and the pains were coming on quick and strong. After several hard pushes, two tiny hooves and a nose appeared, still in the birthing sack. With two more strong heaves, the rest of the foal appeared. All this happened in less than twenty minutes. John, Carol, Karen, and Jim stood at the door, totally transfixed, watching mother nature at work. The mare got to her feet, very aware of the foal still lying on the ground. She was doing such a good job the four people watching decided not to disrupt her. The mare, using her lips, gently pulled the sack off the foal and nickered softly to her new baby. John and Carol crept quietly into the stall and severed the umbilical cord.

The mare, seeing the two people on their hands and knees smearing iodine on her new baby's tummy, totally ignored them.

John couldn't keep the joy out of his voice when he announced to everyone, "It's a boy!"

Karen said, "Oh, I was hoping it would be a filly."

Carol added, "No, Karen, he's a beautiful colt."

The four sat on their cots and watched until the colt finally found his legs and wobbled to a standing position as his mother nickered and encouraged him.

The four then waited, breathlessly, for the colt's first steps and silently cheered as he made them.

Carol couldn't stand it any longer and went into the stall again and gently pushed him up to his mom's belly so he could suckle. After the first taste of milk, he needed no more prompting.

"He's gorgeous," Carol cried. "Dark brown, four white socks and a white blaze right down the center of his face! I believe that he'll be a bay when he's older. His mane and tail are already darker now than his body color; he is truly a handsome colt."

The others, thrilled, agreed.

John, turning to Carol, spoke quietly. "Carol, I'm now going to present you with a special wedding gift."

Carol, still standing at the stall with Karen and Jim, was surprised at John's announcement.

He smiled at her and took her hand. "Before this goes any further," he said, "I need to tell you a story."

Karen and Jim, looking at each other, quietly suggested that perhaps they should leave the two of them alone.

John, however, turning to them laughed and said, "No, I would like you two to stay with us for this story."

Before John could begin his story, they all became mesmerized by the dawn's sudden light spreading through the stall window. The brightness centered on the mare and foal, turning the yellow straw into a spotlight of gold. The mare, even though weary, looked majestic as she basked in this light. The colt, standing by his mother's side, looked tired, but poetically content as the light offered a soft halo, crowning his head. The mare again neighed softly to him, and finding his tiny voice, he answered with a mellow nicker.

It took several minutes before they could pull themselves out of their hypnotic state. The picture washed away as swiftly as it had arrived, but it seemed to them like a dream that would go on forever. And, it left them all in a gloriously uplifted mood.

"Wow!" John exclaimed. "I think we had a beautiful spell cast upon us. Maybe we need coffee," he laughed.

"Or maybe something a bit stronger," Karen suggested.

John, still holding Carol's hand, pulled her over to sit on a cot. Jim and Karen joined them.

John placed his arm around Carol and continued. "Let me tell the story," he whispered.

"It took a lot of trial and error to find the mare that I had given to my first wife, Pat. However, I did finally locate her in South Carolina. Then I went on a more adventurous journey to locate a stallion. I found the one that I wanted in Georgia. Both horses, thank God, were healthy and well. I bred the mare to him last year. I had both horses, well hidden, at New Start for a year, Carol," John said as he stood up and led Carol to the stall. "I want to introduce you to the broodmare, Princess."

Carol, shocked, sputtered, "John, I don't understand..."

"I've not finished the story yet," he grinned. "Your famous horse, Emerson, has a dad named Alley Cat. He is now housed in the stud barn at Loafing Hills. He is the second horse that I found last year, purchased, and hid at New Start Ranch. He is one of the two that I brought and hid from you here at Loafing Hills."

Carol was not only having trouble keeping up with John's story, she was speechless.

John continued, "Carol, this little guy standing so royally beside his mom is...hold on to your hat...*Emerson's full brother!"*

Carol was shocked. She put her arms around John's neck, her head against his chest, and bawled like a baby. She was joined by Karen. John and Jim shed a few tears too.

Once they all calmed down a bit, Carol thanked John for the magnificent gift, and then she reentered the stall, patted Princess' neck, and placed her arms around the little guy. Tears streaming again, she whispered to the colt, "I'm so glad you are here. Loafing Hills will always be your home."

It wasn't long before Ned and Ellie came to join in on the news.

"I think, Dad," Carol said, "you must have known what was going on. I remember that day when all you guys were whispering in the stud barn. And now I know why."

Ned answered, "Yes, we knew. Mike, Dan, and I helped John with the horses and kept our mouths closed. But, Carol, what a wonderful surprise for you!"

Carol answered, "Dad, I'm not mad. I'm delighted! He is a magnificent colt, and I love him. I think he already looks like Emerson." She laughed. "In fact, I'll take the name Prince, from his mom, Princess, Alley, from his dad, Alley Cat, and Em from his great full brother, Emerson. His name is Prince Alley Em." Everyone liked and approved the name.

Later in the morning everyone else on the farm came down to greet the new colt. Mike, Dan, Gloria, Pearl, Billy, and Dora who was holding her little dog in her arms. They all had great predictions for the colt. Pearl, looking at him, decided that he was going to be as great as Emerson. Ellie quickly agreed.

Mike and Dan thought him to be as handsome a colt as they had ever seen.

Karen piped up with, "I know now who I'm breeding Penny to."

Ned agreed with Karen and said, "Well, now Sky Cloud is definitely going to have some tough competition here with the Loafing Hills show horse mares."

Smiling broadly, John added, "That's right. We now have *two* fine stallions standing at our beautiful Loafing Hills, Maryland farm."

Gloria stayed busy all morning taking pictures of the new colt to send to Joanne and Mark. Even little Piggy, wagging his tail, seemed pleased with the new family addition.

John agreed to fly Karen and Jim back to Wyoming the next morning. Karen and Jim planned to bring Penny back to Loafing Hills in June to have her bred. Penny and Princess both would be bred to Alley Cat.

CHAPTER 36

That afternoon, Karen and Jim left the barn and went to the house to pack. When the packing was done, John took Jim to the barn to check out Alley Cat, leaving the girls to talk about their upcoming June visit and more visits later in the year.

Karen, knowing how much they would miss each other, smiled at Carol, her very dearest friend, and gave her a heartfelt hug. She then laughingly reminded Carol that if she was ever feeling blue, to please call her. She would sing to her, "Going out to the garden to eat some worms!"

Carol grinned and said, "Yes, I'll do that, and I'll do the same for you too."

The two hugged each other and giggled like two little kids. "We'll never grow up," Carol laughed and Karen agreed.

Pearl brought some coffee into the living room for the girls. She talked about her and Billy's visit to the ranch this summer to check out the colleges. "Even if we decided to come back to Maryland," she said, "I'm sure that Joanne would stay. She's crazy about Mark, and he feels the same towards her." She continued, "Of course, Granny wants to teach me to horseback ride so we can cook for the guys out on the plains. Now that's a wild picture," she chuckled.

Ellie, Dora, and Gloria joined the girls in the living room. Carol told Gloria how happy she was with her help on the farm. Gloria answered that she loved Loafing Hills and planned to stay as long as she was needed.

Mike and Dan dropped in to wish Karen and Jim luck on the ranch and to inform Gloria that they were happy too that she planned to stay at Loafing Hills. They were hoping that Billy might stay too.

Pearl stated that if she and Billy did decide to stay in Wyoming, she would visit the folks at Loafing Hills often. "I don't want to be forgotten!" She smiled.

Of course, that opened up for funny comments from Mike and Dan.

"Gosh, Pearl," Mike laughed, "with you not here, what will we ever do if a long, long horse comes to visit us again?"

"Or worse than that," cackled Dan, "was when she placed that whoopee cushion on the pew in the church."

"I told you characters, I did not do that. I think it was Billy," she chuckled.

"Anyway, Pearl," both guys declared, "you will not ever be forgotten here at Loafing Hills. "We love you and would miss you very much."

After lunch, Carol left the gang at the house to take a gander at Alley Cat. She was pleasantly surprised. He was a truly good-looking horse. Jim had gone back to the house, and John stayed with Carol.

It was late afternoon when they left the barn, strolling hand in hand, back to the house. Carol looked up at John and whispered, "I love you, John. Thank you so much for this wonderful surprise. I can't wait to start working with this colt. And I promise you this, John, when I have him broke to the halter and lead shank, I'm going to take him for a nice long walk up to the top of that hill," she pointed, "and standing under that beautiful old oak tree up there, we will face the gravestone together." Then, she added through smiling tears, "I will proudly introduce Prince Alley Em to his great, full brother...*Emerson*!"

The next morning's headlines in the little town newspaper read, "Emerson is back at Loafing Hills."

Breinigsville, PA USA
22 September 2010

245803BV00002BA/6/A